2.50

W9-CSQ-012

More praise for Linda Grant and LOVE NOR MONEY

"Among the best of current mystery novels."
The Virginian-Pilot and The Ledger-Star

"Catherine Sayler is a character readers will want to get to know better."
The Denver Post

"Northern California has more than its fair share of fine mystery writers and [one] of the best [is] Linda Grant.... LOVE NOR MONEY provides plenty of action as the story unfolds in various locales throughout the Bay Area.... Catherine is definitely a character readers will want to hear from again and again."
The Monterey County Herald

"Linda Grant is every bit as good as her bestselling peers. Add her name to your must-read list."
The Lexington Herald-Leader

"[A] neatly crafted mystery ... Grant juggles her plot smoothly, keeping all balls up in the air until the very end."
Publishers Weekly

LOVE NOR MONEY

A Catherine Sayler Mystery

Linda Grant

IVY BOOKS • NEW YORK

Ivy Books
Published by Ballantine Books
Copyright © 1991 by Linda V. Williams

Library of Congress Catalog Card Number: 91-22175

ISBN: 0-8041-0947-8

This edition published by arrangement with Charles Scribner's Sons, an Imprint of Macmillan Publishing Company

Printed in Canada

First Ballantine Books Edition: January 1993

To Erin and Megan

Acknowledgments

Many people contributed generously of their knowledge and support to this book. I would like to thank in particular Inspector Glenn Pamfiloff of the San Francisco Police Department, Patricia Melesco of the Alameda County Probation Department, and Mary Waldner Ferris, MFCC, for background on child abuse; Detective John M. Hunt III of the Piedmont Police Department, Michael Berger, and Lynne Houghton, CLI, for legal and procedural information; Elizabeth A. Lynn for help with the aikido scenes; and Andy Williams, Barbara Dean, and Carol Kelly-Thomas for their comments on the manuscript. For her analysis of the Trojan War and insights into teenage behavior, I am indebted to my daughter, Megan.

1

T HE SUN BURNED on the wooden floor like a sheet of white fire. Its brightness stabbed all the way to the middle of my head. I squeezed my eyes shut. I tried to sit up. My head pounded and my stomach lurched. Standing up didn't seem like a good idea.

I waited for the nausea to pass. It didn't. I felt as if I'd been poisoned, which wasn't so very far from the truth. The fact that I'd done it to myself only made matters worse. The night before was a bit hazy in my memory. The reason for it was all too clear.

Orrin Merrick. White male, twenty-seven years of age, blond hair, blue eyes. Deceased. Dead by his own hand in the jail cell that I put him in.

Orrin Merrick had had a wife and two young kids. He'd also had a father with Alzheimer's, and a profound desire to protect the old man from the indignities of institutionalization. The first time he'd helped himself to company funds, he'd thought of it as a loan, but as the need for money grew, his chances of repaying it shrank.

His employer had noticed that something was wrong and hired me to find the culprit. Orrin wasn't a skillful criminal, but he was bright enough to figure out that I was on his trail and to create a computer "accident" that wiped out the proof of his wrongdoing.

He'd have been home free if the company president hadn't decided that confession was good for the soul. He'd asked me to offer Merrick continued employment and the promise of no prosecution in exchange for a signed confession.

I'm good at what I do, sometimes too good. Good enough to convince Merrick I had proof of his crime. Good enough to use his fear of prison to get his confession. But not good enough to protect him when the boss double-crossed us both and went to the police.

I'd acted in good faith, and I'd been betrayed just as Merrick had, but that didn't change the fact that I went home to a comfortable apartment not far from Pacific Heights and Merrick went to a cell.

I was still dressed in the jeans and sweater I'd been wearing the night before. The scotch bottle still sat on the coffee table. I don't even like scotch. Drinking a good part of the bottle had been an act of shameless masochism.

My mouth tasted like old mothballs. My teeth were fuzzy. My face felt stiff and hot, and I had the definite impression that my skin had shrunk. Closing my eyes just made the nausea worse, so I stared at the ceiling. I figured that if I stayed that way long enough I'd either go to sleep or die. At the moment I didn't care which.

I turned my head. Two golden eyes stared back at me. They were not happy eyes. They were full of reproach and that smug superiority that cats manage so well. The eyes said very clearly, "Responsible adults do not get drunk and fail to feed their faithful cats."

I was pondering whether I could make it to the kitchen and find the cat food when I was nearly deafened by the slamming of a door. A tall, broad-shouldered figure appeared in the doorway. My fuzzy brain struggled to fit the image with the fact that I knew that Peter was in Santa Cruz for the week.

"Jesus," he said much too loudly. "What happened?"

"You're supposed to be in Santa Cruz."

He crossed the room and knelt in front of me. "What's wrong?"

"I'm hung over," I said, "very hung over."

"Why?"

I swallowed around the lump that was growing in my throat and told him about Orrin Merrick. He moved up onto the couch and held me against him, and I started crying all over again.

I didn't cry long. It made my head hurt even worse, and I was beginning to tire of exploring the boundaries of self-abuse. It felt good to be folded against Peter's chest. Maureen Merrick had probably felt the same when Orrin held her. I tried not to think about it.

"It's not your fault," he said. "They promised you they wouldn't prosecute. You couldn't know they'd double-cross you. You did all you could for him."

I had testified at the sentencing hearing that Orrin posed no threat to society and would be of far greater use to everyone doing community service than sitting in a jail cell. But the current climate of law and order leaves little room for compassion or common sense.

By all the standards that govern private investigators, my actions had been correct. So why did I feel so crummy? My first boss, Keith Stone, had made a big point of professional ethics. I could remember him holding up three fingers and repeating the words "legal, ethical, and moral." I'd thought at the time that they were pretty much the same thing, but I was beginning to understand the difference. In Orrin Merrick's case I had acted legally and ethically; morally was another question.

"You need fluids," Peter said, gently pulling away from me. "I'll get you a glass of water."

"I'd probably throw up," I said.

He ignored me and came back with a tall glass of water and two aspirin. I didn't feel like drinking anything, but I knew Peter wouldn't give up, so I took a sip.

"All of it," he said.

I groaned and drank some more. I didn't throw up, somewhat to my surprise. "Enough," I said. "Let me just sit here quietly till I feel better."

"That could be quite a while," Peter said, "especially if you keep feeling sorry for yourself."

"I'm dying and all you can think to do is beat up on me. Thanks a lot."

"If you could die from a bad hangover, I'd be long gone," Peter said.

By afternoon, I felt merely wretched instead of terminal, but my mood hadn't improved in the slightest. Peter convinced me not to go to the office, more out of kindness to my staff than concern for me. I half expected him to pack his stuff and move out on me. Instead, he cleaned the kitchen.

I watched him put away the dishes and thought what an unlikely pair we were. We might both be investigators but we were poles apart in the work we did. I operated in the corporate world, where crime was better mannered and less likely to turn violent. Peter worked criminal defense, missing persons, and just about any case where someone could convince him that they were in trouble. I'd always preferred my corporate clients with their relatively neat, nonviolent problems to the assortment of desperate and needy people who sought Peter's help. Today I was no longer so sure.

I'M NEVER ONE of those people who leap out of bed full of enthusiasm for the new day. Under the best of circumstances, I rise grudgingly and hope I can get through some yoga stretches and several sets of sun salutations before I wake up.

The next morning I had even less desire to get out of bed than usual. Peter tried sympathy, then teasing, sarcasm, and finally brute force. He pulled the comforter off the bed and tickled me. I'd have killed him if I'd had the energy.

I went to the office because I always go to the office. I

walked because I didn't trust myself behind the wheel of a car. Fortunately, my office is only four blocks from my apartment. One of the reasons I chose the graceful Victorian on Divisadero was that I could walk to it. The other was that I liked the funky neighborhood with its ethnic groceries and restaurants.

The weather fit my mood perfectly—gray and dismal. I've given up trying to figure out the difference between high fog and low clouds. Both mean gray skies, no sun, no rain. Typical San Francisco weather.

For the last five years, the weather has been even screwier than usual. We'd just spent another winter that looked like summer, and the water department was simultaneously dunning us to cut back on water use and raising the rates as a reward for the great job we'd done.

At the office I discovered that word of my condition had preceded me. Everyone treated me like a recently released mental patient. I knew I'd have to put up with sympathy from my secretary, Amy. She's the only one in the office who doesn't think she's a stand-up comedian, and she takes it upon herself to make up for everyone else's lack of social grace. On occasion my assistant, Chris, has been known to curb her tendency to go for the jugular, so her good behavior wasn't a complete surprise. However, when my partner, Jesse, started acting like Mr. Rogers, it was too much.

He looked a good deal more respectable this morning than I did. Since I'd offered him a partnership three months ago, he'd taken to wearing a suit to the office, and he was looking increasingly like an ad from *Black Enterprise*.

We were scheduled to spend a good part of the morning reviewing our latest case. A firm in Santa Clara that made parts for computer manufacturers had found too many of those parts disappearing. Their security people had identified some of the culprits, but they suspected that the gang was much bigger and that they might be working directly for a competitor. They wanted us to nail the link to the competitor and prove the other company's involvement.

When they got the proof, they might not ask for the rival CEO's underwear; they'd certainly go for everything else.

Jesse was excited. He'd been over the reports and he had a plan. "There's this guy Harold in the warehouse. Security has tagged him as in the gang. We have the company fire him and hire me for his job. The gang needs someone on the inside. They see this smartass black kid with a taste for coke and fast women, how can they resist?"

His eyes shone as he described it, but the light faded when he failed to get any kind of response from me.

"What's the matter? I miss something? We got a problem here?"

I shook my head. It still felt fuzzy from Sunday night.

"Catherine, I've gotten more reaction from mannequins in Macy's. For godssake, talk to me."

"I'm sorry, Jesse," I said. "I just can't seem to get into it. It's like my mind is in neutral. Maybe it's just a hangover from the hangover, but I can't seem to focus."

His expression had changed from mild annoyance to deep concern. I preferred the former.

"This Orrin Merrick thing really got to you, didn't it?"

I nodded.

"It wasn't your fault."

"It doesn't matter whose fault it was, he's still dead."

"You need to take some time off. Why don't you let me mind the store for a while?"

I considered it. I sure wasn't much use to anyone the way I was. On the other hand, I wouldn't be any better off sitting around by myself at home. The flood of exhaustion that washed over me when I tried to think about the new case convinced me. Jesse really could mind the store if necessary. "Can you handle this case alone?" I asked.

He considered. "Sure. I'll use Chris for backup, and I can always call Harman if things get sticky."

The thought of Peter and Jesse operating *my* agency was enough to focus my attention. Peter had as little respect for the law as he could get away with, and Jesse found Peter's free-wheeling style much too attractive for my taste.

"No, if things get sticky, you can call *me*," I said.

"You don't trust us?" Jesse asked with a twinkle in his eye.

"I trust you and I trust him. I do not trust the two of you together."

The rest of the day was a lesson in how slowly time can pass when you're trying to relax. It was also a humbling opportunity to discover how poorly I handle messy emotions. I didn't enjoy my own company; I was fairly sure Peter wouldn't have, either. I was glad he'd gone to Santa Cruz.

By five o'clock that night I could hardly wait to get to the dojo. I train in aikido, a Japanese martial art, two or three times a week and teach a beginners' class on Saturday. When I screw up and allow other things to get in the way, my body lets me know it. Tonight it was fairly screaming for me to get moving.

I made a point of getting there early so I'd have time to do some stretches. All that scotch had had the usual bad effect on my muscles, and it took twenty minutes to get them stretched out enough so that I wasn't courting injury.

There are always plenty of black and brown belts on Tuesday night, enough to guarantee a good workout. I paired off with the biggest, toughest guys so I didn't have to worry about hurting anyone. It felt good to shut my mind off and let my body take over. By the end of class I was covered with a satisfying layer of sweat.

Lou Boone, one of my favorite partners, came over after we bowed off the mat and gave me a hug. "You work off whatever was bothering you?" he asked.

"Not completely," I said, "but I'm getting there."

I felt better Wednesday morning. Enough better so that when the second cup of coffee hit, my brain kicked in for the first time in days. I called the office and caught Jesse before he left for the peninsula.

"Can you give me twenty minutes?" I asked.

"Long as you want. I don't start till tomorrow. Today I rent an apartment and get set up."

"I'll be right over," I said.

Amy greeted me with a still-warm sticky bun from a bakery on Fillmore. She's a firm believer in the tenet that there are few ills that can't be healed by gustatory indulgence. I encourage her since I am a frequent beneficiary.

Jesse and I split the sticky bun. "You're looking better this morning," he said.

"I'm feeling better, and meaner," I said. "I figured out that I don't need a vacation, I need revenge."

Jesse looked startled.

"Not a very admirable motivation, I know. But there it is. I want the bastard to pay for his treachery." I paused. "And I want to be the one who makes him pay."

"Anton Glosser?" Jesse said.

I nodded. Anton Glosser was the man who'd double-crossed me on the Merrick case. He was president of Consumer Electronics, a medium-sized firm that he'd built from scratch. Like so many self-made men, he remembered the hardships he'd overcome more clearly than the people who'd helped him along the way. Such selective vision led to an overinflated estimate of his own worth and an attitude of disdain for others who had accomplished less than he.

I'd have preferred to think my desire for revenge came solely from a thirst for justice or outrage at Orrin Merrick's fate, but there was also an element of pride. I hate to be played for a fool, and I hate it most of all when I suspect that I was chosen for the role because I'm a woman.

"Glosser works from a basic street-fighter mentality: Do unto others before they can do unto you," I said. "He went after Orrin because he wanted it known that no one gets away with crossing Anton Glosser. He also strikes me as the kind of guy who believes that the rules apply to everyone else. I didn't pick up any corporate misconduct from their books, but they cut every corner they could get away with and I'd bet that there's dirt someplace. I plan to find it."

"Hold it," Jesse said. "Glosser was a client. We had access to privileged information. If you were to disclose or use that information, we could be in big trouble. *No one* wants to hire an investigator who reveals privileged information."

"I don't plan to use *that* information. I thought I'd just check on Glosser's personal finances and dig around a bit. See where the bodies are buried. I don't even know what I'll do when I find something, but it sure would be sweet to find some way to get Glosser to take care of Orrin's family."

"You're talking dangerously close to blackmail," Jesse warned.

"And I'm making you nervous."

Jesse shrugged. He likes to be the cool one; it made him uncomfortable to be the voice of reason. "I just think you should think about it a bit before you do anything. How about you wait a week before you start digging around? You could use a vacation."

"I could go stir crazy with a vacation. I'm ready to start now."

"A week, as a favor to your new partner."

Partner. The magic word, subtly selected to remind me that we'd made a deal when we signed the partnership papers that neither of us would take any major steps affecting the agency without consulting the other. I'd suggested it to prevent Jesse from doing anything too wild, and now he was using it against me.

"A whole week?"

"Only a week. Seven days."

I didn't want to wait a week. And when I realized how much I didn't want to wait, I knew Jesse was right. "Okay, a week." I said.

Jesse smiled.

"But only because I like to let you win one occasionally."

I tried to work on other things, but I wasn't in the mood to do anything except go after Anton Glosser. I was so grouchy that even McGee, the office cat, abandoned his favorite spot on my couch in search of a more congenial environment. If

I stuck around much longer, the plants would start to wilt. Finally, I went home.

Home wasn't much better than the office. My cat, Touchstone, was so confused by my arrival in the middle of the morning that he decided it must be mealtime. He and Amy have a lot in common when it comes to strategies for dealing with stress. He fussed and whined and threw himself against my ankles. Other cats rub against your leg. Stone goes for a full body press. I think his real goal is to trip me.

I had started and abandoned at least four projects by noon. By the time the phone rang just after one, I'd have been grateful for anything that would occupy my mind. Later, I'd reflect that you've got to be careful what you wish for.

"Catherine, it's Joe . . . Joe Girard," a familiar voice said.

"Joe, how are you?" I said. "It's been too long."

"Yeah, I need to see you, I mean professionally. Is that possible?"

Same old Joe, no social chitchat, just cut to the point. I could see his intense dark eyes and imagine him drumming his fingers in nervous energy. I'd met Joe over ten years ago at a benefit for some good cause, and ended up recruiting him to help a young Guatemalan friend who was having trouble with immigration.

We had gotten to know each other during the many hours we spent sitting in the outer offices of bored bureaucrats. He was incredibly gentle and comforting with my friend and an absolute tiger with the opposition. At five feet six, lean and wiry, he was possessed of abundant energy, sharp wits, and a sharper tongue. That's what the bureaucrats saw; I got to see the huge heart beneath it all.

I'd helped him out with investigations a couple of times, and he'd helped me on several pro bono cases. The last time we'd met he was working for Greenpeace, but I hadn't heard from him for several years. I figured that whatever he wanted to see me about was bound to be interesting.

3

JOE GIRARD ARRIVED promptly at four-thirty, wearing the same expression I put on for the periodontist. He was thinner than I remembered. His features seemed sharper, the bones of his face more prominent. But the eyes were the same. Dark and intense, they dominated his face, drew people to him or pushed them away. Today those eyes were underlined by dark circles, and Joe Girard looked much older than the years since I'd seen him could account for.

"Thanks for seeing me," he said as he sank into a chair. I'd have liked to know what he'd been up to since I'd last seen him, but his mind was on more pressing matters. "Before I start, I don't want you to feel you owe me anything. I mean there's friendship and business, and this is business. Okay?"

Our friendship and business had always been so closely intertwined, that his declaration surprised me. Then I realized that he was about to ask something for himself. I could never remember him doing that before.

I nodded. "What do you need?"

He picked up a paperweight from the edge of my desk. It was a round glass globe with the puffy head of a dandelion inside. He turned it absently in his hands and began. "I have a cousin, Mitch. He's two years younger than I am." He paused, swallowed, and continued. "Or he *was* two years younger. A couple of weeks ago, he came to me. He wanted me to help him expose a man who had molested him when he was a child."

He paused, watching closely for my reaction, then contin-

11

ued. "I turned him down. Me, who helps every sad-eyed case with a good story, I told him I was too busy. Truth is, he was an alcoholic and a drifter, and I'd bailed him out enough times that I wasn't anxious to do it again." Joe stared down at the floor and retreated into some private place for a minute. When he looked up again, his eyes were moist. "God help me, I just didn't want to be bothered."

He paused and studied the paperweight as though it were a crystal ball, then continued. "He didn't even get mad at me, just said he'd take care of things himself. Five days later, he was killed in the parking lot of a sleazy bar."

His eyes locked on mine. "The police are calling it a robbery attempt gone bad. I don't buy it."

"You think someone killed him intentionally?"

"Yeah."

"What do you know about the killing?" I asked.

"They found him last Thursday morning behind a place called Jerry's in west Oakland. That's a tough section of town. Robberies and even shootings aren't so unusual there. He'd been shot, and his wallet and watch were gone. That's all the cops would tell me. I don't think they know any more than that, and I don't expect them to come up with more because they've already decided that it was a stranger shooting."

"What makes you think it wasn't just a robbery?" I asked.

Joe set the paperweight back on the desk and leaned forward. "It's going to sound stupid, but I just have this feeling. I can't explain it, but when I get a feeling for something, it's almost always right. Like, remember that Laotian refugee who the cops picked up for armed robbery? As soon as I met the roommate, I knew it was him."

I remembered the case because I'd done some checking on the roommate, and Joe's "feeling" had proved correct.

"You have anything beyond this feeling?" I asked.

"Okay," Joe said. "They haven't found his car. He had a bad leg, and he drove everywhere, but his car wasn't in the parking lot. And there was no reason for him to be there in the first place."

"You said he had an alcohol problem."

"Yes, but he was on Antabuse. That stuff makes you nauseous if you have any alcohol, so he wasn't drinking. Besides, he was too streetwise to wander into that section of town accidentally, or to let some stranger come up on him."

Plenty of drunks have taken Antabuse only to drop it when the craving for a drink gets too strong, and it didn't sound as if Joe knew his cousin well enough to predict what he would and wouldn't do. "He could have gone there with someone he knew."

"He wouldn't have gone to a bar when he was trying to stay sober," he said impatiently. "And if he went with someone, why did they leave without him?" He stared at me intently, challenging me to refute his arguments.

"What did the police do when you told them this?"

"What do the cops always do? They pretended to listen, took some notes, and explained about the difficulties of catching this type of killer. 'This type of killer' being a stranger who has no connection to the victim. They're not going to investigate the guy my cousin was watching. It'll be a cover-up, nice and neat."

"Why a cover-up?"

"Because the man who killed him is Judge Samuel Reiter. He has plenty of friends in high places. The cops aren't about to mess with him."

A cover-up. If the cops covered up all the crimes that citizens think they do, they'd have no time to abuse all the guys who complain of police brutality.

"So you want me to prove that Reiter killed your cousin," I said.

"I want you to look into it, tell me if it looks funny to you. I'm too close to this to trust my instincts very far. You tell me it's robbery, I'll go back to sleeping at night."

"And if I find something?"

"We go to the police. I'm not taking things into my own hands. You got my word on it."

I considered it. Joe's eyes never left my face. The intensity of his scrutiny made me uncomfortable. "I don't work murder cases," I said. "I wouldn't even know where to start."

"It wouldn't take you long to figure out," Joe said. "I've worked with you. I know what you can do. Besides, there's more than murder at stake here. Even if Reiter didn't kill Mitch, he screwed up his life. He's still a child molester, and he ought to be punished for that.' "

"And you want me to help you do that."

"Yes."

"How do you know that Reiter molested Mitch?"

"Mitch told me."

"When?"

"When he came to see me. Why?"

"Look, Joe," I said. "This is serious stuff. Just the rumor of it can ruin a man's career. You admit you weren't close to your cousin. Yet you're willing to take his word that he was molested. Do you know what kind of trouble we could both get into if you're wrong about this?"

"I'm not wrong," he said defiantly. "And of course I know. That's one of the reasons I came to *you*. I know you won't do anything indiscreet. I just want justice."

No, I thought, you want to get even. I understood the thirst for vengeance far better than I liked, but I also knew that it is a dangerous ally and rarely an honorable one.

"Let's back up a bit," I suggested. "Tell me about the alleged abuse."

Joe Girard sighed. His manner said that the whole subject was distasteful to him. "Mitch was nine. Reiter was the coach of the chess club. He was a lawyer with a big name firm, smart, rich, sophisticated. Had a big house, beautiful wife, sailboat, sports car. Mitch was really flattered that Reiter liked him. He took him to ball games, movies, fishing on the bay. Anything Mitch wanted to do, Reiter'd take him. Mitch started hanging out at his house a lot. His dad drank too much, and his parents fought a lot, so he needed a place he could get away from all that. Then one day his good friend wanted to be more than friends."

"Do you know how it happened?"

"Not really. Mitch didn't want to talk about it. I know

Reiter didn't hold him down or force him physically. It was closer to seduction. Mitch just felt he couldn't say no.''

"And it happened more than once?''

"It went on for a couple of years.''

"Do you have any proof of that?''

"Nothing you could take to court, but I know Mitch was telling the truth. I remember how he changed a couple of years before he became a teenager. He was incredibly talented as an artist when we were kids. When the rest of us were drawing stick figures, he was drawing people who looked real. He used to carry a little notebook, and he'd whip it out and scribble on it for a minute or so, and there'd be this sketch that was like a cartoon but really captured the person he was drawing.

"Then when he was around nine or ten, he stopped drawing. He became more and more withdrawn. His family wrote it off to acting like a teenager, but I can see now that there was more to it than that. I didn't help him when he was alive, the least I can do is see that he gets justice now. Will you help me?''

Say no, the little voice of reason said. You may know a lot about corporate crime, but you know next to nothing about homicide and even less about child abuse.

The little voice of reason was no match for Joe's eyes. They were so full of pain that it hurt to look at him. Another time, when I understood less intimately the burden of guilt, I might have missed it, but today it was like looking in a mirror.

"All right," I said, "I'll give it a try.''

"This is business," Joe said again. "I expect to pay for your time.''

"I'm on vacation anyway," I said. "I'll do it for expenses and the next favor I need from you. Now, what else do you know about this?''

He started to object, then read the look on my face and shrugged. "Thanks. This one's worth a slew of favors." He reached down for the battered briefcase he carried everywhere and began riffling through it. Joe's briefcase is enough to destroy one's faith in the tight logic of the legal mind.

Finally, he found the folder he was looking for and pulled out a newspaper clipping. The headline read JUDGE HONORED FOR COMMUNITY SERVICE; beneath it was a portrait of a man in his late fifties, with a squarish face and a pleasant smile.

"This article started it," Joe said. "Mitch saw this, and it drove him crazy that Reiter was being hailed as a good citizen and a children's advocate after what he did. If you read the article, you see that most of his good deeds involve organizations of young boys."

"Tell me about him."

"He's a superior court judge, Alameda County, appointed six years ago. He's also the only son, and heir, of a socially prominent family in Piedmont. I don't know how much he's worth, but he lives in a mansion in the Piedmont hills, has box seats at the symphony, gets mentioned in society columns; you get the picture. He's also well connected politically. His name appears on the endorsement lists of a number of politicians."

Position, wealth, and power. This guy had it all. Yet if Joe was right, he was about to lose it all. I wondered if his arrogance was so great that he believed the rules of normal humans didn't apply to him, or if he was driven by a compulsion so deep that he was willing to risk everything to fulfill it.

Joe pulled a three-by-five snapshot from the folder. "I took this about five years ago," he said. "I think it's a pretty good likeness of Mitch."

The snapshot showed a slender, dark-haired man of about thirty. Plain, regular features set in a thin face with a high forehead. Nothing that stood out, nothing to make you notice him in a crowd or remember him after a brief encounter.

"Did he have any distinguishing marks, anything that would make people remember him?" I asked.

"Yeah. You can't see it in the picture, but he had a big scar on the back of his right hand, about two inches long, shaped like a crooked V. It was less than a year old and still fairly red and angry. And he had a stutter. *M*'s especially gave him trouble. People might remember that."

"Address where he lived?"

Joe shook his head. "I know it sounds weird, but I don't even have a phone number. I used to have one, but he moved a couple of weeks before he came to see me. And after our conversation, I forgot to ask and I doubt he'd have told me, anyway."

"But surely the police have figured out where he lived?"

"Not when I saw them, and I haven't heard anything to indicate they even looked for it."

I didn't share Joe's jaundiced view of the police, but it seemed very odd that they hadn't found his cousin's address.

I dialed information and asked for a new listing for Mitch Morrison. There wasn't one. "Would he have had an unlisted number?" I asked Joe.

"Yeah. He was sort of paranoid sometimes, probably from all the booze and drugs he'd done."

The unlisted number was a dead end for me. It wouldn't be for the police. Either they hadn't followed up on it or for some reason they didn't want Joe to know where Mitch had lived. "Do you know anyone who might have the address?" I asked.

"I gave the police everyone I could think of, and they didn't find anyone who knew."

"Think, Joe," I said. "Is there anyone else, or anyone who'd talk to you but might not talk to the police?"

Joe studied the ceiling. Finally, he said, "Artie Fishel. Artie and Mitch go way back. I gave his name to the cops, but Artie wouldn't give a cop the correct time. He'd know if anyone would."

"Talk to him," I said. "We need that address."

I went back over my notes once he was gone, with the peeved voice of reason repeating "You'll be sorry." But I wasn't. In fact, I felt great. There's something refreshingly unambiguous about child abuse and murder, no danger that you'll end

up feeling sorry for the perpetrator or guilty for catching him.
The idea did cross my mind that guilt was not the best basis
for making decisions, but I let it go.

THE OAKLAND POLICE weren't going to tell me much. I
knew that before I started. I knew it because my dad is
a cop and my ex-husband is a cop, and cops don't do show-
and-tell. They take information very seriously. They pay for
it. They trade with it. But they never give it away unless
they're forced to.

I needed someone who owed me a favor or who wanted
me to owe them one. I could ask my ex. He was a homicide
detective in San Francisco, so he was sure to know the guys
in Oakland. People were always anxious to do Dan Walker
a favor, but I wasn't anxious to ask for one.

The main reason he's my ex is that he doesn't approve of
my choice of career. When we were dating, he took a real
interest in my investigative work, but once he'd put that ring
on my finger, he turned protective and decided it was time
for me to find a safer occupation. If I asked him to help me
investigate a murder, I could sell tickets to the explosion.

I decided on the quieter, less-exciting approach of asking
a former student to help me out. Carol Bailey had been in
my aikido class for just over a year before she moved across
the bay. She was an Oakland vice detective, and I figured
she was probably good for a favor.

I called and told her what I needed.

"Do you know who's handling the case?" she asked.

I didn't, but she could find that out from Records. "I'd

like to actually meet the officer if possible," I said. "In fact, I'd like to see the paperwork."

"You don't want much, do you?"

"An arm, maybe a leg. Whatever you can manage."

She laughed, a wonderful rippling sound that was far too light to come from someone who worked the sewers she did every day. Away from work, she looked like a college student or a secretary, but if you talked to her for long, you bumped into the hard shell that cops build up. She was still there behind the shell. Too many of them forget what's inside and become the shell itself.

"I'll call you back when I've got something," she promised.

Peter spent the evening in Santa Cruz, looking for witnesses who might confirm his client's version of a bar shooting. For me it was a long evening without him, too much time to think. I considered opening another bottle, wondered whether I was becoming an alcoholic, pondered the implications of alcoholism, decided I was a real bore. I tried not to think about Orrin Merrick, which meant that I thought about nothing else.

Carol called at seven the next morning. She'd found out who was handling the Mitch Morrison case. It wasn't good news. "Your case has been assigned to John Warren," she said in the funereal tone doctors and mechanics use to announce the need for big-ticket work. "His wife left him last month, he's been passed over for promotion, and his hemorrhoids are acting up. In short, he is one mean son of a bitch. Also, I don't think he likes women, especially not uppity ones."

I groaned.

"That's the good news. The bad news is he *hates* private investigators." She laughed. "He says he's much too busy to see you, for which you should thank your patron saint, but he did agree to discuss the case over the phone. He'll be in the office this morning till eleven o'clock."

"Great," I said. "I don't suppose he'd be any more receptive to seeing a member of the family?"

"Not if it's the lawyer cousin. Warren hates liberal lawyers even more than he does investigators. I'll spare you the colorful adjectives he used to describe your client."

"It's too early in the morning for this kind of news," I complained.

Carol laughed again. Cops have a warped sense of humor. "I have a half-million reports to file this morning, so I'll be around. Call me after you talk with John and give me the gruesome details."

I called Warren at nine-thirty. He had a rough, gravelly voice, like a man who'd smoked too much for too long. I tried to sound cheerful and properly deferential. That used to come easily; lately it's gotten harder.

"We don't give out information on homicides," he growled.

"I understand," I said. "And I'm not asking for the kind of thing you need to keep confidential."

"So what do you want?"

"I'm looking for any evidence that the murder was something more than a botched mugging. Carol tells me you're real good at going beyond appearances. Have you picked up anything funny on this case?" It was only a small lie, and a bit of flattery never hurts.

"Not a damn thing," he said. His words were tough, but his voice was a bit less hostile. "Everything we got points to this being exactly what it seems. I know your client thinks his cousin was killed to keep him from making trouble for a judge, and I'm checking on that angle, but there's no evidence that the victim and the judge even knew each other."

"Anything on the allegation of child abuse?"

"Not yet, but we're checking on it. That kind of stuff takes time." He paused. "Look, I know it's hard for families to accept this kind of thing, but it happens. That's a bad neighborhood. Those kids on crack, they'd just as soon shoot you as look at you. They get the money either way; it doesn't matter to them." He gave a dry, hoarse cough.

"I see that," I said, "but just suppose you wanted to kill someone and get away with it. You could do worse than take him to the parking lot of a bar in a tough section of town, shoot him, and steal his wallet. Especially if the town was in the midst of a crack war that had the police department stretched so thin that they wouldn't have much time to investigate the homicide."

"Sure, that's possible. Just like it's possible that last night's drive-by shooting was really the result of a lover's quarrel. But it's a lot more likely that the dealer was shot for dealing and Morrison was shot for his wallet." Another dry cough. "Aside from the allegations of child abuse, which, like I said, I'm looking into, have you got anything to indicate that the murder was premeditated?"

"How about the victim's car? It wasn't found in the vicinity of the bar."

"The killer could have stolen it. Or someone else hotwired it and stole it. It took us three days to ID the guy and find the cousin. That's more than enough time to steal or strip a car."

"I assume you're looking for it as a stolen vehicle, but what if it's been abandoned on the street somewhere?"

"We'll be notified," he said.

"If you find it, could you let my client know?"

"Yeah, sure, but we can't release the car till we're sure it doesn't contain evidence."

"Of course," I said. "Can you tell me the name of the bartender who was working the night Mitch was killed?"

He paused; paper rustled. "Carl Edwards," he said.

"Any witnesses?"

"No."

I switched tacks. "How did you ID Morrison?"

"Fingerprints. He had a rap sheet in San Francisco, minor stuff sometime back, not a hood but hardly a model citizen."

"Do you have his address?"

"Just a minute." More paper rustling. "Not yet," he said.

"Your client wasn't very helpful on that. DMV only had an old P.O. box, and we haven't heard from the phone company on the unlisted number."

I did a bit of quick mental arithmetic. There'd been plenty of time to get the number from the phone company, if anyone had considered it important. I'd bet that the request was sitting on someone's desk under a pile of more pressing demands.

Warren seemed to read my thoughts. "Look, we're doing what we can. We don't write anyone off here. And let me tell you one more thing,"—he paused and I waited for the cough—"some people think that when there's somebody important, like a judge, involved, we might not look so hard. That's not true. There'll be no cover-up. You find something on Morrison's murder, and I'll be on it doubletime. The same for the child abuse. But till you have something more than rumors, don't go around shooting your mouth off. There's a man's reputation at stake here."

"Inspector," I said coldly, "I'm a professional investigator, not a gossip."

I got another cup of coffee and thought of all the things I'd have liked to say to Warren. When I was calm enough not to start ranting, I called Carol.

"No one ever accused Warren of being Mr. Charm," she said when I finished my recitation of our conversation. "But he is honest and you don't get where he is by being stupid. Also, I think he has a couple of kids, so he'll take the child-abuse charge seriously."

"Maybe," I said. "I sure don't get the feeling he's taking the murder seriously."

"Look, Catherine, how would you feel if you were in his shoes? No one has given him any proof that Mitch's death was anything more than a botched mugging. I'm afraid that unless you can do that, you really can't expect him to do more than he has already."

She was right, of course, which only made me grumpier.

"Morrison's car is missing," I said. "It could be important. You have any suggestions on how we might find it?"

"You could put word out on the street that there was a reward," she said.

"How much?"

"Two hundred."

"And would you know who to tell about this reward?"

"I would, indeed. And I'll do it this afternoon if you'd like."

"I'd like very much," I said. "Thank you."

If Mitch had been murdered by someone connected with the judge, I didn't expect to find any witnesses. But that didn't mean I wasn't going to look.

I put on my grubbiest jeans and the sweatshirt I wore to paint the kitchen, stopped at a bank to pick up forty dollars in single bills, and headed for west Oakland.

I T WAS A gorgeous day—blue skies, bright sun, and just enough breeze to sweep the air clean so that the city almost sparkled in its clarity. It wasn't warm, but then it seldom is in San Francisco. The Chamber of Commerce likes to refer to "natural air conditioning." Tourists realize too late that it's a euphemism for "bring your coat."

Traffic was light on the freeway. It was after rush hour and the heavy commute is westbound in the morning. KKHI was playing Vivaldi's *Four Seasons* and the tall buildings of the business district rose on my left like models from a train set.

Freeways are a visual blight on the landscape, but they provide some of the greatest views in the world.

The view disappeared as the road dipped onto the lower deck of the Bay Bridge, and when I emerged it was into the wasteland of industrial Oakland.

It took considerably longer to get to Jerry's Bar than it would have a couple of years ago. Then I'd have taken the Cypress Expressway that ran through west Oakland. But that was before the Loma Prieta fault shrugged and reminded us of the limits of engineering. For a few terrifying seconds the earth rolled and pitched, and the expressway collapsed upon itself, sandwiching smashed cars between its decks.

The signs of carnage had been removed, but the neighborhood was still pretty grim. It reeked of the hopeless despair of people shut out of the future. An urban prison where no one was ever really safe. Even in the daytime it was enough to make me glad I'd kept up my skills in aikido.

Jerry's was your basic sleazy bar. Dark and rank with the smell of stale smoke and old sweat, a grimy Coors sign worth something on the antique market, and the usual four old guys who look like carved fixtures on their bar stools. A place where it's always night.

The bartender was an elderly black man who didn't look pleased to see me in his bar. He was not Carl Edwards, the bartender who'd been on duty the night Mitch died, but he was willing to give me Edwards's address just to get me out of there before I caused any trouble.

Edwards came on duty at five o'clock, which meant that he was probably home in bed. Waking a night person in the middle of the day was not a good way to get him to talk to you. I figured I'd have to wait till at least three-thirty before I knocked on his door. He hadn't told the police anything, but I figured he might talk to me. I was willing to pay.

The bar was in an area where plenty of people lived on the streets. In a four-block radius, I encountered the usual variety of street people—crazies, druggies, drunks, and prostitutes—those left behind when the Great Society gave way to the Supply Side. One guy thought someone named Roger might have seen something, but it's hard to interrogate an invisible extraterrestrial, and that was as close to anything useful as I came.

I passed out cards and dollars and garnered goodwill and promises to keep an eye out for Mitch's car. The promise of a finder's fee for anyone who came up with information about the killing or the car netted me a whole army of street investigators, though I doubted that many of them would remember our conversation past the next bottle or fix.

That left driving around the neighborhood looking for Mitch's car. I didn't expect much success, and I wasn't surprised.

I still had a couple of hours to kill, so I decided to call Marjorie Domingo. Marge is a therapist, but I knew her from her former life as a phys. ed. teacher. We'd worked together to set up a self-defense class for girls in the Catholic high school where she worked. I knew that her practice was mainly kids and hoped she might have some insights into child abuse. I also knew that she had a six-week-old baby and would probably be at home and desperate for adult company.

The Rockridge area where she lives is a lot farther from Jerry's than the odometer would indicate. The shops along College Avenue are full of delicacies you used to find only in France or Italy sold from shops that try hard to look as if that's where they are. The patrons, however, are not dressed a whole lot better than some of the folks that live near Jerry's. This is probably the effect of being on the border of Berkeley, where the general rule is that the more money you have, the scruffier you look.

Marge greeted me at the door with a bundle in her arms. The bundle had large brown eyes, a rosebud mouth, and her mother's silky black hair.

"Catherine, come in. Talk to me about something other than breast-feeding and diapers."

I made appropriately appreciative noises over the baby

while she studied me with serious dark eyes. Not all babies are beautiful, but this one certainly was.

"We named her Melissa Andrea Domingo," Marge said. "I was about to feed her and put her down. We can chat while she nurses." She settled down on the couch and gave the baby her breast. I don't often regret the life I've chosen and more than fifteen minutes with any child other than my nieces drives me nuts, but there's something about watching a woman nurse a baby that makes me wonder if maybe I'm missing out on something.

We caught up on old times while the baby nursed, and after a while the little black head bobbed to the side. Melissa was clearly asleep. "Let's go out on the back deck," Marge said, leading the way through the kitchen. "There's coffee in the thermos. Pour me a cup, too."

The coffee was a strong French roast, the Berkeley influence again. In Berkeley, they take coffee almost as seriously as politics, and they brew it strong enough to qualify as a controlled substance. If Marge had been drinking much of this, I didn't expect Melissa to stay asleep for long.

I poured two cups of the marvelous brew and followed Marge onto the sunny little deck just behind the kitchen. She put the baby into a wicker basket in the shade and we settled down in the sun.

"I need your expertise," I said.

"Expertise," she replied. "What an appealing idea. After six weeks as a full-time mommy, I don't feel like an expert at much of anything."

"Not even at being a mommy?"

"Especially not that."

"I've got a case that involves a man who was sexually abused when he was nine. Do you ever handle cases like that?" I asked.

Something subtle shifted in Marge. I've seen it in cops socializing in a bar when someone suspicious comes in, the switch from private to professional. "Not many recently," she said, "but I did my internship with a county agency that counseled both victims and juvenile offenders."

"You mean kids who molested other kids?"

She nodded. "Not so unusual, unfortunately. Someone did a study based on interviews with abusers in prison, promised them immunity, and many admitted that they started acting out when they were eight or nine."

I must have looked skeptical, because she hurried on. "We're not talking about playing doctor here. We're talking force or coercion with a younger child."

Melissa stirred and Marge turned automatically in response. After a second, she turned back to me.

"Where does it come from in that young a child?" I asked.

"Usually, these are kids who were abused themselves at a younger age. You hear some pretty awful stories. And the abuser is usually a parent or relative. Is your case incest?"

I shook my head. "No, this was a man who befriended the boy."

"Could be a pedophile."

"What can you tell me about this sort of thing?"

"If it's pedophilia, I see it as a lot like incest, really. It's a devastating betrayal of trust. The child loves someone, trusts them, feels loved by them, then that person demands sex. The adult can give them all kinds of fancy reasons why it's fine, but the child senses that it's not. The adult keeps pressing, and the kid gives in because even if he doesn't want to do it, he can't face losing this adult who is so important to him. You can imagine what that does to a child's head."

"Be pretty hard to trust anybody after that."

"Absolutely. If someone you love can do that to you, it makes the world a very dangerous place. And that doesn't go away. You have thirty-year-old men and women walking around who can't form a relationship because they can't stand to get too close to anyone."

I thought of Joe Girard's description of Mitch—a drifter, an alcoholic, a man who had to turn for help to a cousin he hadn't seen in years. It all fit.

Marge took a sip of coffee and continued. "It reduces a kid. He felt loved and valued, now he feels like a sex object.

He couldn't put that in words, but that's what it is. It makes the child feel pretty worthless.''

How many times had I warned my niece, Molly, not to be too friendly with strangers, never considering that one's friends could be as great a danger? It galled me in my feminist soul to realize that I thought of girls as more vulnerable than boys.

Marge seemed to read my mind. ''In a way it's harder for boys,'' she said. ''Girls are treated as victims and get all kinds of sympathy. But boys don't get that kind of support. They're often blamed as nasty little perverts looking for sex or put down for being victims. Boys aren't supposed to be victims, even little boys. They feel powerless, unmanly, deeply shamed. They doubt their masculinity, wonder if they're gay. Just like many rape victims, they're apt to feel that they're responsible for what happened.

''It's terribly confusing for them. They don't understand much about physiology. If someone strokes them, and they get an erection, they feel like they must have wanted it, where in fact it's a purely physical reaction. Sure, they enjoy the actual orgasm, but they hate themselves for enjoying it.''

The baby stirred again and began to fuss. This time Marge got up and went to her. She rocked the cradle gently, and the fussing subsided. She stood gazing down at the sleeping baby for a few moments, then returned to our conversation.

''What can you tell me about the pedophile?'' I asked.

''Not as much. They're often guys who've been abused themselves. They're not usually gay; that's a misconception.'' She paused. ''Some people might argue that, but they often have wives and families of their own and they're not interested in adult men, so in my book, they are not gay.''

''Do they repeat over time?''

''Oh yes, especially if they're fixated. We categorized them as either fixated or regressed. The regressed pedophile can have a fairly normal sex life, but when he's under a lot of stress—divorce, loss of a job, some other strain—he may turn to kids for sex, and he'll select a victim based on availability—boy, girl, younger, older, it won't matter so much.

"The fixated pedophile has a much narrower range. He's attracted to kids of a certain age, and when they mature beyond that age, he loses interest."

"My client's cousin was molested when he was nine, and the relationship ended when he was eleven."

"That fits. Many abusers are fixated on prepubescent boys. As soon as their victims develop adult characteristics, they lose their appeal. See, if the abuser was molested as a child, adult sexuality is scary to him."

I raised my cup to take a drink of coffee and found it empty. I'd been so intent on what Marge was saying that I'd been unaware of finishing it.

"All this happened twenty-five years ago. Is it likely that the molester is still active?"

"If he's fixated, there's a good chance that he is. And his victims will be about the same age."

"Will he be involved with more than one boy at a time?"

"Probably. That prison study I mentioned earlier estimated that each pedophile averaged over three hundred victims."

I left Marge's a half hour later knowing more than I wanted about the victimization of children. I wasn't convinced that Samuel Reiter was a child molester, but I understood more clearly the importance of finding out.

Carl Edwards, the bartender, had an apartment in a three-story brick building below Broadway in a neighborhood that was just hanging on to respectability. There was a parking place in front, always a sign of good luck, and as I approached the door, a woman with a small child in tow was on her way out.

The child wanted to stay home and was working up to a full-scale tantrum, so the woman didn't even notice as I slipped past her and through the door. The bartender's apartment was number 23.

A large black man in his midfifties opened the door. He had powerful shoulders and a large gut. His right hand was missing a finger. He did not looked thrilled to see me.

"You try to serve me with a goddamn paper and I'll toss your ass down the stairs," he snarled.

"Not me," I said, holding my hands palms out. "I don't bounce well enough to go serving papers."

He made a snorting sound that was probably as close as he came to laughter. "So what do you want?"

"I want you to invite me in so I don't have to stand out here in the hall."

"Yeah, why?"

"Because I need some information, and I'm prepared to pay for it."

Pay was the magic word. He stepped aside and made a vague gesture that was probably intended to welcome me to his humble abode. Inside was neater and better-furnished than I'd expected, not luxurious, but neat enough to make me think he didn't live alone.

I sat down on an armchair covered with a green-and-brown plaid that could only have been bought by someone who was color-blind. He sat on the couch.

"So, what kind of information and how much?" he asked.

"A guy was killed in your parking lot last week. What do you know about it?"

"Not much. Nobody I knew."

"Had he been in the bar that night?"

"Not that I saw."

"Do you get many white guys in Jerry's?"

"Some. Neighborhood guys."

"But not strangers."

He shook his head. "Not usually."

"Hey, come on," I said, "I'm not a cop. I'm willing to pay for anything you can tell me, but you'll have to come up with more than three-word answers. It sounds to me like you'd have noticed if a new white guy had been there that night."

"Yeah, I probably would have. I don't think he came in."

"You know the neighborhood. Does it make sense to you that this guy, who is supposed to have been streetwise and was taking Antabuse, should have been in your parking lot that night?''

"Could have been there to buy drugs. Them cokeheads don't have a lick of sense. Danger don't mean nothing to them."

"There's no evidence of drug use," I said.

"Beats me, then. Hell, I wouldn't hang out down there if I had any choice. That neighborhood's changed. It's always been tough; now it's crazy."

"You know anything you didn't tell the police, something worth me paying you for?''

"Not a thing," he said, clearly regretting it.

"What about the guys who hang out at the bar or in the neighborhood? Could any of them have seen anything?''

"It's possible."

"You find someone who knows something, I'll pay you both. How much depends on what you find."

He nodded. "Sure, I'll ask around, but don't expect a lot. Most of these guys learned long ago that it don't pay to know too much."

6

I COULD HAVE questioned the patrons of Jerry's myself, but I wouldn't have gotten anything more than frustration out of the experience. I'd wait a couple of days, then have Jesse stop by and ask about the shooting. He could do his street-thug act or his FBI impersonation. If Carl called to let me know that someone had been asking around, he'd be twenty dollars richer, and I'd know there was a good chance I could rely on him.

I got back to the office just after five, a miracle commute at rush hour in postquake San Francisco (Peter would have called it freeway karma). After the quake, Caltrans had managed to repair the Bay Bridge in just two months, letting cars once again flow into San Francisco. But since they hadn't repaired the damaged off ramps, those same cars just sat on the freeway once they got there.

"Your sister called about an hour ago," my secretary, Amy, announced. "She asked that you call back immediately. She's at home in Palo Alto. She says it's urgent."

My heart went into overdrive, and I thought immediately of my mother and father. My dad, the original Type A, was a prime candidate for a heart attack. I prayed this wasn't it as I punched in the number on the phone.

My sister, Marion, is a couple of years younger than I am. I spent much of my childhood tormenting her, and she spent most of hers running to mom with tales of my misdeeds. She was a prissy kid with a long memory, and she never grew out of it. Neither one of us is the type of person the other would want to know if she had any choice.

"Catherine?" Marion's voice, tight with tension, filled me with foreboding. "Molly's run away."

I felt a rush of relief, then concern. Molly was fourteen years old, and I knew that her relationship with her mother had been stormy recently, but had assumed their battles were a normal part of adolescence. "How long has she been gone, and what makes you so sure she's run away?" I asked.

"We had an argument last night, and she announced that she was spending the night with a girlfriend and stormed out of the house. The school called to say she was absent. The friend's mother told me she hadn't been there. I called a bunch of kids, and one finally told me that Molly had gone to San Francisco."

"Have you notified the police?"

"No. They wouldn't do much, and besides I don't want to make too big a deal out of this."

"So you think she'll come back on her own?"

"Who knows?" I could tell by the tone that Marion was

moving from worry to complaint. I stretched out the phone cord so I could walk around my desk and sit down in my chair.

"It's like she's been a different person since she hit adolescence," Marion continued. "She used to be so responsible and helpful. Now she's full of anger and resentment. I can't ask her a simple question without having her bite my head off.

"She hates Leonard. She's absolutely awful to him. And she's jealous of the baby. I don't know what she'll do anymore."

Marion had remarried three years ago and had had a baby a year later. It seemed pretty normal to me that Molly might resent having a new father and a new baby sister thrust into her life, but I didn't say that to Marion. Not again. She never listened to me, anyway.

"Let me ask Peter what he'd suggest," I said. "He deals with runaways fairly frequently."

"Peter?" Marion's voice was sharp. "Are you still with *him*?"

I clenched my teeth and tried very hard not to respond like a twelve-year-old. It was such a vintage Marion statement; a deft swipe of disapproval for which there was no satisfactory response.

"What do you want from me, Marion?" I asked in as neutral a tone as I could manage.

"I don't know. I just don't know what to do. Maybe I should just call the police and let them deal with it. Maybe that would teach her a lesson."

"If you think she's in danger, by all means call the police. If you think she's just trying to scare you, you could hold off till tomorrow. Give her a chance to change her mind and come back on her own."

"Her change her mind? Not likely. She's just as stubborn as . . ." She paused looking for an appropriate comparison. "As stubborn as you used to be," she spat out. I wasn't sure whether the anger was directed at Molly or at me, but I felt a real stab of pity for my niece.

I hadn't seen much of Molly for the last year or so. Before

that she'd frequently spent weekends at my place. Marion and I are too different to ever be close, but Molly and I are soul mates. She's adventuresome and curious, enthusiastic and mischievous, and she has a wonderful, irreverent sense of humor that her mother hates and I adore.

Her father moved out when Molly was young, leaving Marion to manage as a single parent. I'd taken Molly as often as I could, just to give both mother and daughter a break. The older Molly got, the more I enjoyed her company. She'd been my weekend buddy until her baby sister came along and she became Marion's babysitter.

Peter and I had spent a week with Molly backpacking in the Sierras last year, and I'd had a chance to observe the effects of adolescence up close. She was still capable of enthusiasm and humor, but there was a new self-consciousness and a moodiness. She complained bitterly about Marion and Leonard, school, kids at school, and life in general. I'd chalked it up to normal adolescent alienation and pressures at home. Somewhere along the way, it had become more.

Peter and I arrived home about the same time. I told him about Molly before he got to the kitchen.

"This is the first time she's run off, isn't it?" he asked as he got a beer out of the refrigerator.

"As far as I know, but things have been rocky at home for over a year."

"With Marion for a mother, I can't imagine why."

"I haven't paid a lot of attention to what was going on there, but I know Marion's complained about Molly missing school and hanging out with 'the wrong crowd.' "

Peter leaned against the sink and took a drink of beer. "That'd worry me more if I hadn't been part of the wrong crowd in high school. I can't see Molly enjoying kids who fit Marion's idea of the right crowd."

I had to agree, but when I was in high school the wrong crowd wore love beads; now they wore skulls and daggers. "I don't like the idea of her in San Francisco on her own. She's only fourteen."

Peter nodded gravely. He knew far better than I the dangers runaways faced on the streets of San Francisco. "Did she come alone?"

"I don't know, but I think she has older friends here. I can remember Marion complaining about them."

"Molly's a pretty together kid. I can't see her just jumping on a bus and being picked up by a pimp at the bus station."

I couldn't either. Molly had good sense, and she had always been reasonably careful. She was adventuresome and a bit impulsive, but she didn't take foolish chances. I could see her moving in with a friend for a few days to scare her mom, but I couldn't see her living on the streets.

"The danger is that she'll trust the wrong person or experiment with drugs and get in over her head. What do you know about her friends?" Peter asked.

"Marion's been complaining about that for years. Molly hangs out with a bunch of kids who dress in black and wear skulls and daggers. I always assumed it was just a harmless form of youthful rebellion."

"Probably is, but if one of those kids is a runaway with ties to the street community, it could mean trouble. Then there'd be a place to stay, and it wouldn't be a place you'd want for Molly."

We were interrupted by Stone's lost-cat-from-hell wail at the back door, his friendly reminder that it was time to eat. "So what do we do?" I asked as I let the beggar in.

"I can get out on the street and talk to some kids I know. I'll take the school picture from your desk."

"How about talking to her friends? I can get Marion to give me their names and numbers."

"That'd be good, if Marion knows anything about Molly's friends. Somehow I can't see her inviting the bones-and-dagger set into the 'house beautiful.'" Peter reached for the cat food. I handed him the dish while Stone flung himself against our legs.

"No, but I'll bet she's already been through Molly's room several times. She probably knows where she keeps her phone numbers."

"Undoubtedly. I'd take it easy on the friends. They're not going to tell you where she is, so it's best just to ask them to give her a message, ask her to call you. Remember that in their eyes, you're probably lumped together with Marion and Leonard."

"What an appalling thought."

Peter's rounds took him several hours and produced nothing more than promises to keep an eye out for Molly. My call to Marion got me a list of complaints about my niece, a soliloquy on the trials of parenting a teenager, and finally, seven names and numbers annotated with lengthy dissertations on the character defects of each individual.

I tried real hard to be as patient with Marion as I would be with a distraught client, but it just didn't work. Maybe because we've done this dance too many times. Maybe because no one was paying me to listen. Finally, I said, "Marion, for godssake, don't you feel anything but anger over Molly's disappearance?"

Silence. Then a choked sob. "I'm so worried, Catherine. Those kids she hangs around with scare me. I don't know what they might get her into. It's so dangerous to be a kid now. Everything, the drugs, the gangs, even sex. She could decide to experiment and end up with AIDS. Oh, God, I just don't know what to do."

I tried to comfort Marion, which was a whole lot better than listening to her complain, and wondered why I never remembered that beneath her fiercest anger is usually fear. Her first response is to be pissed off, always has been, even in situations where she ought to be scared. I handle my fear by trying to stay in touch with it; she handles hers by refusing to feel it. By tomorrow she'd be back to anger again, and she'd be particularly mad at me for making her feel the fear.

I called the seven friends and was able to reach five of them. They responded as Peter had suggested they would, in truculent monotones and single syllables. None of them even faked surprise at Molly's disappearance, and I was sure that they all knew where she'd gone, but they weren't about to tell anyone over sixteen.

7

WITH MOLLY MISSING, I didn't sleep much that night. That was just as well since it spared me my dreams. A vivid imagination can be a real curse, especially when unleashed by sleep. I spent the night listening for the doorbell to ring. It didn't.

I'd decided to wait twenty-four hours before doing anything more about Molly. That left me with only one thing to do. I went to work. At least, my body went to work. It took over an hour for my mind to get there. When it did, I realized I needed to know more about child molesters if I was to investigate Judge Samuel Reiter.

I'd talked to a therapist; the next step was to talk to a cop in the Juvenile Division. I called some friends in the SFPD to find out who to contact. Steve Marley seemed to be the man. I left a message for him, and he called back later in the morning.

Marley's voice was pleasant and his accent put him from someplace in the Midwest. He was willing to see me but was leaving Monday for two weeks' vacation.

"Is there any chance of seeing you today?" I asked.

"Today's not so hot. I'm waiting for a search warrant, and once it comes, I'll be tied up, probably for the rest of the day."

"Could I talk to you while you wait for the warrant?"

"Sure, so long as you understand that we could be inter-

rupted. You know where we are? Not down at the Hall of
Justice. Over on Greenwich, near the Marina.''

Greenwich Street is over the hill from my office, and I'd
driven past the SFPD Juvenile Division often enough to know
where to find it. The building itself is a tasteful one-story
Spanish style, but it is adorned with two giant iron lighting
fixtures that look as if they came from someone's idea of a
Middle Eastern palace.

I rang the bell and was admitted to a cluttered office where
metal file cabinets lined the walls and covered the windows.
A large vending machine full of junk food provided a bit of
color in the otherwise gray room. The dark-skinned woman
sitting behind the desk was anything but gray. She wore a
bright purple dress and was attractive enough to inspire many
trips to the vending machine.

I told her I had an appointment with Steve Marley, and
she made a call and informed me that he'd be right out. A
couple of minutes later, a tall, slender man in his mid-forties
appeared in the doorway. He was wearing jeans and a sport
coat over a blue-and-white-striped sports shirt.

''Catherine Sayler?''

I nodded and put out my hand. ''Inspector Marley?''

''Steve, please. Come this way, but watch out for the file
cabinets. For some reason, they've decided to move them
today.''

I followed him through a large room that seemed absolutely full of file cabinets, and down a narrow corridor to his
office. Like every other police office I've seen, this one was
too small for its occupant and all his papers. However, Steve
Marley dealt with the problem by organizing his space as
neatly as a ship's cabin. Boxes of materials and files were
stowed under the desk and table. Hanging files and stacked
trays covered the table and much of his desk.

On the wall next to his desk hung a poster board filled with
snapshots of faces, mostly male, with a paragraph of text
next to each one. He caught me trying to read the type.

''That's my rogue's gallery,'' he said. ''I keep it for the

brass who can't figure out what it is we do down here. I figure that every one of these guys we put away means maybe a hundred kids that are safe, at least for a while.''

''A hundred kids for each guy?''

''Depends, but for some of them, sure. That guy there,'' he pointed at the photo of an overweight, balding man, ''Doug Duarte. Doug had names of a hundred and twenty kids he'd molested over the last few years. You should have seen his place. It was like a fantasy world for preteen boys—jars of candy and snacks, computer games, a VCR with every movie any kid ever wanted to see, a fridge stocked with ice cream.''

I peered at the photo and reflected on the banality of evil. Like so many of the men who are arrested for heinous crimes, Doug looked more like the checker at your corner grocery store than a man who wantonly destroyed lives. If he wasn't someone you'd invite home to tea, he sure wasn't anyone you'd pay any attention to on the street.

''Are all those men pedophiles?'' I asked.

Marley nodded. ''But there are differences. Some prefer boys, some girls. Some like little kids, others go for teenagers.''

''Are they violent?'' I asked.

''Not if you mean do they grab kids in the park and drag them into the bushes. They handle those guys downtown. But you have to understand that with a kid there are subtle kinds of force that an adult has just because he's an adult. Kids are taught to obey—they feel powerless—and these guys play on that.''

''Let me tell you about a client, and you tell me what you think of the story,'' I said as I sat down.

Marley settled into his chair, leaned back, and put his feet up on a box of files. ''Shoot.''

I repeated what Joe had told me about his cousin Mitch, omitting the name of the molester but identifying him as a judge. Marley nodded occasionally. When I finished, he said, ''It's possible, though I've got to tell you that in a situation like this you have to be very careful. We're getting the story secondhand from an adult. And that adult could have lots of reasons for wanting to smear the man he's accusing, especially since that man is a public figure. I'd be very careful about saying anything publicly until I had a lot more than an accusation.''

Getting more than an accusation was exactly what Joe had hired me to do. I hoped Marley had some suggestions on how to do that. Before I could ask, he continued. "But let's assume what your client told you is true. The story does make sense. The molester was into prepubescent boys; when the kid hit puberty, he lost interest in him. Were there other kids?''

"You mean did he molest other kids before or after?''

"No, I mean was this Mitch the only one, or were there other boys around at the same time? Frequently, these guys will encourage a whole bunch of kids, and they'll have the kids bring their friends. The guy doesn't go after all the kids, he picks the one he wants, the ones he knows he can get to.''

"Joe didn't mention other boys, but I'll ask. How do they choose a kid? Do you know what they're looking for?''

Marley nodded. "They're like any predator. They hone in on the vulnerable ones. A lion doesn't go after the biggest buck. He watches the herd and picks out the sick or the old or the lame. These guys are the same. They watch for a kid who's alone, the one on the edge of the crowd.

"They're very good at spotting what a kid needs and providing that. Sometimes it's friendship; this guy becomes his best buddy. Sometimes it's a father figure; the guy becomes the greatest father a kid could imagine. He offers love, attention, respect, all the stuff the kid doesn't get at home. The sex doesn't come till the kid is really attached, so attached that he can't give up the relationship. Even then it comes slow. We're talking seduction, not force.''

"He told Mitch he'd teach him about being a man," I said.

Marley nodded. "That's fairly common. But I'd bet that even that didn't come out of the blue. There were probably weeks of jokes about sex, maybe more touching than before, maybe watching porno movies, stuff that sets the stage and lets the molester know that the kid isn't going to bolt.''

"It really is a kind of seduction, isn't it?''

"You bet it is. And it can go on for a long time. This isn't just about having sex, you see. These guys are obsessed with kids. They fantasize about kids, they're completely focused on them.''

"But the judge was married at the time,'' I said.

Marley shrugged. "Not so unusual. So are some of the guys on the wall. Some even have families. The ones that are really fixated don't have a lot of time for a relationship with another adult, but a lot of them manage. It's like they have two lives.''

"And the wife doesn't know?'' I asked incredulously.

Marley shook his head. "Two lives,'' he repeated, holding up two fingers and spreading them apart. "They keep them separate.''

"But he brought Mitch to his house.''

"Maybe she was off working, or she was a high-society type who was always playing golf or going to tea. And probably she didn't *want* to know. Lots of people just don't see what they don't want to see. You should hear some of the child abuse and incest cases; the wife sits there and sobs about her poor baby and how she didn't know, and you think, how could she *not* know, but they can't because they don't let themselves.''

My mind jumped back to Orrin Merrick. Had there been signs I didn't want to see that should have told me what was going to happen? Had I let my desire to close the case blind me to the games the company brass were playing?

"From what I've told you, what are the chances that the judge is still molesting kids?''

"If what you've been told is true, very good, I'd say. If we're right that he's fixated on one type of kid, one age, then he's not going to change. It isn't something he'll outgrow. It's a compulsion.''

"But now that he's a judge, that he's in a fairly visible

position where he stands to lose so much, maybe it's just too much of a gamble.''

Marley shook his head. ''We're not talking a preference for chocolate ice cream here. This is a basic part of a guy's personality, especially if it's been going on for a while. Besides, you said he was active with boys' clubs. If he had been a molester and been able to stop, he sure wouldn't be putting himself in that kind of temptation. No, he's still doing it.''

''Steve.'' A loud voice boomed out just behind my head and made me jump in my seat. ''Sorry to interrupt, but the Armstrong warrant just came through. Jordan'd like to move on it as soon as you can.''

Marley swung his feet to the floor and sat up straight in his chair. ''I'll call you when I'm through here,'' he said to the man who'd appeared at the door, motioning him away.

''I won't take much more of your time,'' I promised. ''If the judge is still molesting kids, how do I prove it?''

''You'll need to find a victim. We have to have an incident report before we can act, it's the same in Piedmont. And given the status of your man, that he's a judge and has friends in high places, you'll need something pretty substantial.''

''How do I find the victim?''

''Find out where the judge meets kids. The boys' club is an obvious starting place, but he may be involved several places. He may have several kids, all from one place or each from a different one.''

''And once I've found one of these kids?''

''That's the toughest part. The kid isn't going to just tell you what's happening. Victims feel a lot of shame and guilt about this. They don't want to talk about it. Even though they don't like what's happening, they'll deny it.''

''So how do you get them to talk about it?''

''It takes time, time and a lot of trust. I let them know that I understand what's happened and why they don't want to talk about it. I tell them about other kids so they feel less alone. Try to reassure them that it's not their fault. Takes hours, sometimes days to get through. They *really* don't want to talk about it.

"But it's the only way. If they don't admit it, don't get it out there where you can deal with it, it just stays inside and festers. You can't get them any help till they've taken that step. There isn't any other way."

I nodded, touched by the depth of feeling I heard in his voice. "So the first step is to find a victim."

"As many as you can get, because the more kids you have, the better your chances that one of them will cooperate."

"If I succeed, I'll need someone to help get the kids to talk. Do you ever work as a consultant?"

He considered it for a moment, and said, "It's tempting, but my vacation starts Monday, and I promised the wife I'd paint the kitchen and do all the other stuff I've put off."

"I pay fifty dollars an hour for consultants. You could work for me and hire a painter to do the kitchen."

He smiled broadly. "You got a deal. I'll have to check it with Oakland, since it's their jurisdiction. But I don't think that'll be a problem. With luck I might even get time for some fishing."

As I stood to go I thought of one more question. "Mitch's cousin doesn't believe that his death was an accident. I don't have the evidence to know either way. Is a guy like this more likely to kill someone?"

Marley considered it. "Being a pedophile doesn't predispose them to violence if that's what you mean. But anyone involved in a crime has a lot to lose if they're caught. You got someone desperate to protect a secret, there's always a chance they'll freak out. Then anything can happen."

8

THERE ARE FEW things harder than blocking an insistent thought. I knew there was no point in worrying about Molly, but that didn't keep me from doing it. She sat at the edge of my thoughts and my mind raced back to her in defiance of my wishes. My interviews with Marge Domingo and Steve Marley did not contribute to my peace of mind.

I hurried back to the office with only one thing on my mind, the possibility that Molly had called. Amy informed me she hadn't and that there were no messages on my answering machine at home. I could see that this was going to be a long day.

About that time, Jesse arrived wearing jeans and an Oakland A's sweatshirt. "You've got some nerve wearing that around here," I said. Amy and I are faithful Giants fans. Every year we ride the rollercoaster with them. Most years the ride down is a lot longer than the climb up.

Jesse had taken his share of merciless ribbing when the Reds swept the series, but it didn't make up for what we'd had to put up with during the regular season.

"How's it going in Sunnyvale?" I asked.

"No bites yet, but someone paid a very discreet visit to my apartment yesterday. Real professional job. I figure they were checking me out. If I passed, I'll hear from them soon."

"Any reason you might not have passed?"

"Nope. Nothing there that would indicate I'm anyone but who I claim to be. Boy, I hope they bite soon. This warehouse job is absolutely mind-numbing. I spend all day checking numbers in a logbook against numbers on boxes, and the numbers in the logbook are smaller than print in a phone book. I do hate honest labor.''

We all laughed. "So, Catherine, Amy says you're working on something. Just couldn't stay away, huh?''

"Like the old firehorse.''

"What is it?''

I told him, and his grin faded. When I finished, he said, "Catherine, I'm supposed to be the wild one around here. You are supposed to be responsible and prudent. You are forgetting your place.''

"This doesn't look responsible and prudent to you?''

"Not by a country mile.''

"Good,'' I said. "I was never too fond of responsible.''

After Jesse left, I went back over my notes on the case. What's missing can often tell you more than what's actually there. I'm good at spotting what's missing in a corporate setting. It took me a bit longer here.

What was missing was Mitch's address. Joe should have spoken to Mitch's friend Artie by now, yet I hadn't heard from him. He knew the apartment might hold clues to Mitch's activities. It was time we had another talk.

I called his office and got a secretary who was in protect mode. I told her I was from the IRS. She had Joe on the line in less than sixty seconds.

"What's Mitch's address?'' I asked.

"Jesus, Catherine, don't joke around about the IRS. That's no laughing matter in the movement.''

"Mitch's address?''

"Artie did have it. I got it here someplace.'' His tone was just a bit too casual.

"Joe, what's going on here? I thought you wanted me to work for you.''

"I do; I do.''

"Then why are you holding out on me? What's in that apartment that you don't want me to see?''

"Nothing. There's really not much there.''

"Joe,'' I said sharply.

There was a pause, then he said, "Oh shit, you're right. There was some stuff there I didn't want anyone to see."

"What sort of stuff?"

"Pictures. Pornography . . . with boys. Some of it is pretty offensive."

"Mitch is dead, Joe. That's pretty offensive. He's not around to be embarrassed. I'm not going to be embarrassed, and the police aren't going to be embarrassed. That leaves you. I'll pick up the keys in ten minutes."

Joe managed to clear his calendar and was waiting in front of his office when I got there.

Mitch's apartment was in a better part of town than I'd expected, not affluent, but a step up from skid row. The building was old, and the carpet had been there since before the '06 earthquake, but the halls smelled of curry instead of urine, and there was no graffiti on the walls.

"He'd been working in Alaska in the oil fields," Joe explained. "Till he messed up his leg. He'd saved enough to think maybe he could get a new start. He was off the booze, going to AA. I'd like to think he might have made it this time."

The apartment itself was obviously just a stop on the way to somewhere else. Mitch had invested in as little furniture as he could get away with—a mattress, a card table and two chairs, and a secondhand couch and chipped coffee table. The television set in the corner was probably on its third or fourth owner.

Mitch handed me a black binder. "I found this hidden under the mattress," he said.

I think of myself as an openminded person, tolerant of others' ways. The black binder reminded me that tolerance has its limits, and it's a damn good thing. The pictures were eight-by-ten glossy photos of naked boys in provocative poses. The youngest were barely out of diapers and gazed out at the camera in awkward innocence, holding poses that someone else had arranged for them. The older ones who looked to be in their early teens had a conscious seductiveness, like hookers on a street corner, but their eyes were flat and dead.

The boys were all Hispanic. There were twenty of them, all posed against a whitewashed brick wall. After the portraits, there were a half-dozen pages of candid photos of men and boys engaged in various forms of sexual activity. The men's faces had been blacked out; the boys' had not.

I sat and stared at the last page, in a place of pure emotion beyond the reaches of rational thought. I'm used to thinking in terms of right and wrong, legal and illegal, but these pictures went far beyond that. They spoke of a side of human nature that I didn't like to look at.

I knew why Joe didn't want me to see them. He was afraid I'd be so revolted that I'd refuse to work on Mitch's case. The book certainly complicated things, but I don't bail out that easily. If anything, the case had just become considerably more important, and if I had less sympathy for Mitch, I had plenty for the boys in the pictures.

"You think these were Mitch's?" I asked.

"They must have been. How else did they get here?"

"You realize that your cousin may turn out to be a pedophile?"

Joe nodded glumly.

"And you want me to go ahead, even if that's what we may find out?"

"Yes." His voice was hoarse. "I don't believe he could have been. There must be some other explanation."

"That's possible," I said. "Mitch could have come across them when he was investigating Reiter. Or they could be part of a setup. He could have decided to plant them at Reiter's house."

"I suppose they could be from Reiter." That possibility seemed to cheer Joe substantially. "Do you think we can prove that?"

I doubted it, but I got out my tape recorder and described each of the pictures in as much detail as I could stand. The candids were tough going, especially those involving young boys. Amy was not going to like transcribing this tape.

My interview with Steve Marley was still fresh in my mind. He'd shown me some pornography seized from the home of a pedophile. The pictures he'd seized were grainy Xeroxes, and there'd only been six or eight of them. The album was high-quality work, probably shot and printed by a professional. I wondered what Marley would make of it.

I'd have to turn it over to the police when they searched Mitch's apartment, but after all this time, an extra day wouldn't make much difference. Especially if they didn't know about it.

Mitch's sparse life-style made the search fairly easy. There wasn't much out in plain sight, and there weren't a lot of places to hide things. A bottle of Antabuse sat in the kitchen and a plastic pillbox divided into sections for each day of the week sat beside it. The compartments for Friday and Saturday contained pills; the others were empty.

"What day of the week was Mitch killed?" I asked Joe.

"Thursday."

"Then he was still on his Antabuse."

"See, I told you he wouldn't go to a bar," Joe said.

We found further indications of Mitch's efforts at sobriety in the AA booklets that seemed to be the main reading material in the apartment. There were two copies of *One Day at a Time*, one next to the couch, the other in the bedroom, and numerous other AA titles in various locations. A blue hardcover book, known as the Big Book, lay open next to the bed. It had a well-thumbed appearance that suggested Mitch had turned to it often.

I checked the book for telephone numbers, the lifeline that recovering alcoholics establish to help them through the hardest times. But the last page had been cut out. I wondered where it was and why it had been removed.

The phone was in the bedroom, and beside it, the red light on the answering machine blinked. I pushed the playback button and a gruff voice said, "I got those magazines you wanted. Don't ask me to do any more of this shit." There was a pause, and a slightly gentler voice said, "It's Mel. I haven't heard from you for a while. How are you doing?

We've missed you at meetings. I'm here anytime you need me." That was the last message.

"Who's Mel?" I asked.

Joe shook his head. "I don't know. I didn't know his friends."

The reference to missing him at meetings made me suspect that Mel was someone in AA, maybe even Mitch's sponsor. I've had some experience with AA. Drinking problems often go right along with stealing and embezzling problems, and part of the restitution deal can involve solving the former so these guys have some chance of earning money to repay their employer.

Once people have been in AA for a while and are really committed to recovery, they're urged to choose a sponsor, someone who possesses whatever it is they want to achieve. It's a good plan: Set a goal for yourself, find someone who's already attained it, and have them help you figure out how to succeed at it yourself. The relationship requires absolute trust and truthfulness. If anyone knew what Mitch was up to, it would be his sponsor.

I pulled the mattress off the springs and found something Joe had overlooked, a spiral-bound notebook of drawing paper. The pages were covered with pencil sketches; most were of faces, though there were some figures and a few landscapes. I stopped at a full-page sketch that was unmistakably Joe. The drawing was rough, but in remarkably few strokes it captured not only its subject's features but the intensity of his gaze.

There were a number of sketches of boys, but the sexual charge of the photographs was missing in the drawings. These were simply portraits, catching their subjects in a variety of moods ranging from gleeful to contemplative. Some were quick sketches of only a few lines, others were more fully developed. All had a vitality and rough honesty that set them far above the work of a Sunday painter.

"I thought he'd quit drawing," Joe said quietly as he looked over my shoulder.

"He really was very talented," I said.

Joe nodded. "He could have done so much." There were tears in his voice.

I turned one more page and found portraits of two men staring out at me. One man was unquestionably Samuel Reiter. The other was a man in his mid-forties with a square jaw, wide-set eyes, and a bland but pleasant-enough face.

"Do you know him?" I asked.

Joe shook his head. "Never saw him before."

It could be random chance that Mitch had drawn the two men on the same page, or they could be connected. If they were linked in some way in the artist's mind, I wanted to know more about Reiter's mysterious companion.

With each revelation, Mitch became a more complex and contradictory character, and nothing we had found made it any easier to judge the truth of his allegations against Samuel Reiter. I put both books—the photographs and the sketches—aside. I'd want a copy of the sketches and a professional opinion of the photos.

I sat Joe down on the couch and had him tell me exactly how he'd learned of Mitch's death and everything he'd done in connection with it. We went over the funeral arrangements, his search for the car, and his visit to the apartment. He'd told me most of it at our first meeting, and there weren't any contradictions. The words were all right, but the nonverbal messages didn't fit.

"Joe," I said, "there's something I need to know. Why are you holding out on me?" I didn't ask if he was holding out or what he wasn't telling me. That would have gotten me a denial. Instead, I asked, "Is there some reason you don't want me to find out what happened to Mitch?"

"No, no, it isn't that," he said. Then realizing he'd admitted to more than he intended, he snapped his mouth shut.

"Does it have something to do with Judge Reiter?"

It must have looked like a brilliant bit of deduction, but I'd just stumbled into it. It wasn't until his face registered alarm that I had any idea where this might be going.

"Tell me about it," I said.

For once Joe avoided making eye contact. He stared at the

stained beige carpet on Mitch's floor. "Mitch wasn't the only one," he said, his voice so low I could barely hear him. "He wasn't the only one Sam molested. And he didn't meet Sam through the chess club. I met him there."

He looked up at me and now his gaze challenged me to look away. "I was sort of a lonely, nerdy little kid who didn't fit anywhere—not school, not my family, no place. Sam understood me. He took me to plays, the symphony, the ballet, art galleries. He opened up a whole new world for me. And he told me how he'd felt just like I did as a kid.

"Here was this terrific, successful man telling me that I wasn't an ugly duckling but a swan, and showing me how great the world could be for people like us. I worshiped him."

He stopped, and looked down quickly. "He had this collection of *Playboys* and other nudie photos that he'd let me look at. He said he wanted to teach me about being a man. He'd taught me so much else—what to read, how to eat at a fancy restaurant, what to wear to a play—it didn't seem as weird as it sounds.

"I wanted to please him," he said desperately. "I loved him so much and he'd done so much for me that I couldn't say no."

"And Mitch?"

"Mitch was two years younger than me. He stayed with us for a month one summer because his dad was drinking and his mom couldn't handle them both. Sam suggested I bring him along on an outing, and I did. Mitch didn't like the plays and cultural stuff, but we did a lot of hiking and boating that he loved. Pretty soon he was part of the scene."

"Weren't you jealous?" I asked.

"Not really. Sam still had plenty of time for me." He paused, then jumped up and began to pace. "To tell the truth, I was glad. It made it seem more okay somehow that we were both doing it. As if, I don't know, as if everyone was really doing this, but they just didn't talk about it.

"That fall I turned twelve and my voice and body started changing. That was when Sam told me it was time for me to give up the kid stuff and start paying attention to girls. He took me out several more times, but the sex stopped and the closeness was gone.''

Joe was pacing with such intensity that I was afraid I'd get a crick in my neck from following him. I wished he'd sit down, but it was clear that he couldn't.

"It was awful," he said. "Like losing your lover, only worse, more like losing a parent. I was depressed for most of that year. *Then* I was jealous of Mitch, really jealous, because he'd taken my place. We were never close after that."

"Is that why you wouldn't help him unmask the judge?"

"No. Maybe a little, but mainly it was because I've worked hard to put that behind me. I've been in therapy for years. It was only a year ago that I could finally manage a relationship with a woman without destroying it when we started to get close. I just didn't want to bring all that back up. I wanted to get on with my life."

"Why haven't you gone to the police with this?"

He lit temporarily on the arm of the couch, and his eyes bored into mine. "I can't have this come out," he said fiercely. "How could I go into court with everyone looking at me and knowing what had happened? It's bad enough that it happened; I don't want to be reminded of it every time someone looks at me funny or I hear laughter from two guys in a corner."

I nodded. "I understand," I said, knowing that without actually being there you don't really understand. "Do you have any proof of the relationship, even if you won't take it to the police?"

Joe hesitated, then pulled out his wallet. "I found this in my old stuff after Mitch died. I don't know why I kept it. I put it in my wallet to remind me not to back down on this." He took out a snapshot and handed it to me.

The photo showed a man and a boy on a sailboat. Samuel Reiter's face hadn't changed so much over the years; recognizing Joe was only a little harder. In the picture Joe sat stiffly on Reiter's lap. Though they both wore swimsuits, there was something in the way Reiter held him that was seductive and sensual. It was nothing you could use in a court of law, but the feeling it generated in my stomach was proof enough for me.

"Mitch took the picture," Joe said. "And I took some of him. Sam made us take our suits off for the others."

He wasn't looking at me now, and his usual manic energy had drained from him, leaving him hunched and defeated. I knew more than he wanted anyone to know about him, and I feared that the price of that knowledge might be our friendship.

"Is there anything more I should know?" I asked.

"No." Joe shook his head. "That's it. It's enough."

I spent the afternoon talking with people who didn't know Mitch Morrison. The manager of the building could tell me that he'd moved in about a month ago, but that was all. It wasn't the kind of place that kept much information on its tenants. His neighbors had seen him come and go, but they didn't know anything about him.

A check of the neighborhood shops brought the same response. A few people remembered the scar and the stutter or thought maybe they did, but none of them knew anything about the man himself. The afternoon was an exercise in urban anonymity. It left me sad and vaguely depressed.

I headed back to the office to check for a call from Molly. The Morrison case, which should have distracted me from my worry, only fed it. Mitch's sketches were a painful reminder of how easily children can be robbed of their future.

9

S TEVE MARLEY'S PLANS for his vacation probably didn't include an invitation to look at dirty pictures. I was glad to be competing with a paint brush instead of a fishing pole. I didn't mention where the photos came from, just told him that I needed a professional opinion and asked him to come by after work. For fifty dollars an hour, he was happy to oblige.

He was in high spirits when he arrived, but his expression was grave as he looked through the photo album. As he turned the pages he automatically touched only their edges. He studied the candid photos carefully, then looked up at me.

"Where did you get this?"

"At Mitch Morrison's apartment."

He put on an official cop expression and said, "This is evidence in a homicide. You should have known better than to handle or move it."

"The Oakland police would already have that book if they'd done their job," I said. "Since they didn't, I did it for them. They're not going to tell me what I need to know. I hoped you would."

Marley studied me for what seemed like a long time. I met his eyes. What we decided about each other in those moments would determine whether or not we could work together.

Finally, he nodded. "Okay," he said slowly. "I'll help you if I can, but I won't be involved in any screwing around."

"I *never* screw around," I said.

He nodded again, then turned to the front of the book and went back through it.

"I don't know any of them," he announced. "Not the kids, and probably not the perps, though with the faces blackened out, it'd be hard to tell."

"What do you make of it?"

"Well, it's not your usual type of porn, that's for sure. I've never seen anything like it. With the portraits, it's almost like a sales catalog, maybe for a brothel. But if there were something like that around here, I think we'd have some hint of it. The kids are Hispanic. It could be in the valley or down in L.A."

"You're sure there's nothing like that in the Bay Area?"

"Not sure, no. Hell, there could be. I've broken a case where stuff's been going on for years, and I didn't have a clue about it. You wonder how the hell you could have missed it, but the guys who do this are working to keep it secret as hard as we're working to find out. And there are a lot more of them than us."

"What about the little ones? There are kids in there who aren't even in school yet."

"Yeah, ones that young, someone else has got to get them started, someone from the family or who's trusted by the family."

"A preschool or day-care provider?"

"Could be, though I think the danger of that is overplayed. After you turn this over to the homicide guys in Oakland, I'll ask them to let us make copies of the portraits and check them against runaways, kidnap victims, and kids with jackets in the juvi division. Then we'll run them by other departments as well. All we need is to ID one kid, and we'll have a place to start."

"Any idea why Mitch would have had the book?"

Steve shook his head. "It's not something a victim would keep around. This is a perp's book. Makes me wonder about your client's story, or at least his cousin's story. This thing may be a whole lot more complicated than it appears, and

I'd be careful making assumptions about bad guys and good guys till you have more information."

I thought about Joe's confession that afternoon. Could it have been faked? Anything can be faked. But I tend to trust my gut feelings, and I had a strong visceral sense that Joe had not lied when he described his childhood experience. Whether he'd lied earlier or been lied to by Mitch, that I didn't know.

I called the Oakland PD to give them the location of Mitch's apartment. John Warren was gone for the day, but another officer took the information and my name and number.

"I hope it doesn't put you in a difficult situation with the Oakland police," I said to Steve.

He shook his head. "Stuff happens."

I had checked my home answering machine several times, but there was no message from Molly. I called Marion as soon as I got home to confirm that she knew no more than I did. She'd decided to call the police if Molly wasn't back by the next morning. By then, Molly would have been missing for forty-eight hours. I tried not to think of the awful things that could happen to a kid alone in San Francisco. I wasn't very successful.

I poured myself a glass of white wine and collapsed on the sofa. Peter came around behind me and began to rub my neck. "Ouch," he said, "your trapeziuses are like steel. No wonder you get headaches."

I closed my eyes and tried to relax as his thumbs worked the knots out of my shoulders. It felt good to have his hands on my body. "We haven't had much of a love life lately, I'm afraid," I said.

"Pain and tension are not great aphrodisiacs," he said. "I do a fine full-body massage, and have even been known to muster the great restraint to avoid erogenous zones."

I reached up, drew his face down to mine, and gave him a kiss. "You are a saint."

"No, Saint Peter is someone else. I don't think he did massage."

Peter has great hands, but his willpower has its limits. It wasn't entirely his fault that he forgot his promise to avoid erogenous zones; I helped distract him from it.

We had a late dinner, and since it was my turn to shop, there wasn't a lot in the fridge. I scrounged up four eggs, a tomato, the last of the cheddar, and Greek olives that had been in the fridge forever but looked okay. Peter pinched some leaves from the oregano and marjoram that he'd been growing in a window box on the back porch, and we made omelettes.

We avoided the subject most on our minds, Molly, since there was nothing new to say and neither of us could face rehashing the dangers. Instead, I told Peter about Mitch's apartment and the mysterious book. "I don't know what to think of Mitch's story, or Joe's for that matter," I said. "My gut feeling is that Joe's telling the truth, as far as he knows it. Mitch is a wild card. He was a real loner, but he did go to AA regularly. If he was on to something, my best chance of finding out about it is there."

"That could be tough," Peter said. "Tough to find the meetings he attended, and even tougher to get anyone to talk to you. AA's a very tight circle; they don't talk with outsiders about what goes on in meetings."

"Would they talk to an insider?"

"Possibly. But you'd probably have to attend a couple of meetings before they trusted you. And remember we're not talking Rotary here. People don't go to the same meetings every time."

"It's my only lead."

"Then you're going to get to spend a lot of time reflecting on the effects of strong drink and your own indulgences. You want some help?"

"You'll come with me?"

"It's not my idea of a hot date, but it's better than some

of the things you've asked me to do. Besides, you'll need someone to go to the men-only meetings."

I nuzzled his neck. "Ah, kind sir, how can I ever thank you enough?"

"I'm sure you'll find a way," he said. He gave me a long, sexy kiss, and said, "You could start by doing the dishes."

"You wretch."

"I have to save myself for more important efforts, like attending AA meetings and being thanked," he said. "But to show you what a good guy I am, I'll dry."

Peter's approach to dirty dishes is to ignore them until you're out of clean ones. Mine is to avoid them by eating out. The result is a kitchen sink that we could rent out for dishwashing commercials.

I scraped a gluelike greenish substance out of a saucepan. "This may be alive," I said.

"Try not to think about it," Peter suggested. "Tell me more about the late Mr. Morrison."

"I've told you all I know, which is appallingly little. If I don't find someone who knew Mitch through AA, I'll have drawn a complete blank on the murder investigation. The AA connection is iffy at best, and it could take a long time to trace down. I don't think I can face eight or ten AA meetings a day."

"I *know* I can't."

"Then there's the other part of the case, the child abuse. I wasn't convinced that Reiter was a pedophile when the only proof was Mitch's story, but I do believe Joe, and the snapshot clinches it. From what Steve Marley told me, there's a good chance Reiter's still molesting kids. If that's true, it's just a matter of finding the boys and convincing them to file a report."

"Piece of cake. Except that you can't slander the judge while you're doing it."

"That's the tricky part," I said.

"Tricky and risky," Peter said. "You'll need to find out where he meets the kids."

"Yes, and I know where to start." I dried my hands and

went to get the newspaper article that Mitch had shown Joe. I gave it to Peter and said, "Youth Services, the organization that gave Reiter the award."

"I don't know the group, but I can ask around, see if LeRoy or someone else does," Peter said as he looked over the article. LeRoy is a friend of Peter's who works with runaways and knows the social service scene from what he calls a gopher's-eye view (you can see who's kicking dirt in your face even if you can't understand what they're saying).

"Thanks. I have Chris checking on it, but your sources may know something that the more official channels don't. In the meantime, I think it's time for a feature article on the judge, a piece that will highlight his many contributions to the community."

"Ah yes, the inquiring-journalist gambit." Peter poured more wine.

"No, more the let-me-make-you-famous gambit."

"Irresistible. Who among us can resist tooting his own horn?"

"I'll need some press credentials."

"I might just be able to help on that. If Mike Monroe's still at *Bay News*, I could get him to write a letter indicating you're a free-lancer on special assignment. In fact, that arrangement might work out very nicely all around. You promise to give him a crack at whatever you come up with, and he'll be delighted to back you all the way."

Bay News is one of the Bay Area's most lively small papers. It has a reputation for good investigative journalism and occasional juicy gossip about local figures.

"I have to clear it with Joe first," I said, "but I think he'll go for it."

Joe was in favor of anything that would expose the judge without involving him. He loved the idea of a newspaper article. Mike Monroe was less enthusiastic, small wonder since all I could offer him was a very vague outline of the story and no indication of the identity of the prominent man who might be involved. He was talking fast and saying nothing, which I figured was a lead up to turning me down, when he stopped suddenly. "Say, you're the lady in the First Central case, aren't you? The one who caught the guy with the scheme to rob the computer?"

When I admitted my role in that case, his whole tone changed. The case had been sensational enough to catch the interest of the media, and coverage of it had blown the low profile I try to keep. I'd prefer to forget the whole thing since it very nearly got both Peter and me killed, but Mike Monroe remembered, and that was enough to convince him to co-operate in my plan.

The doorbell rang at ten o'clock that night. It was Molly. She was dressed entirely in black—black jeans, black turtleneck, black jacket. I was always amazed by how big she was whenever I saw her in Palo Alto, but standing on my front porch with nothing but her backpack, she looked awfully small.

"Molly, thank God you're all right. Come in." I gave her a big hug, which she received as if she'd been carved from wood, and she allowed me to walk her into the living room.

"Where have you been?"

"Around. I came up to the city with a friend. I'm leaving home."

"It must have been quite a fight."

"No worse than usual. I don't want to live there anymore. Can I live with you?" She said it with a studied casualness, as if she were asking for a glass of water.

"You can stay here for a while," I said, "until you get things worked out with your mother."

"There's nothing to work out. She doesn't really want me there now, with her new husband and her new baby. She'd be only too happy to have me move in with you. It'd save everybody a lot of trouble."

Peter came in just then. Molly looked a little surprised, and I realized that she probably didn't know we lived together. She hadn't spent the night since he moved in four months ago, and Marion certainly wouldn't have told her.

"Molly, good to see you." His voice betrayed none of the emotion her disappearance had generated. "Come to see Reepecheep?" Reepecheep was the gray mouse Molly had bought in defiance of her mother's ban on pets. It resided in my study while negotiations for its release continued between mother and daughter.

"Molly'd like to stay here for a while, till things get straightened out at home," I said.

Peter nodded. "Sure. I was about to make some cocoa. Want some?"

Molly nodded and sank down into a chair. I was watching Peter. We don't drink cocoa. I don't keep it in the house. He'd not only expected Molly to come to me; he'd planned for it.

"Want to tell me what happened?" I asked as Peter headed off to make the cocoa.

Molly shrugged. "You know my mother. She's Missus Perfect Suburban Wife. She wants me to be the perfect suburban teenager, and I'm not. I don't even want to be. She doesn't like my friends, she doesn't like my clothes, she doesn't like my attitude. She doesn't like me. And the feeling is mutual."

I could remember thinking that my mother didn't understand me, but never that she didn't like me. That had to be a painful feeling. I wanted to assure Molly that it wasn't true, but my conversation with Marion didn't give me much support for that. I'd heard more anger than fear in my sister's voice when she discussed her daughter's disappearance.

Peter came back with the cocoa and some chocolate chip cookies. There was something in his manner that seemed to help Molly relax. As she sipped her cocoa and munched on a cookie she lost her wild-animal wariness and began to look more like the girl I'd spent so many Saturday afternoons with.

"Do you mind if I call your mother and tell her you're here?" I asked.

Molly frowned. "Okay, but I'm not going back."

"Understood."

I called Marion from the study. She was relieved to know that Molly was with me, but that only lasted a short time and was quickly replaced by irritation. As I listened to her blow off steam about all the trouble Molly had caused her and how thoughtless the child was, I lost my illusions about any quick reconciliation.

"Maybe Molly should stay with me for a while," I suggested, even as an inner voice shouted, "Don't do it."

Marion didn't want Molly at home, but she didn't much like the idea of her staying with me.

"She has to go to school," she said.

"There are schools in San Francisco," I pointed out.

"But the public schools are terrible."

"They're better than the streets."

"I ought to put her in a boarding school. It's too bad they don't have military schools for girls."

I thought it was too bad they didn't have personality transplants for people like Marion, but I didn't say it. What I did say was "You both need some time away from each other. I'll come down tomorrow to get some of Molly's things."

"Don't you get bossy with me, Catherine. I'll decide what's right for my daughter."

"You can decide whatever you want, but Molly's just let you know that she can decide things, too, and if she decides she'd rather be on the streets than in your house, that's where she'll end up."

"She wouldn't," Marion spat out, but her voice lacked conviction.

"So do you want me to drop her off in the Tenderloin or leave her on the front steps till you pick her up?" I asked. I knew that the only way to handle Marion was to be tougher and meaner than she was; any sign of weakness or emotion and all was lost.

I could practically hear her pouting. When she spoke, it was simply to say, "You two deserve each other."

10

I PUT MOLLY to bed on the couch in my study. She'd spent the night with me before, but we could both sense that this time was different. I gave her a hug, and told her how glad I was that she was safe. She told me that I shouldn't have worried. "I'm not a baby; I can take care of myself," she said.

"Yeah, but at fourteen, you shouldn't have to," I said.

As I closed the study door and started for the kitchen the emotions I'd been carefully suppressing surged to the surface. I was furious with Marion, and more than a little angry with Molly for putting us through two days of worry; grateful that she was safe, and totally overwhelmed by the idea that she'd become my responsibility.

I went to the kitchen, pulled the bottle of gin from the freezer, and poured myself a glass. Peter came in as I was pouring the second.

"You have a short memory if you're working on another hangover," he said.

I put the glass down a bit too hard. "What the hell am I going to do?" I said. "I can't send her home, can't put her out on the street, and I sure as hell can't take care of her here."

Peter put his arm around me and held me against his chest. "We could look after her for a few days."

"A few days. A few days aren't going to make things okay with Marion. It could be months before we get this thing straightened out, and where's she going to stay in the meantime?"

"I could talk to LeRoy," Peter suggested.

I pulled away. "LeRoy? You can't be serious. LeRoy's kids are at the last stop before jail or the morgue. Molly's just a suburban kid having trouble at home. The last thing she needs is to live with kids who are more alienated than she is."

"Your mother?"

"I put my mother through enough when I was a kid. She doesn't deserve to have to do it twice. Besides, she'd be on Marion's side. She's always preferred Marion's conventional approach to life. Molly's too much like me to get along very well with her."

I could see where all this was leading; so could Peter, and neither of us liked it.

"You're talking yourself into taking her in," he said.

"I guess I am. Could you handle it if I did?"

Peter poured himself some of the gin, took a drink, and grimaced. "How can you drink this stuff straight?"

"Could you handle it?" I repeated.

"I'm supposed to say, 'Sure, no problem,' but I just don't know. I haven't lived with anyone for years; sometimes it takes all my energy not to bolt."

I knew what he meant. I was having the same problem. We'd both been on our own too long to find it easy to adapt to another's rhythms. We were like porcupines in winter, wanting to get close, but knowing the risks of any quick movement.

"We could try it. Maybe things'll clear up in a couple of weeks. Molly will find that living here isn't as easy as she imagined, and Marion will cool off and realize that she misses her."

Peter nodded, but he didn't look convinced. "One step at a time," he said. It made me think of AA. It wasn't a flattering comparison.

I put my arms around him and we gave each other a hug that had more desperation than eros in it. "How sure are you that this is just adolescent rebellion?" he asked as he held me.

It was a question I'd been asking myself. I'd heard too much about abused children recently not to wonder if Molly was a victim. Puberty and a new stepfather had arrived about the same time, and it was hard to tell what was responsible for the changes in her personality.

"I don't know," I said. "And I'm not sure I even know how to ask. This stuff is easy to talk about until it gets close to home. It's hard to dig for something you don't want to find out."

I teach a ten o'clock aikido class on Saturday, so I decided to take Molly along. She woke with all the grace and good-will that I do.

"It's Saturday," she complained. "I get to sleep in on Saturday."

"Come on, sleepyhead," I said. "I'd really like to have you come with me."

Her brows pinched together in a frown and she started to say something, then thought better of it.

The Saturday class is a beginners' class. I hoped I could get Molly to participate. I suppose I thought that because it had been good for me, it would be good for her. I figured it couldn't hurt.

I tried to treat Molly like any other newcomer to the class, but I was aware that a part of my attention was always drawn to her. Even as I spoke of the importance of keeping the mind focused on the present, my own attention skittered off in her direction.

We were practicing *shomen uchi iriminage*, a strike to the forehead. I noticed that a number of people were concentrating so hard on the throw that they weren't paying enough attention to moving out of the way of the attack. The first step in many defenses in aikido is to get out of the way. In other martial arts you block and counter, in aikido you move out of the path of attack and direct the opponents' energy against them.

"If you don't get out of the way first," I pointed out, "you're not going to be around to worry about the throw."

I motioned one of the brown belts to help me. She attacked; I moved only a short distance, and she demonstrated that she could still strike at my face or kick my knee. "But when I do this"—I pivoted fully away from her—"I'm beyond her reach." I had the class partner up, then had one person walk slowly toward the other with an outstretched arm. When the attacker came close, the defender was to pivot out of the way.

As they got the hang of it I had them speed up the action so that the attacker lunged. A number of people who'd thought this was kid's stuff got poked in the stomach.

"It's not so easy to step out of the way of an attack," I said. "You have to be alert enough to sense it coming, and the movement has to be immediate. We're taught never to run away, and we miss the difference between running and simply stepping aside. When you step aside, you place yourself in a position where you can direct what happens next.

"You might pay attention over the next week to how you respond to conflict. Do you counter it, run from it, or do you just step aside?"

Molly was not exactly bubbling over with enthusiasm after class. I don't know what I expected, probably something along the lines of "Gee, that was wonderful. I want to go back to Palo Alto, make up with my mother, and become a black belt." I got gum-chewing silence.

"So what did you think of it?" I asked.

"It was okay, but I hate getting up early on Saturday mornings."

"You'd rather not go, right?"

She sighed. Teenagers are great sighers. "Look, I know it's real important to you, and you'd like me to do it, too; but it's not my thing. My mother is all the time trying to make me do stuff she thinks I ought to do—join clubs, go to football games. That's her thing, not mine. Why won't anybody just let me be me?"

"Okay," I said, "so what *is* your thing? What do you want to do?"

Another sigh. "I don't know. Maybe if everyone weren't always on my case, I could figure it out."

Ho, boy, I thought, here we go.

Molly hadn't been thrilled by the idea of going back to Palo Alto, but she needed to pick up clothes and some other things if she was going to stay with me. I'd hoped that the drive would give us a chance to talk.

When we got into the car, I asked her the question that had been on my mind all morning. "Does your running away have anything to do with Leonard?"

"Some, I guess. He's such a drag. But mostly it's my mother."

"What I'm asking is, Has he ever bothered you sexually?"

"Sexually? Leonard? God, no! How gross!"

Her absolute shock and disbelief was the best evidence I could have asked for. I breathed a sigh of relief while she stared at me in shock.

"It happens," I said. "I had to be sure."

"Well, not to me," she said. "Leonard has plenty of faults but he's not a pervert."

"So tell me what's been going on at home that made you want to leave," I said as I headed for the freeway.

The next hour was a litany of refreshingly familiar teenage complaints. Marion didn't understand, didn't want to under-stand, didn't like Molly, didn't like Molly's friends, Molly's attitudes, Molly's ideas. "They're on my case all the time," Molly complained. "Nothing I do is right, nothing satisfies them. They want me to be like Becky Norton down the street. Perfect Becky Norton who gets good grades, has nice friends, kisses up to adults, and is a total shit."

I had a little trouble hearing all this because Molly had turned on the car radio and selected a station that played loud music with unintelligible lyrics. I'd have asked her to turn it down if I hadn't spent most of my adolescence fighting with my mother about my passion for acid rock. It made me feel terribly old to dislike Molly's music so much.

I did manage to extract from her a little information about

what she'd done between the time she left Palo Alto and when she showed up at my door. She'd stayed with two girlfriends who were a couple of years older and had moved to San Francisco. Molly was distressingly vague on where they lived and what they were doing.

As we approached her house I said, "You might try stepping aside as a way to handle your mother."

Molly looked confused, then realized I was talking about what we'd done in aikido. "How do I do that?" she asked.

I realized that I was into the dangerous area of giving advice that I myself was seldom able to follow, but I guess that's an adult's prerogative. "Don't let her get to you. When she says something to provoke a response, just let it go."

"I'll try," Molly said grudgingly.

"Yeah, me too."

Molly actually did better than I did. She gave her mother the silent treatment, which wasn't exactly stepping aside but at least didn't provoke a blowup. Unable to get a reaction from Molly, Marion began issuing instructions to me. She managed to combine not so subtle complaints about aspects of Molly's behavior with an inventory of the character defects that made me an unsuitable parent substitute.

I tried stepping aside till I felt as if I was doing the Mexican hat dance. Finally, I blew up just as I'd always done and said something satisfyingly nasty. It was not a mature, adult way to handle the situation, but it sure felt good. In fact, the fight we had, in which we screamed at each other pretty much the way we'd done as kids, also felt good. It was not an edifying sight for Molly, but she enjoyed it thoroughly.

"Step out of the way, huh?" she said once we were back in the car. "Is that what you call stepping out of the way?"

There was a teasing quality to her voice, so I didn't have to fake a responsible, adult answer. I just grinned. "Haven't you ever heard of 'Do as I say, not as I do'?"

When we got back from Marion's, I was ready for a good stiff drink. Peter pointed out that it was probably time for our first foray to AA. I'd have killed him, but I didn't want to go alone.

We checked the meetings that started at four and found one close to Mitch's apartment. The plan was for me to make a short statement that might catch the attention of Mitch's sponsor. I'd tell the group that I'd come to AA because I was going through a rough period and had started drinking again. The story was basically Joe's—a friend who'd asked me for help in unmasking the man who'd molested him, my refusal, his murder outside a bar in Oakland, my guilt. I knew enough about guilt to be convincing on that score, and if I had any trouble feeling like an alcoholic, I need only remember the Sunday night I'd heard of Orrin Merrick's suicide.

The meeting was in a church social hall a few blocks from Mitch's apartment. It was a large cavernous room that I suspected never felt warm, the kind designed to serve a number of purposes with the result that it was not quite right for anything. A circle of folding chairs had been set up at one end and beyond them a long table held a coffee urn and a pink bakery box.

There were about sixteen people in the circle. I found myself wishing there were rows so I could hide in the back. Peter came in a few minutes after me and sat several seats away.

The meeting went pretty much as I'd expected, but saying the words "I'm an alcoholic" gave me a little trouble. Not a good sign.

I waited around after the meeting. Several people came up to me to offer encouragement, but no one mentioned the friend I'd betrayed. Peter had ducked out after the meeting and was waiting down the block in a doorway.

"No luck there," I said as I met him.

"We've got fifteen minutes to get to the next one," he said. "Or we could find a nearby bar."

"Or we could go home and keep Molly company. I vote for that."

"Find the AA meeting a little tough?" Peter asked as we drove home.

"I like wine far too much to be entirely comfortable at AA," I said.

"I know exactly what you mean."

Molly was in the study listening to the same loud music I'd endured on the ride to Palo Alto and back. Peter grimaced and suddenly remembered something he needed to get at the store. I headed for the kitchen and closed the door to shut out the noise.

I'd brought a street map, and I spread it out on the kitchen table and drew three concentric circles around Mitch's apartment; the first had a half-mile radius, the second a mile, the third two miles. At Mitch's apartment I'd found a book that listed the times and locations of AA meetings. I went through it, paying special attention to the dog-eared pages, to find all the places he might have attended meetings.

Molly came in as I sat over the map and meetings book. "Whatcha doing?" she asked.

I explained. "Can I help?" she asked.

I'd like to say that I considered the child-labor issue here, but I truly hate this kind of work, so I accepted her offer with enthusiasm.

We worked until my eyes began to cross, than I made a batch of popcorn. The smell drew Peter to the kitchen.

"Look who's home just in time for popcorn and eye-strain," I said.

He suggested that the job would be easier with a magnifying glass. "Damn print seems to get smaller every year," he said, pulling out the reading glasses he'd recently bought at the drugstore. "You might want to try these."

I didn't want to try them. I didn't even want to think about the fact that I might need them.

"Leonard has a pair of those," Molly said. "He says it's 'cause his arms got shorter. I think that's supposed to be some kind of dumb joke."

"Only amusing to those with long arms," Peter said. Molly looked confused, and I tried not to choke on my popcorn.

Two batches of popcorn and many cups of coffee later, we had a full list of the times and locations of all the scheduled mixed or men-only meetings within a two-mile radius of Mitch's apartment. It was an appallingly long list.

11

S UNDAY PROVED TO me that four AA meetings in one day was enough to produce the opposite of the desired effect. It was all I could do not to reach for the bottle when I got home.

Peter had good news. He'd called around to ask about schools for Molly, and found one that he thought was perfect. A friend of a friend, Gil Matthews, was starting his own school for dropouts and other kids who didn't fit in the public system. The Phoenix School was Gil and fifteen kids; its curriculum covered the standard subjects, but in a hands-on, real-world setting.

"She'll get lots of personal attention and a supportive environment to work on both academic and social issues," Peter said.

We discussed it with Molly, who didn't share Peter's enthusiasm but agreed that if she had to go to school, Phoenix sounded okay. I realized as we talked that she was still on her good behavior with us. The time would come when she'd feel comfortable enough to let us see the anger and hostility that had gotten her in trouble at home. I wasn't looking forward to it.

Chris's report on Youth Services was on my desk Monday morning. She'd left it off before heading to Palo Alto on some job Jesse'd given her. I felt guilty for not keeping closer tabs on that case, then reminded myself that Jesse was my partner now, not my assistant. It'd take a long time before either of us felt comfortable in our new roles, but it would happen sooner if I backed off a bit.

According to Chris's research, Youth Services had been around for almost twenty years. It had started in the early seventies when the federal government still believed in spending money on kids. In their usual manner, the feds had tossed money at every group that could employ a sharp grant writer, without giving much thought to how it all fit together.

Youth Services had been started by several frustrated social workers who had the radical idea that the system might work better if everyone knew what everyone else was doing. They began collecting information and helping groups coordinate their efforts. Then the politicians decided if you couldn't win the war on poverty in ten years, it wasn't worth fighting, and Californians got cranky about paying taxes, and there wasn't much money for kids or anyone else except defense contractors. That Youth Services had stayed in the game testified to a rare combination of dedication and political savvy.

The group was still primarily involved in gathering information about youth and family services and providing referrals. The director was Mrs. Audrey Shay. I dialed the number Chris had written down.

Audrey Shay's voice was so soft that it took an effort to hear her. She was delighted that I was interested in the "Good Citizen for Youth" award, and told me that this was the third year it had been offered. The award had been started both to recognize the efforts of volunteers who gave unselfishly of their time and to make the public more aware of the programs that relied on volunteers to make them function.

"We ask the organizations to nominate candidates, then a special committee made up of representatives from community groups and city and county agencies selects the winner. There were over thirty nominees this year," she informed me.

"You must gather a great deal of information on the nominees," I said.

"Oh, we do. It's a tremendous amount of work, but very gratifying to see the good work that some people are doing."

I asked if I might come by to get background information for my article on the judge, and she told me that she'd be there any afternoon between one and five. She was so enthusiastic that I felt guilty when I thought of the likely outcome of my story.

The Youth Services office was in downtown Oakland, in an area that hadn't been prosperous for twenty years. If you looked closely at the buildings, you found some real jewels, much more interesting architecturally than a lot of the modern cubes they were throwing up downtown.

Youth Services shared a building with a number of other worthy-but-impoverished causes. Walking through the door was like stepping back into 1968. The walls were covered with copy-shop posters and signs announcing a variety of meetings on subjects ranging from homelessness to child care. Paint peeled from the high ceilings, and the halls smelled old.

A hand-printed directory read like a reminder of the social ills that have grown worse rather than better over the last twenty years. I admire people who continue to work on problems that the government gave up on long ago. Sisyphus and his rock would have been right at home among these folks.

The number of entries crossed out on the directory testified to high attrition in the good-works department. Youth Services was still there, in room 201.

Audrey Shay was a tall, slender black woman dressed in a white blouse and dark skirt. She was too well dressed and too well groomed for her surroundings. She'd have looked more at home in the corporate offices across town than in this throwback to the sixties.

The room was large and square, with gracious high ceilings. Someone, probably Shay, had made a valiant attempt to make it homey and inviting. Colorful curtains framed a window made almost opaque by decades of urban grime. An aging sofa sat against one wall, a braided carpet covered the scarred wood floor, and black-and-white photographs of smiling children decorated the drab walls. But the heavy oak desk in front of the window and a bank of metal file cabinets were the real heart of the office.

I introduced myself, and she was so pleased to see me that I felt guilty all over again. She pulled a thick folder from one of the file cabinets and presented it to me.

"I can't let you take anything from the file, but the drugstore down the street has a copy machine, and you're welcome to copy whatever you need. And, of course, I'll be happy to answer any questions you have."

I spent the next hour on the couch getting to know Samuel Reiter. The man described in the letters and articles was a community treasure, a man of wealth and power who gave freely of his time and money in a variety of charitable and social causes, many of which did not involve young boys. He served on the boards of the symphony, the arts commission, the museum, and an organization that set up halfway houses for the mentally ill.

Letters from local leaders extolled his virtues. He was a man who could get the job done, always willing to help in a good cause, dedicated, and wise. I began to wonder if this was the same man Joe had described to me.

Then I listed his activities, and the pattern emerged. Over half of the judge's good works involved agencies working with young boys, and while he served the symphony and arts commission as a board member, he worked with the YMCA, Big Brothers, and other boys' groups as a volunteer. Newspaper clippings showed him coaching a chess club in east Oakland and a computer club in Piedmont. I separated out everything involving boys and headed for the drugstore copy machine.

I'd hoped to be home before Molly got back from her first day of school, but traffic was slow and I knew by the time I got off the bridge that I'd never make it. She was fourteen years old and had her own key to the apartment, so I don't know why I felt so concerned. Being a substitute mother wasn't going to be easy.

I needn't have worried about being late. Molly had made herself at home. I tripped over her backpack just inside the door and found a half-full soda can and the remains of a bag of potato chips on the coffee table in the living room. Rock music blared from my study. I cursed Marion for not raising a more responsible child.

Molly had never acted like this when she visited me. She'd always been careful to clean up after herself. If she was playing some kind of game, it was time to get clear on the rules.

I walked to the study and turned down the radio. Molly looked up from a paperback book she'd been reading.

"How was school?" I asked.

She shrugged. "Okay, I guess."

"What do you think of the other kids?"

"Some of them are okay; the others are sort of dweebish."

"How's the work compare to what you were doing in your school in Palo Alto?"

She raised one shoulder slightly in what I began to suspect was the universal answer to any question asked by an adult. "Okay."

"Well, things here are not okay," I said. "I don't know what you do at home, but here we have a few basic rules. First, you do not leave your backpack on the floor where someone can break a toe on it. Second, what you get out, you put back. I know that Peter doesn't always follow that one, but we're working on it, and I'll never get him trained if you set a bad example." The corners of her mouth twitched in what might have been the glimmer of a smile.

"I'd prefer not to have the neighbors call the police about your music, so you'll have to keep the volume down, especially when Peter and I are home. It makes us feel out of date not to recognize the songs or even the groups. And finally, we have a policy that junk food is only eaten outside the house. Otherwise, I'd weigh four hundred pounds. Okay?"

She looked uncertain, caught between a pout and the giggles. Before she could decide which way to jump, I said, "How'd you like to help me on a case?"

It was pure impulse, but I knew she'd always been fascinated by my work, and I wanted to reach out to her in some way. Maybe if we had something neutral to talk about I could get more than five-word responses out of her.

"Sure," she said, before she could censor the enthusiasm in her voice. "What do you want me to do?"

That was the point when I realized that this might not be such a great plan. I'd been careful not to discuss the case when Molly was around. She was a bright kid, but she was still a kid, and I couldn't trust her discretion. I thought for a minute and decided that she didn't need to know anything confidential to dig out the information I wanted.

I gave her the stack of papers I'd brought home. "These contain information on a man named Samuel Reiter. I need to put together a list of his activities." I pulled out a résumé that Audrey Shay had compiled listing Reiter's community service. "I don't know if this is complete, but it's a starting point. We'll start with the organizations listed on the résumé and add any others we come across. For each organization, copy down any information you can find: names of other people—adults or kids—dates if you can find them, places, any comments on Reiter's activities."

"Is he a bank robber?" she asked, her eyes shining.

"No, he's a judge. I've told you a dozen times how boring my work is. Now you get to find out firsthand."

Molly set to work with more enthusiasm than she'd shown for anything since she'd arrived, which made the project a success as far as I was concerned. I didn't expect much in the way of results. I figured that I'd do the real work tomorrow at the office.

In the meantime I needed to get started on dinner. Peter and I normally cook together, usually with an open bottle of wine, and meals are often late, but with Molly around it was time to clean up our act.

When Peter got home an hour later, I had dinner on the table and Molly had my stack of papers laid out into fourteen piles in the study. She'd booted up the computer and was entering information on the Piedmont computer club.

"You really should have dBASE," she said. "Word-Perfect has a data-sort function, but it's fairly primitive. DBASE would be much better."

I watched in amazement as she explained the way she thought the data should be arranged. This was a side of Molly I'd never seen. I wondered if Marion knew of it.

"This way I can sort the data to give you a list of organizations with the people in each and any information we have on them, and I can pull out just the names and alphabetize them so you can see if anyone appears in more than one organization. I can also sort the organizations by city or county if you'd like."

No doubt about it, I had a junior Jesse on my hands. Same brilliant mind, same smart mouth.

Molly would have happily given up homework to work for me. She was obviously disappointed to discover that I was just as old-fashioned and inflexible as her mother on that subject. I spent the evening entering information the way Molly had shown me while Peter and Molly explored the mysteries of algebra.

She went to bed at ten, complaining that *no one* goes to bed that early and her homework wasn't done and at home she stayed up till eleven. With Molly's presence, my apartment seemed to have shrunk. She and her ever-present companion, rock radio, occupied a good deal more than physical space.

Peter and I went out for a long walk. In my neighborhood you can walk on Clay Street or hike up one of the perpendicular streets that climb hills better suited to mountain goats than cars. Mostly we walked.

We talked about his cases, my case, Molly, and how we both felt about becoming instant parents. Peter's one of the few men I know who both talks and listens; I think that's one reason I fell in love with him. His impossibly blue eyes, sexy

smile, and marvelous body are other reasons. And his laugh.
And the way he combs his hair.

We hadn't talked like this since Molly arrived, and I realized that I'd missed it. We'd been so busy taking care of
her needs that we'd lost track of each other.

Back home, I showered and towel-dried my hair. As I've
gotten older I've become more fond of the natural curl that I
hated as a teenager when straight hair was the rage. It's great
to be able to dry your hair with a towel, push it around with
a brush, and be ready to go out in public.

Tonight my efforts to look good were not for public con-
sumption. I was interested in an audience of one. The audience, stretched out on the bed with a glass of wine in his
hand, looked interested in return.

My bedroom isn't particularly large, and my bed is a king,
so there's not a lot of room for anything else. I figure most
of what you do in a bedroom you do on the bed, so you don't
need a lot of extra room.

I flopped down next to Peter, had some of his wine, and
helped him out of his clothes. Then I remembered Molly and
decided I'd better lock the door.

"Did you ever hear your parents make love?" I asked.

"No. You?"

"Never. I was in college before I even entertained the
notion that they'd done it more than twice."

Peter laughed. "Does it make you uncomfortable, having
Molly in the house?"

"Let's just say I doubt that you can be as quiet as your
father."

"And I'd bet you're nowhere near as silent as Marion. Or
Leonard, for that matter."

"It's a damn good thing Molly's so fond of loud music,"
I said as Peter's mouth found mine and put an end to our
conversation.

12

I'M NOT SURE whether Molly's system for putting things on the computer made the job easier or harder. It gave me more information than I'd have had under my usual system, but it also took longer to type everything in. I suspect that the computer, like so many modern labor-saving devices, makes one job easier while creating several new ones.

The letters and clippings I'd copied spanned a number of years. I was most interested in the organizations in which Reiter was still active, since they were where I'd find his current victims. Steve Marley had suggested I get a full list in order to trace previous victims, so I dutifully assembled all the information I had.

The job turned out to be easier than I'd expected. Reiter's résumé was complete, and while he had been involved in a number of organizations, for the last few years he'd concentrated on chess and computer clubs. He was currently coaching a computer club in Piedmont and chess clubs at a Catholic school and a neighborhood center in Oakland.

I could probably have done the whole investigation without ever meeting Samuel Reiter, and maybe I should have. My desire to meet the man, to know more about him than his name and his crime, was a sign that I was already too personally involved in this case.

I'd heard from Joe the betrayal and destructiveness Reiter was capable of, but I'd also seen another side to him in the Youth Services file. Letters testified to good works that were unrelated to his desire for young boys, and many of those

79

letters had a personal quality that suggested the writers knew the judge well and felt genuine respect and affection for him.

It's been my experience that good and evil are rarely as neat and tidy as we'd like. Too often both can exist within the same individual. Mafiosi can be good family men; cold-blooded killers can be loyal friends, and even Nazis love their dogs. I could invent a reason to meet Judge Reiter, but I knew that my true motivation was curiosity.

It's axiomatic that the more important the person, the more difficult it is to get around his or her secretary. For a superior court judge, we were probably talking a law clerk in the Doberman league. I don't like to deal with Dobermans, so I called Audrey Shay at Youth Services and asked if she could arrange an interview.

I told her that I'd prefer to interview Judge Reiter while he was involved in one of his many activities with children. She thought that would be lovely.

Reiter didn't agree. She explained that he wanted to be able to give his full attention to the children while he was with them. He suggested that I attend a meeting of the Piedmont Arts Commission instead.

I wasn't thrilled with the idea of spending several hours pretending to be fascinated by a business meeting of the arts commission, but Audrey explained that the judge was very busy and that normally I'd have to wait several weeks to get an appointment. The only reason he had consented to an interview this week was because the arts commission needed the publicity.

The commission was meeting at Judge Reiter's house at eight o'clock tomorrow night. He would be willing to talk with me afterward if I needed further information.

I thanked Audrey for her help and got directions to Reiter's house.

I had the names of three clubs that Reiter was involved in; and there was no reason to put off checking on them until after I'd seen him.

Snooping around Fortune 500 companies is a far cry from figuring out which of a bunch of ten-year-olds is being preyed on by their coach. I called Steve Marley. He'd gotten far enough into painting his kitchen to be delighted by an excuse to abandon the job to a professional. I explained that we were supposed to be writing an article about Reiter, a profile of his activities in the community.

"I'll bring my big press camera," he said, "and my tape recorder. You can be Lois Lane; I get to be Clark Kent." I didn't tell him that it was Jimmy Olsen with the camera.

I managed to make appointments for the next day at the two schools and the neighborhood center where Reiter coached chess and computers. The cover story was the key. Everyone was anxious to see Judge Reiter get the recognition he deserved. I assured them that I'd do my best to see that he did.

Carl Edwards, the bartender from Jerry's, called to tell me that a suspicious-looking character had been asking a lot of questions about the shooting in the parking lot. The physical description fit Jesse. Edwards's certainty that his curious visitor had been "on something" told me that my partner had a new persona. I thanked Edwards and told him I'd be sending a check. He assured me I'd be the first to know if he learned anything more about the shooting.

When I got away from the office a little after four, the fog was riding in on icy Pacific air. By the time I walked the blocks to my apartment, I was thoroughly chilled and ready for a fire. I was not ready to find the living room full of cigarette smoke.

Molly and a couple of other kids were all spread out on the couch. A bag of potato chips spilled its contents across the coffee table between the cans of soda, and one of my favorite pottery bowls had been converted into an ashtray. The air was blue with smoke.

Molly jumped up, caught somewhere between guilt and embarrassment. "Catherine, I didn't know you'd be home so early. I was going to clean this stuff up."

Molly's two companions looked up at me with that surly

blankness that teenagers must practice in front of mirrors. They looked bored, much too cool to be caught up in this embarrassing little drama. Both girls were dressed entirely in black. One had shaved half her head and teased and tangled the hair on the other half. The other had a short, unisex haircut and big eyes outlined in black eyeliner. She reminded me of a waif in a Keane print.

Half-and-half stubbed out her cigarette and rose from the couch. "We gotta go, anyway," she told Molly, never even looking my way. The waif followed her lead. She was painfully thin; there seemed to be nothing between her bones and the skin that covered them. Her black miniskirt, tiny and tight enough to be obscene on a better-shaped body, only emphasized the meagerness of her hips.

I was angry, and it wasn't because of the mess or the smoke or even the rudeness of Molly's guests. I was angry because these three teenagers had just made me feel impossibly old. I've always thought of myself as little more than a kid; now I was an authority figure.

Molly came back from the door, looking petulant. "Geeze, you didn't have to make such a big deal out of it," she said.

"I didn't say a word," I protested.

"You didn't have to. You looked like you were on the edge of pitching a hissy fit."

"Now look here, young lady . . ." The words were out of my mouth before I realized it. They weren't my words. They were my mother's, spoken in exactly the same tone of voice I'd heard so often when I was growing up. I stopped in horror.

Molly, who had been waiting for the standard adult lecture, looked startled.

"Oh, my God, I sound like my mother," I said and sat down on the arm of the couch. Molly stared at me uneasily. I looked from her worried face to the mess on the table, and began to laugh.

It was like being caught in a time warp, only I wasn't the kid anymore. I remembered the day my mom paid a surprise visit to my apartment at the University of Colorado and found the air blue with a sweeter, less-legal type of smoke. I wondered if my face had worn the same mixture of shock and outrage I'd seen on hers. The only thing she ever said was a whispered, ''Your father had better never find out about this,'' as she left the apartment.

At least they hadn't been smoking pot in my living room, though Molly's companions looked tough enough to be into almost anything.

Molly looked more unnerved by my laughter than she had been by my anger. I got myself together and said, ''You should be warned that tobacco smoke has a funny effect on me. In certain concentrations, especially inside my own home, it transforms me instantly into the Wicked Witch of the West. Understood?''

She nodded and began cleaning up the chips and ashes. I opened the only window that hasn't been painted shut over the years and the back door. Between fog and cigarette smoke, it's an easy choice in my book.

''So who are the weird sisters?'' I asked.

Molly looked blank.

''The vampire twins. Who are they?''

Comprehension dawned. ''Oh, just friends from Palo Alto.''

''Things must have changed down there since my last visit. I don't remember that black miniskirts were standard dress.''

''They live in the city now.''

''They're the ones you came to visit when you left home?''

''Yeah.''

''Where do they live?''

''Around.''

''Around? As in 'on the streets'?''

''No, they've got a place with some other kids.''

''They have jobs?''

''Geeze, I don't know their life stories. Will you stop grilling me?''

''Hey, this is not grilling, maybe from Marion it's grilling, from me it's catching up. Grilling is what I do for a living. So how long have you been smoking?''

"Cigarettes?"

"For starters, yes, cigarettes."

"A couple of years. I don't smoke a lot, just with my friends. It's not a big deal."

"I'll spare you the lecture on lung cancer. What other vices do you have that I should know about?"

Molly rolled her eyes. "Don't make a big deal out of this, okay? I know you still think of me as a little kid, but I'm fourteen now."

"Which is about halfway between being a kid and a grown-up."

Molly looked offended. "You don't understand at all what it's like."

"I understand exactly what it's like," I said. "Contrary to what you may believe, I was once a teenager myself, and kids were at least as wild in the seventies as they are now. Ask your grandmother sometime."

That got her attention. This seemed the time for a heart-to-heart talk about drugs. I was tempted to wait for the resident expert on that subject, but decided it'd be a lot easier if Peter weren't there. Before Molly could get her sophisticated teen pose back in place, I said, "I think it's time we talked about drugs."

The frown was back. "I know all about that stuff. They're always going on about it in school."

"Do you smoke marijuana?"

"Sure, sometimes, not a lot. Look, it's really not like they say it is, it doesn't lead to other drugs. You don't get hooked or anything."

I decided it was time to close the back door. It was the only way I could handle the fit of giggles that threatened to break through at the thought of Molly lecturing me on pot.

I built a fire and made some cocoa for Molly and tea for me. I'd have loved a good stiff drink, but it didn't seem the proper beverage for a discussion of drug abuse.

Twenty minutes to cool down, a fire in the fireplace, tea and hot cocoa did wonders for both our dispositions. She wasn't a pothead, and she assured me that she hadn't experimented with other drugs. "And I don't drink," she said. "You know alcohol is a lot more dangerous than marijuana. People get drunk and they drive or they get in fights or beat up their families. Smoking dope doesn't do that to you."

Now, there was a line I could have used on my mom in the old days, except that she refused to discuss the issue. She was a firm believer in the if-you-don't-talk-about-it-it-will-go-away approach to life. I wasn't about to defend drinking, and it seemed hypocritical to say much about pot, which left me with not much more to say than my mom.

13

THE NEIGHBORHOOD AROUND St. Stephen's School in east Oakland was the kind where leaving a decent-looking car on the street could cost you at least your hub caps and radio and probably a good deal more. I was grateful that the school had its own parking lot. Steve Marley was glad it was my car we were parking.

My knowledge of parochial schools has not been updated since I was about Molly's age when my friend Mary Ellen Spizer was sent off to St. Theresa's after we were caught smoking. From her whispered confidences, I got the feeling that things hadn't changed a lot since the Inquisition.

St. Stephen's was a pleasant surprise. In striking contrast to the blighted neighborhood that surrounded it, the school was bright and cheerful. Student art projects covered the bulletin boards that lined the halls, the floors looked freshly scrubbed, the walls freshly painted, and there wasn't a spot of graffiti anywhere.

Brother Gregory was responsible for extracurricular activities. He also taught third grade, but he'd agreed to see us during second period while another teacher took the class for music. On the phone he'd had a cultivated, deep voice with an English accent, and I pictured him as a kindly older man wearing wire-rimmed glasses and clerical robes.

I would have walked right by the tall black kid in chinos and a checked sport shirt if he hadn't spoken to me. The voice was unmistakable. It was a full twenty years older than the face.

Brother Gregory was proud of the chess club and very grateful to Samuel Reiter for coaching it. "I teach the beginners," he said. "But we needed someone much more advanced for the better players. Chess is wonderful for these children. It gives them confidence in their intelligence. I tell them, 'If you can play chess, you can go to college.' "

"Have you watched Judge Reiter work with the boys?" Steve asked. "Could you describe how he interacts with them?"

"He's marvelous. Warm, relaxed. You'd never know he was a judge. He jokes with them, takes the time to know each of them, treats them like pals. They're very devoted to him. It takes a lot to get children to show up on a Saturday morning when everyone else is watching cartoons or hanging around on a street corner."

"We'd like to interview some kids for the article," Steve said. "Are there any boys who are particularly close to Judge Reiter? Someone he's sort of taken under his wing?"

Brother Gregory didn't have to think long. "Jon Marcus," he said. "Like so many of our boys, Jon comes from a broken home. I think his father may have abused him, because he's quite a withdrawn child. Sam—Judge Reiter—has made a special point of drawing him out. I've seen substantial changes in the last year."

"Has he done that before, made an extra effort with a boy who has special needs?" Steve asked. It all sounded so harmless, so altruistic, the way he said it. The knowledge of the true meaning of his questions left a taste like bile in my mouth.

"Just over a year ago, there were two Vietnamese brothers. I don't remember the name right now, but it doesn't matter, because they've moved, out to the valley, I think. Sam befriended the whole family, helped them with immigration. I think he even helped the father get a job. That's the kind of man he is."

Brother Gregory asked if we'd like to talk to Jon Marcus. I discovered that Steve was as accomplished an impromptu liar as me when he smoothly suggested he'd prefer to do that at a chess club meeting. I asked for the boy's phone number so we could get the mother's comments on the club.

When we were back in the car, I asked, "So what do you think?"

"I don't know," he said, staring out the window at the school. "I could give you reasons either way. I'd need more proof than that to go forward with an investigation."

I reached for my purse and pulled out the snapshot of Joe and the judge. Joe hadn't wanted to let me have it. It'd taken some fancy talking and letting him black out his own face in the picture before he'd finally let me borrow it. "What do you make of this picture?" I asked.

Marley studied it, then looked up at me. "This is your judge?" he asked.

"Yes."

"He's a ped," Marley said. "You can see it in the body language. And look at his left hand. It isn't resting on the kid's thigh; it's caressing the thigh. If you substituted a woman for the boy, you'd assume right off that they were lovers."

"Does that change your take on what Brother Gregory said?"

"Oh, yeah. You bet it does. Your judge isn't just one of the thousands of dedicated men who work with kids. He's got his own agenda, and this kid, Jon Marcus, is probably part of it." Marley shifted, trying to get comfortable in the confined space of the car. "You noticed how Brother Gregory described Reiter's way with the kids—a pal, just one of the guys—that's classic. You watch most adults who work with kids—Brother Gregory, for example—you see an adult who likes kids, but he's still an adult. The pedophile, when he's with kids, he becomes a kid. It's not like a forty-two-year-old guy and a bunch of ten-year-olds; it's more like just a bunch of ten-year-olds and one of them is a lot bigger and older-looking. There's a peer quality in the interaction.

"See, I think I told you that a lot of these guys get fixated at some age, probably when they were abused, and they don't really grow beyond that. Their bodies do, of course, and they learn how they're supposed to act so they can look like adults, but inside they're still a kid. At an emotional level, they're still eight or ten or whatever.

"I'd guess that Reiter's fixated around nine or ten, right before puberty, so when he's with these nine-year-olds, he really understands them in ways that a normal adult just doesn't. One place you see it is the jokes. Nine-year-old jokes are generally dumb to an adult, but I'll bet Reiter thinks they're a scream. He can even tell nine-year-old jokes. The kids love it."

"And the Vietnamese kids?"

"Victims, too. We're seeing a lot of victimization of Asian immigrants in San Francisco. They're perfect prey for these guys. The guy befriends the family; he's their friend, their protector, then when he hits on the kid, the kid can't say no. He can't tell his family, and if he refuses, he's scared that the family will suffer. So he goes along."

"It's so ugly," I said.

Marley nodded.

The story was much the same at the other two clubs—testimonials to Judge Reiter's warmth and generosity of spirit, accolades for his contributions to the community, and at each, a single boy who was particularly close to him.

I dropped Marley at the BART station so he could get back to San Francisco, and had a quick dinner in Oakland before my appointment with Samuel Reiter and the arts commission.

Reiter's house was in Piedmont, a wealthy enclave completely surrounded by Oakland. I've always wondered how

Piedmont's city fathers got away with carving out a little
island of wealth and privilege for themselves and incorpo-
rating it as a separate city. They'd managed to create a
WASP's dream, a community where the range of income ran
from very rich to well-to-do. Poor people here were the ones
with only two garages.

Steve Marley and I had driven by Reiter's house earlier in
the day when we came to interview the director at the rec-
reation center about the computer club. Even in the daytime
we'd needed a street map to find it. It was on Glen Ellen
Drive, a street that looked like it belonged in Beverly Hills.

The house was an American version of an English manor
house, Tudor style with exposed beams and mullioned windows with tiny panes. This wasn't a large house; it was a
small mansion. It could easily have sat on a hill overlooking
acres of open country. Instead, it sat in the middle of an
immaculately tended yard with a grumpy French chateau
looming over its color-coordinated gardens. The lawn looked
as if it had been brushed instead of mowed, and trees that
were thoughtless enough to drop leaves were probably pulled
out and cut into neatly stacked cords of firewood.

This was not a neighborhood where you did surveillance.
Any stranger who stopped for more than twenty-five seconds
was probably reported to the police department. I wondered
how Mitch had gone about his investigation of Reiter.

It wasn't any easier to find Reiter's place in the dark. I was
glad I knew which house it was. Rich people don't put up
house numbers.

The door was opened by a tall, olive-skinned young man
in a suit. I wasn't sure if he was a butler or a friend. The
entrance hall was paneled in dark wood and was larger than
my entire living room. You could have played basketball in
the living room except that it was stuffed full of furniture.
The drapes and couches were made from floral prints that
contained similar colors but seemed to be subtly at war with
one another. And the exquisite Oriental carpet wasn't speaking to either of them.

My mother would have been shocked that anyone would

put three patterns together and expect them to get along, but the room had obviously been done by a designer, and they play by a different set of rules.

The assortment of people in the room got along about as well as the prints. There were five women and three men; most were in their late forties, early fifties. Two of the women were fashionably close to anorexia, one had clearly stepped over the line, and two had given up the battle and were comfortably overweight. All five wore sweaters and slacks with accessories worth more than most of my better dresses.

The men rose when I entered the room, and the tallest of the three came to greet me. I recognized him from the newspaper photographs, though he was a bit heavier than I'd expected. He was a little shorter than Jesse, which put him just under six feet, not really heavy but with a soft paunch that men develop when they forsake exercise but not wine.

From Joe and the résumé I knew that Reiter must be in his late fifties, but neither his face nor his body gave him away. His hair had receded and thinned, but it was a sandy color that doesn't show the gray, and he moved with the ease and vitality of a younger man.

"Ms. Sayler, we're delighted you could join us," he said, then went on to introduce the others and put in a plug for the arts commission's Mayfest.

The Mayfest was to be a community-wide art festival on the first weekend in May. I heard more about it than I wanted to know, but I took notes faithfully and even asked a couple of questions. At one point in college I'd thought I wanted to be an investigative reporter and had joined the school newspaper. Several weeks of covering meetings like this had convinced me that I'd never get through the apprenticeship.

The meeting lasted about two hours, and my presence probably kept everyone on task and better behaved than they'd have managed by themselves. Four of the women were involved in Junior League and made frequent references to a conflict in that organization, which they found considerably more interesting than the Mayfest. The most stimulating discussion of the evening involved the boundary between art

and craft and the importance of keeping people who cro-
cheted pot holders from exhibiting their wares.

The big surprise of the evening was the arrival home of
Judge Reiter's wife, Aileen. This was clearly not the wife
Joe had mentioned. This was the trophy wife—the gorgeous
younger woman, the payoff for wealth and power.

She was in her late twenties or early thirties with self-
assurance and poise beyond her years, the product of a good
Eastern college, most likely. Her conservatively tailored suit
and briefcase suggested that she was an executive-model trophy wife.

Aileen didn't stick around for the interview. Reiter offered
me brandy, a real step-up from the coffee he'd served for the
committee meeting. It's impossible to have an intimate chat
in a room the size of a small stadium, but Reiter managed to
establish a feeling of intimacy through the intensity of his
attention. The man was a master of sincere eye contact.

We covered his civic and artistic activities. The list
matched the one on his vita. "I noticed that a number of
your volunteer activities involve work with boys. Can you
tell me about the special appeal of that kind of work?" I
actually said that with not a hint of irony in my voice, and I
kept a straight face. I learned it by watching the White House
press corps.

"I think my work with boys is the most important thing I
do," he said, giving me a smile that had helped make some
orthodontist rich. "There are so many boys who don't have
fathers at home anymore. They're desperate for male role
models, and there are less of those available all the time.
When I was growing up, families lived closer together. If
you didn't get on with your father, you had uncles or older
cousins. You could go down to the playground and find a
director who'd teach you to play basketball. There were
sports, boys' clubs, Scouts, lots of places boys got together.

"Today, the uncles live across town or in another state.
The playgrounds don't have money to do more than cut the
grass. The schools can't afford extracurricular activities, and
too many adults are too busy to coach soccer or lead Scouts.

"They don't know what they're missing. Believe me, I get far more from the boys I work with than I give." It was all I could do not to choke at that one, but I must have done a good job of concealing my emotions, because he continued. "I used to coach soccer, but an old knee injury acted up, so now I'm confined to chess and computer, things like that.

"It's terrific to watch these kids develop. I suppose that's part of the joy of being a parent. I missed out on that, but I tell you, I feel like I've had dozens of sons. Boys I coached ten, fifteen years ago still come back to see me when they're in town. It's a great feeling."

Watching his enthusiasm and listening to the obvious pride and affection in his voice, it was hard to hold on to the other reality. I had no doubt that Joe was telling the truth, but I also had no doubt that Reiter believed that he, too, was telling the truth.

"I know your professional activities as a judge must keep you very busy," I said. "How do you find the time for all your volunteer activities?"

"I don't play golf or tennis," he said with a laugh. "No, seriously, I don't know how much you know about my life, but I lost my first wife in an accident, and I spent many years as a widower before I remarried. My activities in the community are what got me through that difficult period. I spend much of my professional life dealing with the darker side of human nature. I find the laughter of children a powerful antidote to the grimness of that reality and to any personal depression that I might be tempted to indulge in."

I had plenty to think about on the drive home. I hadn't expected Reiter to be a monster, but I was certainly not prepared to find him so likable. My investigation would save some boys from exploitation, but it would cost many more a friend and confidant.

14

I ARRIVED HOME to find Peter holed up in the bedroom, reading John McPhee, and Molly studying *As You Like It* to rock accompaniment. Stone had curled up on a sweatshirt she'd dropped on the floor, and was kneading and purring enthusiastically. His face was set in an expression of glassy-eyed ecstasy that bordered on the lewd.

"Steve Marley called," Molly informed me. "Peter took the message."

The message wasn't good news. Marley's mother had fallen and was in the hospital. He'd gone to Ukiah and didn't know how long he'd be there. A better person would have worried about Marley's mother, instead of feeling irritated about losing him at a crucial point in the investigation. I was not that better person.

The alarm woke me from an unpleasant dream in which I wandered through a trackless forest, trying to find a path out. I had the sense of something ominous following me, but never figured out what it was. It was a dream I was glad to leave unfinished.

At the office, over a second cup of industrial-strength coffee, I reviewed my options. The prudent thing to do was to wait for Marley's return. If we'd been dealing with an embezzler or even a spy, I'd have done that, but there was too much at stake to sit back and wait. I couldn't know what a day or two might mean for the kids Reiter was molesting, and I wasn't willing to gamble on it.

The obvious starting point was the boys themselves. I had

three names—Jon Marcus and Ben Sutter in Oakland, and Mark Lashman in Piedmont. I was fairly sure that all three were being molested by Reiter, and equally sure that none would want to admit it. I'd have to talk with their parents and convince them to let someone question the boys.

I could think of several hundred things I'd rather do than tell a mother that her son was the victim of a pedophile, but none of those things was going to put a stop to Reiter's activities, so I poured a third cup of coffee and called Jon Marcus's mother, Sally. She could see me anytime during the day. I suggested later that morning. Irene Lashman, Mark's mother, was terribly busy but finally agreed that she could work me in around one today. Rosemary Sutter worked until five but agreed to let me come at six. I asked if Ben would be home and was relieved to find that he'd be at soccer practice.

My desk calender had the name *Glosser* written across it in red. The week I'd promised Jesse that I'd wait was up. I was too busy to do much about it today, but I could get Chris started on a background search. I called her in and told her what I needed.

"So you're going to do it," she said grimly. Chris is the straight arrow in the office. I could tell that she didn't approve.

"Yes," I said, thinking it was good she worked for me instead of vice versa. I don't think I'd have lasted long in Chris's agency.

The first boy, Jon Marcus, lived with his mother and two younger sisters in east Oakland. The neighborhood had never been a particularly affluent one, but the small, sturdy houses had been the pride of working-class families on the way up. By the eighties the working class was shrinking; more and more families were slipping into poverty, and those who could afford to were fleeing the urban jungle for safer havens. The people left on Sally Marcus's street were the ones who couldn't get out.

Iron bars on doors and windows announced that the occupants were under siege. Some yards still showed the effects of loving care, but most were knee high in weeds. The Marcus's house was somewhere in the middle. Someone had made an attempt to keep the lawn alive and mowed, but the house needed a paint job and the windows were so grimy that seeing much through them would be a real challenge. There wasn't much to see, anyway.

The iron-barred gate that protected the front door made some attempt to appear ornamental. It didn't succeed. I rang the bell, and a dog barked and hurled itself against the door. After a few minutes, the door opened a crack, and a woman peered out at me. The dog—a tan, fifty-seven-variety mutt—struggled to thrust its head out. I was grateful for the bars between us.

"Mrs. Marcus?" I asked. She nodded. "I'm Catherine Sayler. I called about the chess club."

She opened the door wider, grabbed the dog by the collar and unlocked the iron gate. She looked about forty-five, but she was probably much younger. Her limp brown hair was straight; whoever'd cut it hadn't worried much about style. Her pale skin had a sallow cast. She looked tired.

The living room had been furnished from Goodwill. Nothing matched, and none of the furniture looked like anything anyone would choose. I sat down on a hideous brownish-yellow tweed sofa and immediately jumped up when something sharp dug into my thigh.

Mrs. Marcus stepped forward and pulled a battered toy gun from between the couch cushions. "I'm sorry," she said wearily. "I keep telling 'em to clean up their things, but they never listen."

When we'd gotten settled and I'd established that the children were out of the house, I began. "Mrs. Marcus, I understand your son is quite active in the chess club at Saint Stephen's."

"Yes, he's real good at it, too. He can beat lots of grown-ups."

"Does he spend much time on club activities?"

"Oh yes. He's gone one or two evenings a week and often

on the weekends, too. It's a godsend for a kid like Jon, keeps him out of trouble. In a neighborhood like this, there's always plenty of that.''

I felt my throat and chest tighten. I'd found exactly what I was looking for, but there was more grief than elation in it. I did not want to tell this woman that the chess club met only for an hour after school once a week and that actual tournaments occurred only a few times a year. And I didn't want to tell her about what was really happening on all those evenings and weekends that Jon was supposed to be at the chess club. But I did.

She gasped and her already-pale face became even paler. When I finished, she said, ''I don't believe it. Jon wouldn't . . .''

''It's very hard for a child to resist in a situation like this. We teach them to trust and obey adults. This man has probably spent months winning Jon's trust and affection. If it happened, Jon was probably too confused to resist, and afterward he felt too guilty to say anything.''

''But, the school sponsors this club.''

''The school has no idea what's going on. The man who advises the club, the molester, is a respected member of the community. He's been doing this for many years, and he's been very successful at hiding it.''

''No,'' she said, getting up and beginning to pace. ''It just isn't possible.''

''Has Jon brought home any expensive gifts, things he wouldn't have money to buy himself?''

''No.'' The answer came a little too quickly. I looked around the room and into the dining room that adjoined it. On a desk in the corner sat a portable computer.

''What about the computer? Where did he get that?''

''He won it. It was a prize in one of his tournaments. I told you he was good.'' Her tone was defensive. She knew, but she couldn't admit it, even to herself.

''That's an awfully expensive prize. Have there been others?''

The look on her face told me that there had. She was very

close to tears, but she was holding them back. "No, it couldn't be," she said fiercely.

"Jon needs help with this," I said. "He probably won't admit what's going on at first, but it's confusing and upsetting to a child. When someone you trust demands sex in return for their affection and friendship, it's shattering. And every time it happens, every gift he gets, he feels more guilty and confused. If it continues, it can destroy his ability to trust other people or himself."

"No, no," she kept repeating. "It's not happening." There was a fierceness to her face that was unnerving.

"I can recommend a counselor to work with Jon."

"No," she said. "No. You don't have any proof. You're just guessing."

"I don't know for sure, only Jon can tell us that. But we know the man he's been with is accused of doing this before. We know that he's been telling you he's going to chess club when he isn't, and we know he's been getting expensive gifts. Will you agree to having him see a counselor? Will you let the counselor work with him, try to find out what's been happening? It's the only way to help Jon out of this."

She sank into a chair. "It's so damn hard," she said. "You don't know what it's like, you can't, trying to raise three kids on next to nothing and nobody helping and nobody even gives a damn. They sell crack up the street, just three houses from here, and there was a drive-by shooting just a couple of blocks away.

"Jon's dad left when I was pregnant with his sister, the little one. Didn't even stick around to find out if it was a girl or a boy. Just left and never looked back. I try, God knows I do, but he's almost as tall as I am already, Jon is, and he's always talking back and acting up. He's only ten. What's it going to be like when he's fifteen?" She buried her head in her hands, but still she didn't cry. She seemed totally exhausted.

"I just can't handle it," she said. "I can't take any more."

"Now is the time to get help for both of you. Part of Jon's poor behavior is probably caused by the abuse. Kids who are sexually abused frequently become angry and take it out on people around them," I said. "With therapy we can turn that around."

She just kept shaking her head. I told her that the counselor wouldn't charge her to question Jon about the abuse, that the county would provide ongoing counseling for him.

I don't know if she even heard me. She seemed to withdraw into her own misery. Finally, she said, "Well, I just won't let him go to chess club anymore."

"That's a start, but it won't deal with the damage that's already been done. He needs help with this now. If he doesn't get that, he'll continue to have behavior problems. The problems will get worse."

"No, we'll be okay," she said. "He won't go to chess, and that's that."

"Will you let the counselor see him?"

"No. No, it's over."

"Please, Mrs. Marcus. It's not over for Jon, and it can't really be over until he's faced it and worked through all the feelings and confusion it's created."

"I don't hold with all the psychology stuff, and we don't go telling our family problems to strangers," she said stiffly.

"Jon is the victim of a crime, a serious crime. You can help the police put the criminal away. You and Jon can stop him from doing this to any other child."

"Crime? Tell me about crime. They're killing people on the streets and the police don't do nothing about it. Leave me alone, lady. I've already got more problems than I can handle. I don't need more." A bitterness had crept into her tone and a stubbornness. I wasn't going to get any further with her today, so I gave her my card and told her to call if she changed her mind.

15

PIEDMONT APPEARS PARTICULARLY lush when you come from the obvious poverty of east Oakland. It's enough to make a liberal weep and a radical start building bombs. It didn't do a lot for my already sinking spirits.

The Lashmans' house was fairly modest in comparison to the mansions and *Architectural Digest* candidates that make up much of Piedmont. In any other neighborhood, it would have been a nice middle-class house, but its address bumped it up to lower-upper or upper-middle or whatever they call the wannabe rich.

The woman who answered the door was tall, blond, and fashionably thin. She was wearing jeans and a Western-style shirt, but the look was anything but casual, more on the order of *Vogue* does the Old West.

"Mrs. Lashman?"

"Yes?" The voice had a sharpness to it. She probably thought I was selling magazine subscriptions.

"I'm Catherine Sayler. I called about the computer club."

"Oh, yes. Come in, please." Her tone thawed a few degrees. She led me to a living room furnished with metal, glass, and leather, and offered me a chair that looked like it had been designed by the Marquis de Sade.

I took a bit longer getting to the point this time. Irene Lashman seemed made of tougher stuff than Sally Marcus, but I wanted to avoid the reaction my revelations had produced the last time. Where Sally's face had broadcast her every reaction, Irene's was a mask. No emotion was allowed to reach the surface, but the muscles around her mouth tightened as I spoke.

Between her silence and lack of expression, she gave me as much feedback as a statue, making it impossible to guess the impact my words were having on her. She remained that way until I finished. Then she said very coolly, "Those are very serious allegations."

"Yes, they are. The impact of this sort of abuse is very serious. If your son is a victim, he'll need help—a lot of support from you and professional counseling."

Before I could go on, she stopped me. "I don't know who you are or why you're doing this, but Judge Reiter is a good friend of this family, and I won't hear any more attacks on his character. I think you'd better go."

She rose to see me out, but I remained seated.

"I know it's difficult to even contemplate the possibility. No parent wants to think that something like this could happen to their child, but if you don't at least consider it, you risk leaving Mark in a terrible situation."

"I asked you to leave," she said. "If you don't, I'll call the police."

"Then you're not even going to ask Mark?"

"Of course not."

"Let me at least tell you what kind of signs you might look for to tell you that he's a victim of abuse."

She shook her head. "I don't need to know. This is a fine Christian family and my son is a fine young man. Your suggestions are a profound insult."

"A victim is not responsible for what's done to him," I said. "This is not Mark's fault, and it's no reflection on his character."

"I will not have you try to involve my family in this sort of filth. And I won't have you interfere with his relationship with Judge Reiter. If you so much as mention my son's name to anyone, you will hear from my lawyer."

I struggled to keep anger from my voice. "This is not a matter of social standing. This is your son's life. I can understand that you don't want to believe that Mark is a victim.

That's a normal reaction. But I can't understand how you can leave him in jeopardy . . .'' I wanted to add "how you can put your own concern for social status before your child's welfare," but I didn't. Instead, I got up and went to the front door. There I stopped and took out my card. "If you change your mind and want help with this, please call me. I can put you in touch with a juvenile officer who specializes in helping boys like Mark.''

She didn't take the card, so I put it on the hall table and left.

I was shaking with rage by the time I got into my car, but I didn't want to sit in front of the Lashman house while I waited for it to pass. I drove very slowly around the corner and pulled into the curb.

I knew with a sickening certainty that both boys were victims. Jon would turn to a man who offered stability and safety. The gifts, things he could never afford to have, would sweeten the appeal, but it would be the sense of being cared for by a strong, protecting adult that hooked him.

And it wasn't hard to guess what Reiter would offer Mark to win his trust and devotion. Raised in a home where appearance and social position were all-important, the boy would be an easy mark for a powerful man who seemed to like him just for himself.

I could understand Sally Marcus. She had used herself up in the daily struggle of life, and she no longer possessed the strength to protect her son. But Irene Lashman was another matter. Her need to maintain an acceptable facade, a respectable social position, was more important to her than her son's welfare. She seemed to me almost as bad as Reiter.

I had over four hours before my appointment with Rosemary Sutter. It took that long to calm down. I took a long walk around Reiter's neighborhood. The houses were spectacular, yards designed and maintained by professionals—all the beauty money can buy. Another time I might have enjoyed it, but after my visit to Irene Lashman, it depressed me.

All this wealth and we couldn't even give our children
what they needed. I thought of Molly. What did she need?
And could I give it to her? She bounced between pleasant,
easygoing sociability and sullen hostility. I wasn't handling
the hostility well. I was awkward in my new role of surrogate
parent, and in my frustration, I came down on Molly harder
then I intended and created more problems than I solved.

Being a parent was such a big responsibility and the costs
were so appalling if you failed. It was easy to pity Sally
Marcus and feel contempt for Irene Lashman, but I'd been
fitting Molly in around the other demands in my life. She
was far more important to me than this case could ever be,
yet tonight I'd be late getting home and the time I'd been
planning to have with her would get put off again.

It was a short drive down the hill to Grand Avenue in Oakland. Grand runs right up to the end of Lake Merritt, an
urban jewel in a setting that is becoming increasingly tar-
nished by crime and violence. Grand Avenue has a nice
small-town feel to it. Many of the buildings date from the
forties, and while most are well maintained, few have been
indulged with fancy face-lifts.

The Sutters' apartment was in a building a block from
Grand Avenue in a neighborhood no longer grand but still
comfortable. I rang and identified myself. A muffled female
voice told me to come on up to 312 on the third floor. The
buzzer let out a sound like a dental drill from hell, and I
pushed the iron gate open and followed the directions to 312.

Rosemary Sutter was a small woman, barely over five feet.
Her curly black hair was cut short and her large brown eyes
reflected the smile on her lips.

"Do come in," she said warmly.

She offered me a chair and perched on the edge of the
sofa, watching me expectantly. "What's this about the chess
club?" she asked.

The story got harder with each telling, and the stakes got
higher. If I couldn't convince one of the parents to have their
son see Steve Marley, I'd have to start all over again on the

search for victims, and the further back in time I had to go, the colder the trail would become. Without a victim willing to speak up, there'd be no way to stop the judge from seducing and destroying the boys who came to trust him. There'd be no way to get help for Jon and Mark and Ben, no satisfaction for Joe, no justice for Mitch.

I tried a different approach. "Have you noticed any changes in your son's behavior since he joined the chess club?" I asked.

The question surprised her, but she considered it. "He joined about a year ago. I don't recall any changes then."

Something in her tone told me to push on. "How about since then?"

She fidgeted and looked uncomfortable. "Why do you ask?"

"Because I think that something may have happened at the club that could have affected Ben and might well have caused a change in his behavior."

"What?" she asked sharply.

"There has been a change," I said.

"Yes, but what happened?"

I told her as gently as I could. She was a sharp woman; I didn't have to spell it out for her.

"Oh no, God no," she cried. She jumped up and began pacing, rubbing one hand with the other. "Not Ben; please, not Ben."

I let her have a few minutes to absorb what I'd told her. She paced and talked, as much to herself as to me.

"I *knew* something was wrong. I *knew* it wasn't just normal preteen behavior. He was so angry all of a sudden. Angry and hostile. He was like another kid. His schoolwork went downhill, and he got in fights. I should have known. I should have known.

"I talked to his teacher. She said he wasn't so bad, that he was probably just going through a phase. But I knew she was wrong. She has thirty kids, and half of them can't read or have parents strung out on drugs or they're already in trouble with the police. Of course Ben's problems didn't seem serious to her.''

She collapsed onto the sofa, the pain etched on her face. ''What am I going to do?''

''There is help available,'' I said. ''I have the name of a counselor who will work with Ben to find out exactly what happened, and to get him into a treatment program where they can help him deal with it. He can recommend someone for you, too, if you'd like.''

She nodded dully.

''The man who did this has been molesting boys for years. The only way to stop him is for you and Ben to go to the police.''

She nodded again, but I wasn't sure it signaled agreement. ''I know that's what we should do, but what about Ben? Will he have to testify in court?''

''It's possible,'' I said. ''But the police officer I talked with told me that very few of these cases ever get to court. In the vast majority, the molester pleads guilty. Also, once the police are involved, they're likely to find other boys who were molested and other evidence so that the burden doesn't fall on Ben alone.''

I hoped it would work that way. I hated to think of a ten-year-old boy being forced to go into court and face the man who'd molested him, then having to tell that awful story to a group of complete strangers. I had a momentary flash of what it must be like to be that small and vulnerable, sitting in a chair made for grown-ups, with the judge's bench looming over you, and being asked to describe events so private and painful that you wouldn't even talk about them with your parents. I could understand why no mother wanted to put her child through that.

She nodded again—it seemed almost a reflex reaction— but she said, ''We'll see a counselor, then decide what to do.'' Then suddenly her expression changed. She sat up straight, her eyes wide. ''What if he has AIDS? Could Ben have gotten AIDS?''

Another level of horror added to the others. I hadn't even thought of it.

"I don't think it's likely," I said. "This man is attracted to children. It's highly unlikely that he's had sex with infected adults."

"But if he's a homosexual?"

"We have no evidence that he's a homosexual. He's a pedophile, and he likes boys; that doesn't mean he likes adult men."

She considered it. Her face was pinched with worry. "If we go to the police and they arrest him, will they test him for AIDS?"

"I don't know, but I can find out. I think the first thing we need to do is arrange for Ben to meet with Steve Marley. He's a juvenile officer from San Francisco who works with boys like Ben. He'll talk with Ben and get him to tell him exactly what happened."

I could see her relief at having something concrete to do. "Just tell me where and when to bring him," she said.

"I'll be honest with you," I said. "This isn't going to be easy on Ben. He's apt to resist it. It may take some time."

"I understand."

"He'll want to avoid it. There'll be a tremendous desire to ignore it and hope it'll go away."

"You can't do that," she said grimly. "It doesn't work."

I wondered what experience had taught her that, but she wasn't about to tell me, and I wasn't anxious to know. I'd seen enough human misery already today.

I gave her my phone number and told her that I'd ask Steve Marley to call her.

I was so tired that I couldn't face driving back to San Francisco. Three interviews, maybe two hours' total, but so much pain. I found a café on Grand Avenue where I could get something to eat. I hoped that food would give me some energy, but I knew that my exhaustion had little to do with nutrition.

I wondered how many boys Samuel Reiter had abused

during his lifetime. How many lives had he torn apart? How many boys had learned too young that you can't trust anyone?

16

WHEN YOU'RE IN a hurry, it's easy to make mistakes. But when you're in a hurry, you tend to forget that.

I'd been in such a hurry to get the Reiter case wrapped up that I hadn't wanted to wait for Steve Marley's return. When he called that night, he didn't hide his displeasure at my activities.

"You went to see the parents? I *never* talk to parents. You should have gone to the Oakland police and let them handle it."

"I didn't have enough evidence to go to the police," I said, "and besides, I got what I was after. Rosemary Sutter is willing to have you interview Ben. How soon do you think you can do it?"

Marley had already told me that his mother's fall had produced no more serious injuries than a number of ugly bruises. She was not the kind of woman to hang around the hospital, and had gone home and resumed spading the garden as soon as she could bully the doctor into releasing her. Marley could stick around and paint her kitchen or go home and paint his own. I figured I could make him a better offer.

"I could drive back tonight," he said. "If you can set it up for tomorrow, I'll see him then. If not, we could do it Monday."

"I'll try for tomorrow," I said.

Rosemary was as anxious as I was to get moving. She offered to bring Ben to my office the next morning. I warned her that it would take more than a few polite questions to get Ben to admit what was going on with Samuel Reiter.

"Think of the worst secret you know, the most embarrassing thing you could admit about yourself, and imagine what it would take to get you to tell that to a stranger," I said.

It would take getting through every defense that Ben had erected, building enough trust so he could risk telling the truth, wearing down his resistance until it was easier to talk than to keep covering up, and finally, convincing him that his private pain was not his alone. That was the distance Marley had to cross to reach Ben, and it was full of emotional mines.

Marley would begin by establishing rapport and building trust. He'd ask easy questions to get a sense of how Ben reacted when he was telling the truth, then he'd move to the harder ones and watch for the subtle signs that the boy was lying or trying to hide something. His questions would tell Ben that he already knew what had happened, that he'd heard the same story from other boys. Slowly, in the hours they spent together, Steve would create the safe space in which Ben could finally open up.

Rosemary brought Ben to my office the next morning. She hadn't confronted him about Reiter, and he was happy enough to miss a day of school that he didn't ask too many questions about where they were going.

Steve took over my office. McGee had already settled in on the couch and saw no reason to leave, and Ben immediately took to the lazy tom and began stroking him. McGee is a shameless hustler. He rolled right over on his back and began purring like mad. I figured Ben could use all the support he could get. For once McGee was actually earning his keep.

I finally convinced Rosemary that there wasn't any need to hover outside the door. She couldn't think of anywhere to go, so I suggested a museum. "Go to the De Young. You can walk around the Japanese Tea Garden when you're feel-

ing too restless. Call every hour or so, and I'll tell you how
it's going."

She went, but only because she couldn't think of a good
excuse for staying.

It was a long day for all of us, probably longest for Ben.
Steve Marley came out after about thirty minutes. "He's a
victim, I'd bet on it. But I don't know how long it'll take to
get him to admit it," he said.

I played waitress, taking in cider and doughnuts, sand-
wiches, and other munchies. Each time Ben looked tighter
and more drawn. Rosemary called every half hour. My heart
went out to both of them.

Since Jesse was still in Sunnyvale, I'd taken over his office
just down the hall from mine. I still had plenty of work to
catch up on, but I didn't get much done, and I'd guess that
Amy's productivity was also near zero. Around eleven
o'clock I got a call that focused my attention.

"Ms. Sayler, this is Lawrence Chilton of Pacific Rim."
Pacific Rim imports mechanized toys and other low-tech
goodies from the Far East. Lawrence Chilton is its founder
and president. He'd hired me last year to find out how crates
that contained highly sophisticated toy robots when they left
Japan arrived in San Francisco full of cheap copies from
Indonesia.

"Yes, Mr. Chilton. What can I do for you?"

"I'm calling because I understand that you've made some
very serious allegations against a good friend of mine, Samuel Reiter. I'm sure there must be some mistake here."

It sure hadn't taken long for word to get back to Reiter,
and it hadn't taken him long to counterattack. I could see the
Old Boys circling up to protect their own.

I wanted to ask Chilton if he had children and how he'd
feel about a man who befriended them and then demanded
sex. Instead, I said in as neutral a tone as I could manage,
"I appreciate your desire to help, Mr. Chilton, but I'm sure
you understand that I can't discuss a case with anyone other
than my client. I owe him that same confidentiality that I
promised you."

"Yes, of course," he said. The irritation in his voice said, "Who the hell are you to defy me?"

"I'm glad you understand," I said before he could tack on a "but." "Let me assure you that I will conduct this investigation with the same integrity and discretion that I provided Pacific Rim."

"This doesn't seem an appropriate kind of case for your agency," Chilton said. "I doubt that I'd have selected you as our investigator if I'd known you were also involved in this sort of thing."

"That would certainly have been your right, just as it's my right to decide which cases I choose to take."

I got two more calls before lunch. I gave them both the confidentiality speech I'd used on Chilton. They didn't like it any better than he did. One, a bank vice-president, took the avuncular approach and warned me to beware of tales scoundrels tell. The other came very close to warning me that I'd never work in this town again.

My dad used to say that when you pull on a snake's tail you'd better watch out for the other end. This snake was proving to have sharp fangs and a long reach.

I was surprised by Reiter's reaction. I'd known when I left Irene Lashman that there was a real danger she'd call him, but I'd assumed that he'd want to keep my investigation a secret and hope that none of the boys would talk. Instead, he'd taken the offensive, recruiting his powerful friends to warn me off.

It was an aggressive move. It made me wonder about how he would have responded to Mitch. The threats of influential businessmen wouldn't have been of any use there. Would he have ordered up a hired killer with the same cold calculation that he'd called his friends about me? And if so, would he try the same solution on me when he found out that threats hadn't worked?

A little after three, I was startled by a loud shout from my office. Ben was screaming at Steve. The words were muffled by the door but the fury behind them came through. The angry shouting was followed by sobbing, as loud as the shouts at first and slowly quieting down.

After what seemed forever, Steve came out. He looked emotionally and physically exhausted. "Ask his mother to come back when she calls," he said. "Ben could probably use something to drink."

I took Ben a Coke and some chocolate chip cookies. His face was streaked with tears, and he looked terribly young and vulnerable. He was clutching McGee on his lap and stroking him absentmindedly, a liberty that the big tom had never allowed an adult.

Steve was planning to wait until Monday to talk to the Oakland police, but when I told him of the phone calls from Reiter's friends he changed his mind.

"Damn, I was afraid of that. It means we have to move fast," he said. "There's a good chance he's already gotten rid of any evidence in his house. We have to hope he doesn't realize that we're ready to move. Guys like Reiter usually keep mementos of their affairs—photos, cards and letters from the boys, little presents—stuff that helps us make the case and identify the other victims. We really want to get there before he disposes of that stuff."

"How fast can you move?"

Marley looked at his watch. "Friday afternoon. Boy, I don't know. Especially when we're asking for a search warrant for the residence of a superior court judge. Let me make a couple of calls."

Marley got lucky; an old friend in the Oakland PD agreed to wait for Rosemary and Ben to come down and file a report. "The judges'll be gone by the time we get the warrant written up, but we can get one of them at home to sign it. There'll be a lot of bitching about the screwed-up weekend, but we'll get it done."

Steve went with Rosemary and Ben. He put an arm around the youngster and spoke gently and encouragingly to him.

"I'm going to tell you exactly what to expect over there," he said as they headed out my door. "You've already been through the worst part."

I picked Marley up at the BART station at eight-fifteen. The sigh he heaved as he settled into the seat spoke of more than fatigue.

"They're getting a warrant to search Reiter's house. They wanted to do more investigation and line up a couple of more kids before they asked for the warrant, but I convinced them that we couldn't wait, not now that he knows we're after him.

"Ben did great. He's bouncing between guilt and anger. One minute he feels he's betrayed his best friend; the next he wants the cops to take Reiter out and shoot him. But he's holding it together. And the guys on the case are good. They believe Ben. They'll work hard to make a case."

We drove up Market Street. Homeless men and women were settling into doorways and any other space that might offer a night's uneasy sleep. The temperatures in San Francisco in April might not be cold by comparison to much of the rest of the country, but they were a long way from anything you'd want to sleep in, if you had any choice.

"When will they search his house?" I asked.

"Tonight or tomorrow morning. I asked one of the guys to call me when they have the results."

"At least you'll get a week of fishing in," I said, feeling guilty that I'd used up half of his vacation.

"I'm ready for that."

I dropped him at his car and headed on home, hoping that by tomorrow the case would be over. I was ready to go back to some nice, quiet corporate crime.

I was also ready to give up my daily round of AA meetings. I'd sat through at least a dozen of them, telling my story and listening to others, and all I'd gotten from it was more opportunity for self-scrutiny and reflection than I found comfortable. I don't know that I was drinking less, but I sure wasn't enjoying it the way I used to. That seemed like a heavy price to pay for the possibility that I *might* find some-

one who *might* know something about a man who *might* have
been murdered.

17

MOLLY HAD BEEN adamant about her desire to sleep in
Saturday morning, and I agreed to let her miss aikido
in exchange for her promise that she'd do something with me
in the afternoon. She was living in my house, but I'd been
busy enough with work that we hadn't had nearly enough
time together. It made me nervous that the black-eyeliner
crowd was waiting in the wings should she not get what she
needed from me.

Th aikido class went well. We had a couple of new women
who were attending regularly and with growing enthusiasm.
One was fifty and had gray hair and smile wrinkles, the other
was fifteen. The fifty-year-old was feisty and exuberant, the
fifteen-year-old, shy and retiring. They'd adopted each other,
and we all enjoyed watching their friendship develop. I wondered if the older woman ever felt awkward with her young
friend the way I did so often with Molly.

Molly was in the kitchen eating breakfast when I got home.
She'd made scrambled eggs, a welcome change from the junk
food she ate in prodigious amounts. The counter was piled
with more dirty dishes than I would have dreamed you could
use making such a simple dish.

"Steve Marley called," she said. "The number's next to
the phone."

The number wasn't next to the phone. It was over by the
sink. Molly couldn't figure out how it got there. Marley an-

swered on the fifth ring. Background sounds suggested that the home improvement of the day involved some form of demolition. His voice was grim. "They've done the search, and they got zip. He must have cleared out the house as soon as he heard that you were asking questions."

"Damn," I said. "What does that do to the case?"

"Makes it harder, of course, but not impossible. We still have Ben's testimony, and the juvenile division will start tracing down every contact past and present. Sometimes you get a list of kids and acts and dates, and then it's real easy. This way is harder."

"Do you think he destroyed all the evidence?"

"I doubt it. Could you just burn up all your scrapbooks, old letters, and snapshots? And I'd bet Reiter is much more attached to his mementos than you are to yours. We're talking compulsion here. I'd bet he hid them somewhere."

"It's not the type of thing you box up and ask your neighbor to store. Where would he put it?"

"He could have an apartment somewhere, though Ben didn't mention one. Could have given it to another ped. Maybe he has a summer cabin."

"Or a boat," I said, remembering Joe's snapshot. "Did Ben say anything about a boat?"

"No, but I can ask him. A man in Reiter's position might well have a summer place and a boat. I'll ask about both."

I made some fresh coffee and sat down at the table. "So what would you like to do this afternoon?"

She shrugged. "You don't have to entertain me, you know."

"I wasn't planning to. But I was looking forward to spending a few hours with you. How about the Museum of Modern Art? There's a new photography exhibit there. Or we could go walking on Mount Tam or at the beach."

Neither possibility seemed to enflame her with enthusiasm. I wondered what had happened to the cheerful little girl who was in love with the world a couple of years ago. The first horror writer to create body snatchers must have been the parent of a teenager.

I made some more suggestions. She worked on perfecting her shrug. Finally, I said, "Let's hold up a bank."

She looked surprised. At least she was listening. "Just checking," I said. "How about we change sides? You make the suggestions and I'll shrug for a while."

"I know you're trying to help me," she said, "but I'm not into those things anymore."

"What are you into?"

"Hanging out with my friends."

"So why don't we invite your friends to go along?"

"Catherine," she said, in the tone I'd used to say "Mother," "my friends aren't into the kind of stuff you want to do."

Having met the friends, I wasn't sure I wanted to know what they were into.

A dish crashed to the floor just behind me. It was followed by a large, very guilty-looking cat who made a dash for the door. "Stone," I yelled, and threw a paper at him. "Bad cat."

Touchstone can move remarkably fast for a grossly over-weight animal. He was under the bed by the time I'd finished swearing at him.

I don't believe you can train a cat, that's part of why I like them so much. They have a bad attitude toward authority. With a cat, you learn to practice preventive behavior. With Touchstone, that means never leaving any form of food within his reach. It had taken two months to get Peter to accept that dishes had to be rinsed before being abandoned on the counter. Now we had Molly. Molly who seemed to believe that dirty dishes magically cleaned themselves. When Molly arrived, Touchstone must have thought he'd died and gone to heaven.

Molly was working hard to suppress a giggle. She was saved by the phone. I answered it. A voice I didn't recognize said, "Molly?"

I gave her the phone and tried to decide whether I should

leave the room. I settled for doing the dishes. "You can take it in my study if you want," I said.

"It's okay," she said, and took the phone. Eavesdropping is an occupational hazard. I didn't mean to do it; it's just an automatic reflex.

"Uh, no, I can't, not today. I'm supposed to do some stuff with my aunt. . . . Yeah, well, I'll try. . . . Yeah, I'll call you." Not a lot of words, but the tone said, "Mental cruelty practiced here."

I was just finishing the dishes when the phone rang again. It was Marley with the news that Reiter had a sailboat that he kept at the Berkeley marina, and a cabin in Pinecrest. "I'll get the Oakland PD to get warrants for both of those," he said. "Maybe we'll get lucky."

The morning had been cold and gray when I went to aikido, and it had progressed to a miserable thin mist. Just enough to make outdoor activity unpleasant, and not enough to help with the drought that had scorched the state for four years. We'd had too many mornings like this.

"Get your swimsuit," I said.

"What?"

"Get your suit, your bathrobe, and a couple of towels. And dress warm."

"Where are we going?" she asked suspiciously.

"You'll see."

The town of Calistoga is about an hour north of San Francisco, in the middle of some of the most beautiful grape country in the world and right on top of a bunch of hot springs. Sam Brannan, who'd dreamed of creating a Western spa that would rival New York's Saratoga, had built quite a resort there in the 1850s, but the scheme had drained his wealth and a nasty divorce had taken the rest of his assets and left Calistoga a sleepy little town, until a few years ago when the yup people discovered it.

Back East, sitting in hot water may be regarded as a cure for what ails you. Californians take a more hedonistic approach. Hot springs in the middle of a valley full of wineries is pretty close to our idea of heaven.

The drive itself is worth the trip. The upper Napa Valley is covered with neatly tended rows of wine grapes, interrupted occasionally by ancient volcanic cones that rise like tree-covered islands from a sea of vineyards. Thickly wooded hills frame the valley to the west and their arid, starkly rocky cousins form its boundary to the east.

Downtown Calistoga is four blocks long and lined with buildings old enough to be picturesque. I turned at the second block and took us to the Roman Spa Motel. I love the Roman Spa because it makes no pretense of being in the health business. The pools are surrounded by palm trees and flowers, and at night steam rises from the outdoor pools in great dramatic clouds.

Molly hadn't said much on the way up. She was looking at me as though I'd completely lost my mind. "Come on," I said. "At the worst you'll have a good story to tell your friends."

I bought day passes and we changed into our suits. The "cool" outdoor pool is somewhere around comfortable bath temperature. We started there, worked our way to the hotter indoor pool, and ended up in the small, very-hot pool under the palm trees. The lightest of rains brushed our faces, and even Molly couldn't suppress a sigh of contentment.

I leaned back with the rain on my face and felt all the tension of the last couple of weeks drain away. When I'd reached cooked-noodle status, I dragged myself out into the delicious coolness of the air. "You want a late lunch or a massage?" I asked.

"I've never had a massage."

"Always a first time."

We put on robes and headed to the long, low building in back. They'd redone the office since my last visit, gone upscale, but the girl at the desk still looked like it was 1968.

"I can get you in, in about an hour," she said. "Would you like a mud or an enzyme bath before the massage? We're offering a special on them this weekend." Immersing my body in hot mud, even healthy hot mud, has never particularly appealed to me, especially after a friend told me it felt like dying. That's an experience I don't pay money to have.

"What's the enzyme bath?" I asked.

"It's a Japanese practice," she explained. "We put you in a tub with specially blended cedar fibers and plant enzymes. It's very warm and relaxing, stimulates the circulation and metabolism."

"Sounds better than mud," Molly said.

I was going to pass on the shredded cedar, but Molly looked interested, so I signed us up. Fifteen minutes later we were climbing into large boxes of what looked like sawdust. I grumbled. Molly said, "Relax, at worst you'll have a great story to tell Peter, or better yet, my mom." The enzyme bath was a success before we ever got in it.

It was relaxing and it smelled good. I don't know what the enzymes did, but I had a short snooze and felt great when I climbed out. Getting all the little shreds of bark off my body would have been tedious as hell except that Molly developed a fit of the giggles, and we ended up clowning around and laughing like a couple of ten-year-olds.

After the massage, we had an early dinner at a little restaurant that reminded me that yuppification is not all bad. It does improve the quality of the food and wine. Molly has fairly conservative tastes, which is part of being a kid, but she tried some duck sausages that were absolutely exotic for her.

Sunset comes early in the valley, so much of our ride home was in fading light, but nothing could dampen our spirits. We were both a bit euphoric—lots of "Look, there's a hawk on the fence" and "Jeeze, that's beautiful." I wondered why she'd locked that side of herself away for so long.

In Marin, where houses had replaced the open country, she said, "You know, that really was fun. Mom never does anything for fun."

"Maybe her idea of fun is different," I said. Marion's idea of fun had always been different from mine.

"I guess," Molly said.

"You're different people. You like different things."

"Yeah, well, I just wish she'd stop trying to make me into something I don't want to be. She doesn't know who I am, and she doesn't want to. She wants me to be just like her. And when I'm not, *I'm* wrong."

I remember saying something similar to my mother. I also remember her sighing and telling me it wasn't so easy being a parent.

"She treats me like a baby, for chrissake," Molly complained. "For all those years before Leonard came along, I was her 'big girl.' I was mature enough to be home alone, to fix dinner for myself, to listen to her troubles. Now that I'm really old enough to take care of myself, she's decided that I'm 'still a child.' "

I remembered how Marion had praised Molly's independence and maturity when she was younger. Molly had had to be mature. There wasn't much choice. Her daddy took a hike when she was six years old, and Marion was ill equipped to be on her own. There were times when Molly had seemed more responsible than her mother. She'd relied on herself too long to become "Mommy's little girl" now that Marion was ready to take charge.

"You're pretty grown-up, all right," I said, "but it's a scary world out there. I wouldn't like to think of you having to face it all alone."

"I know kids who do."

"I know you do," I said, "but it seems to me that no one cares enough about those kids to want to protect them. They have lots of freedom, but I don't know that they have much else."

Molly was silent for a while. I didn't know whether she was thinking about what I'd said or had dismissed me as a creature from the Dark Ages. I did know that teenagers do not say, "You're right."

18

THE RED LIGHT on my answering machine blinked to tell me I had a call. Steve Marley's voice on the tape sounded excited. "Call me when you get in. I've got news."

He was excited. "I think we got a live one here," he said. "The sailboat isn't at the Berkeley Marina. Reiter's slip is empty. He claims a friend is sailing the boat to Mexico, but I've got a hunch it's closer than that."

"Are the police checking the local marinas?"

"I don't know. It may take them a while to get around to it."

"I'll give them a little help," I said. "Give me a description of the boat."

"It's a thirty-foot Catalina sloop, white. The name is the *Jolly Roger*, California registration number 360964."

Tracing boats isn't my specialty, but I'd done it once before as part of another case, so I had a starting point. My starting point was Larry Davis, the harbor master at Oyster Point. I called him first thing Monday morning.

Larry remembered me. "You're the gorgeous creature who resisted my efforts to get you in the sack, and destroyed my self-esteem forever," he said.

"I prefer to think of it as saving you from being decapitated by your lovely-but-jealous wife," I replied. "How's my favorite sex maniac?"

"Better for hearing from you. When you coming down, so I can chase you around the desk?"

"As soon as I get a new pair of running shoes. In the

meantime, I need some help.'' I explained my problem to him. ''So if you had a thirty-foot Catalina you didn't want found, where would you put it that would still be within an hour or two of Oakland?''

''Well, not one of the bigger marinas. We check registration and all that stuff pretty carefully. I'd go to an older, private marina, one where they want your money badly enough not to ask too many questions.''

''And where would you find such a place?''

''There's one or two on the Bay, but I think I'd go up the Sacramento River to someplace in the delta. There's plenty of private places up there. I might scrape the registration numbers off my boat, maybe even the name, but unless there was time to repaint the sucker, you'd probably still be able to read them from where the paint faded.''

''Is there a directory with the names and phone numbers of those places?''

''I don't know of one offhand, but I have a bunch of numbers here. You planning on calling marinas?''

''That was the plan,'' I said.

''I don't know how much luck you'll have. We harbor masters don't just give out information, especially not on paying customers.''

''Actually, I was going to identify myself as your new assistant.''

He laughed. ''The day I make enough to hire an assistant, I'll be too old to enjoy the interviews.''

It was my turn to laugh. ''So how do I get these guys to tell me if the missing boat is in their marina?'' I asked.

''You can tell them you're a friend of mine, that might help. But the truth is never as much fun as a good fib. Why don't you tell them that the owner of the boat stiffed me for fees and you're helping me find him.''

''Sounds good to me,'' I said. ''Thanks, I really appreciate it.''

''Think nothing of it. I'm planning on calling you the next time some guy really does stiff me.''

I couldn't see asking Larry to read me all the telephone

numbers he had over the phone. Jesse would have suggested that he fax them, but I knew Larry. He probably didn't own a microwave; he definitely wouldn't have a fax.

It's my belief that almost anything you want to know can be found in some book, and the real challenge is finding that book. A call to Rand McNally confirmed that there was a book that listed marinas, public and private, on the West Coast, and they had one copy in stock.

I sent Amy for the book, and asked Chris to come give me an update on what was happening with Jesse's undercover job. "This is taking longer than it should. What's going on?" I asked.

"We think something spooked them," she said. "Jesse's playing it extra careful, that's why he hasn't come in since last week. He's coming up tonight to see Claire, so he'll stop by here sometime after six. He was hoping to meet with you then."

"I'll be here," I said. "Do you need anything from me on this case?"

She shook her head. "We just need these folks to make a move."

"Well, when that happens, let me know. It makes me nervous to be sitting this one out."

Chris handles Amy's desk when she's out, and while she can be Ms. Charm when she wants information, she's just slightly more pleasant than Leona Helmsley as a receptionist.

"There's a Kevin Doyle here to see you. He says he's a reporter. He does *not* have an appointment," she announced. The tone of her voice was only a few degrees above freezing.

I figured that the poor guy would never get up the courage to come back, so I told her to send him in.

Kevin Doyle had more freckles than I can remember seeing on a grown man. He was covered with them—face, arms, hands. I don't know about anywhere else, but I'd bet they were there, too.

His hair was red and sort of curly, and he had a Tom

Sawyer grin. His parents obviously hadn't believed that boys
needed their teeth straightened, so his upper jaw looked like
it had too many teeth competing for too little room. Instead
of detracting from his appearance, the crooked teeth came
across as a badge of individuality.

Doyle was probably in his mid- to late twenties. He was
surprisingly well dressed for a newspaperman. His pants had
a single crease down each leg instead of the spider web or
wrinkles that my friend Max Siedman manages to impress
on every pair of slacks he owns. His shirt was actually tucked
in all the way around.

He handed me his press credentials and explained that he
was a reporter for the *Chronicle* on special assignment. "That
means they put me on a slightly longer leash," he confided.
"I'm doing a series on child abuse, and I've gotten interested
in pedophiles. The stereotype is that these are guys in dirty
raincoats who lurk around bus stations, but they're often
highly respected members of the community. But then you
know that," he said with a knowing look.

What I know is never to tell a reporter anything you don't
want to see in print. I kept my expression neutral.

Doyle was undeterred. "I understand that the juvenile sex-
crimes unit executed a search warrant of one Judge Samuel
Reiter," he said. "And I understand that you had something
to do with it."

"Mr. Doyle," I said, "I *never* comment on my cases to
anyone outside my office, especially not to reporters."

He waited for me to say more. I didn't. He just kept sitting
there looking at me expectantly. He was waiting for me to
get uncomfortable with the silence, so I'd say something to
fill it. I use that maneuver all the time. I didn't appreciate
being on the receiving end.

I stood up and extended my hand to signal that the interview was over. "I'm sorry that I can't help you. I'll look
forward to reading your articles."

He remained seated. I remained standing. "Ms. Sayler,
from what I hear, you care deeply about abuse of this kind.

Surely you won't just turn your back and let this man get away with his crime.''

"I told you, Mr. Doyle, I don't discuss my cases with reporters.''

He shrugged his shoulders, gave me an engaging can't-blame-me-for-trying grin, and finally got up to go. At the door, he stopped and took out a business card. "If you change your mind, or you know someone who wants to make sure that the truth gets told, please give me a call.''

I had the feeling as he left that I wasn't going to get rid of Kevin Doyle that easily. It had taken less than forty-eight hours for him to learn about the search warrant. I expected that rumors must be flying around the courthouse, but I also knew that only the insiders would hear them. Kevin Doyle had excellent sources someplace.

There were more marinas in the Bay Area than I'd guessed, especially when you included the ones in the Sacramento River delta. I spent so much time on the phone that my ear hurt, and I began to fear that the telephone would grow onto the side of my head.

It took the better part of the day to call them all. Most were friendly and cooperative when I mentioned Larry's name, but none of them had seen the *Jolly Roger*. Several harbor masters at smaller, private facilities didn't know Larry and wouldn't talk to me.

I could drive to each of those marinas, or I could take the easy way out. I could send Chris. She'd prefer being out of the office to going over Anton Glosser's financial records, and she'd actually enjoy flirting with strange men and getting them to tell her things. I got tired of that one a long time ago.

I asked her to bring me the Glosser file and catch me up on what she'd found.

"Hard to say yet," she said. "Most of what I've found looks pretty clean, but there are a couple of things to raise questions about. They have to do with some limited partnerships where Glosser's listed as one of the general partners. Two of these partnerships have ownership structures that look like Chinese boxes. You know, X is owned by Y and Z, who are owned by A, B, and C, who are owned by . . ." She shrugged. "When things get that complicated, you have to wonder why."

"The other partnerships look solid—property management, real estate, a couple of small electronics ventures, that sort of thing. Ownership's pretty straightforward. I've checked on the other general partners, and they're just who you'd expect—a couple of relatives, his wife, and the major investors in his company. There's only one guy who doesn't fit, a Milton Diesman." She shuffled through the file, and pulled out a sheet of paper.

"Diesman is himself the general partner in a long list of limited partnerships, many of which are obviously real estate deals. I haven't had a chance to check on them, but one name was familiar—Sunnyside Properties. Ring any bells?"

"More like sirens," I said. The name's familiar because those are the folks we nailed in a pro bono case just after you came on staff almost three years ago. Remember the Tenderloin SRO hotel where the owner cut off the heat in December? That was owned by Sunnyside. They're slumlords."

She gave a low whistle. "You mean our boy's a slumlord?"

"His friend Diesman could be. It's worth checking on Sunnyside and Diesman."

"I have one more thing for you," Chris said. I waited while she pulled out another paper. "I checked the newspaper file on Dialogue. Two references to Glosser in the *Chronicle* in the last six months. He was elected president of the German-American Association, and he's involved in trying to put together some kind of trading deal with Germany. He's been working with the State Department, might be headed into politics."

"Really," I said. "A place where the appearance of propriety is required, at least in order to get in."

I called Molly at four and got the answering machine. When I picked up my messages, her voice informed me that she was going to "hang out" with some of her friends and would be back that evening. I wondered about the friends. Were they the vampire twins or someone from school? And what exactly did *hang out* mean to kids in the nineties? I was beginning to feel real empathy for Marion.

Jesse got there about six-fifteen. He was wearing a black T-shirt and jeans, and he'd gotten a haircut that made him look very hip and about nineteen years old.

"Is this the International Harvester look?" I asked.

"You like it? I wanted to catch people's attention, maybe speed things up a bit. Claire hates it."

"You look like someone I'd cross the street to avoid," I said. That's a compliment in our business.

We went over what was happening down in Sunnyvale. The answer was not much. "I been making lots of noise about having a new lady who's running me into the poorhouse. And I know they checked out my room over a week ago, so I don't know what's holding them up."

"Any chance they've made you?"

"Nah. I don't think so. It just doesn't feel like that. The guys I figure as contacts, they're still real friendly, and they're still dropping hints that maybe they know how a bright, not-too-straight guy could make some real money."

"Just be careful. Maybe I should be running backup. I think things are about to come together up here, at least on part of the case."

Jesse shook his head. "Sometimes it's more dangerous to have backup than to go it alone."

I knew he was right. When you're working alone, you only have to worry about not screwing up; add another person and you have to worry about them, too.

"So tell me about Anton Glosser. *That's* the situation I'm worried about," he said.

"Nothing yet. Chris has found enough to make me think I might find something if I dig deeper. Peter's talked with an attorney who thinks that Maureen Merrick may have cause to sue the county for negligence. I'd rather see her get the money out of Glosser."

"Where does this thirst for vengeance come from? I thought you didn't believe in that sort of thing. How does that square with your aikido?"

"Aikido is about experiencing the consequences of your actions. You try to hit me, you end up on the floor. Glosser took an action when he double-crossed Orrin Merrick. I just want him to experience the consequences."

"No turning the other cheek, huh?"

"Not when it encourages a man like Glosser to hit the next poor soul who irritates him."

I AWOKE TUESDAY morning to the sound of rain. Four years of drought have sharpened our appreciation of what used to be regarded as a general nuisance. Now heavy, dark clouds are a cause for celebration. On barren hillsides in Marin, New Agers perform rain rituals, and I have friends who refuse to carry umbrellas out of the superstitious belief that their lack of protection will somehow hasten a downpour.

Molly seemed unusually cheerful at breakfast, and even Peter managed a minimal effort at conversation. Stone took the rain as a sign that he'd better store up more fat for winter, and made a nuisance of himself until I dumped him out the back door. He took one look at the puddles in the backyard and dashed between my legs back into the kitchen. Stone believes that water should be confined to bowls and toilets.

I took my umbrella to the office, just to be ornery and

because I find the rain a whole lot more pleasant when it's not dripping down my neck.

Larry Davis called around ten. "A friend of mine, Charlie Milkin, from up the delta, called. He'd lost your number, but he thinks he's found your boat."

"Terrific. Where?"

"He was driving over to his cousin's yesterday and went by a place upriver used to be owned by a family with two boats. Present owners just have a small motor boat, and the second slip is usually empty. Only right now it has a pretty little Catalina sloop there. Charlie went over to take a closer look, and the name's gone, but you can still see where the paint's faded around the letters. It's the *Jolly Roger*, all right."

"Larry, you're a prince. I'll take you *and* your lovely wife to dinner the next time I'm down your way. What's Charlie's number?"

"Pam's on a diet, but I know a great place with candlelight and soft music."

"Dinner, Larry, no dessert. Now, what's the number?"

Charlie Milkin was delighted to help. He told me all about the last guy who'd slipped out without paying for repairs. "Guy said he was a doctor. His check bounced like a rubber ball. But he'd been talking about going to San Luis, and I got friends down there. They called the cops. Turned out this guy owed marinas up and down the coast. He'd even used fake papers to get the loan to buy the boat. He'll be making license plates for a while."

Charlie gave me directions to the boat and promised not to let anyone know we were onto it. I passed the information to Steve Marley. He tipped the cops in Oakland. He asked if I'd like him to tag along on the search. I figured that meant he was anxious to escape cleaning out closets at home, so I said yes.

I didn't get a lot of work done during the next several hours. My attention kept straying to the phone. We must have gotten a dozen calls before the one I was waiting for.

Steve Marley's voice was jubilant. "We found it," he announced. "Boxes and boxes of stuff. They'll go through it back at the station, but just the stuff from the first box would be enough for an indictment. There's a diary. Reiter was into flowery descriptions of his affairs. His own writing'll be enough to convict him. And the diary seems to have some kids' names, so tracing recent victims won't be that hard."

"Did you tell them to look for anything that might tie him to Mitch's death?"

"I did, and they'll contact homicide if anything at all shows up. I should think that Judge Samuel Reiter is only a few hours away from being arrested."

Joe was not as excited by my news as I'd expected. He gave a long sigh and said, "So it's finally over."

I hated to tell him that it wasn't anywhere near over. Reiter would probably plea-bargain, but he was a public figure and the media were bound to make a circus out of the whole thing."

"I don't think you need worry about being dragged into it," I said. "That is, unless they find something linking Reiter to Mitch's murder. It sounds like they have more than enough to make the child-molestation charges."

I hate to admit it, but I'm just a bit superstitious. A part of me believes in omens and runs of luck. When things are going my way, I buy a lottery ticket. When they're not, I'm especially careful in crossing the street. Today I bought a lottery ticket on my way to another AA meeting.

The lottery ticket wasn't a winner, but the meeting made up for that.

It was led by a short, dark-haired man with a pockmarked face who introduced himself as Mel R. I closed my eyes and listened to his voice to see if it matched the one on Mitch's phone tape. I couldn't be sure.

The topic of Mel's talk was transcending the past. As he related how his uncle had gotten him drunk to draw him into sex play and bind him to silence, I knew I'd found Mitch's sponsor. Who else but a former victim could have served Mitch in that role, and who better than the quiet self-assured man who was leading today's meeting?

Mel finished his talk with a plea to let go of past wrongs. "The past is a great excuse when you're looking for a reason to drink," he said. "But you have to let it go. Living in the present is hard enough without carrying the burdens of the past along, too."

When he asked for questions or comments, I ran through the speech I'd made at earlier AA meetings. I tried to change it each time, since I'd seen some of the same people at several meetings, but I didn't have to change it a lot. This was a group that understood that problems don't go away fast and some wounds need a lot of telling to be cleansed.

After the meeting, Mel R. came up to me and took my hand. "Your friend is dead," he said. "You have to go on."

"I feel so guilty," I said.

"All that doesn't matter. You have to put it behind you." His voice was warm but authoritative; he was just the kind of person I could see a man like Mitch turning to for help. "You can't let the past become an excuse for taking the next drink," he continued. "A drunk can always find an excuse."

"I feel like if I could just—"

A tiny, almost elfin man in his fifties broke in. "I'm sorry to interrupt, but I need to talk to Mel," he said. "It's really an emergency." Mel let himself be led aside, and was immediately drawn into an intense interchange that didn't look as if it'd be over soon.

After more than a week of searching for Mel, it was all I could do not to grab him and drag him away from the little guy. Drawing on my dwindling reserves of self-control, I took my sorrows to the coffee table, and hung around trying to resist the urge to reach for one of the doughnuts. A young woman wearing more makeup than she needed drew me into conversation, and in the moments that my attention was distracted. Mel disappeared.

I tore outside, then back in to check for other exits. I'd lost him. I knew where to find him again, but I'd have to wait a week to do it. Just barely managing not to swear out loud, I took a doughnut to soothe the frustration and headed for home.

The judge's arrest wasn't on the six o'clock news, but it made the ten o'clock broadcast. The police had managed the arrest without alerting the media, so Reiter was spared having television cameras pushed in his face while he was being led from his home. This would be the last time he was granted that little bit of dignity.

The reporters hadn't had enough time to put much of a story together. They'd dredged up some old footage of the Good Citizen for Youth Award and made a big thing out of the irony of the situation, making Youth Services and a lot of other valuable organizations look foolish. I fervently hoped they wouldn't go around to the chess and computer clubs and harass the already-confused boys there.

"You look pretty glum for someone who just won," Molly said.

I felt pretty glum. "I'm glad they caught him," I said. "I'm just sad for all the kids and their families that were betrayed by him."

"But aren't they better off with the judge out of the way?" she asked.

"Sure they are, but it's like having someone tell you that you need a tooth pulled. It's a good thing to find out before it does any more damage, but it still hurts like hell."

Molly nodded, but I doubted that she really understood. One of the virtues of being a kid is that you can still think in terms of doing good, instead of worrying about not causing too much harm.

Reiter's arrest made the front page of the *Chronicle* the next morning. The byline was Kevin Doyle's. He'd done a good job with the story. I had to give him credit for that. He'd hit all the sources I had, and had quotes from most of them, and he hadn't gone for the cheap shots. He'd made an effort to portray Samuel Reiter as a complex man instead of a monster, and he'd tried to provide some information on pedophilia. It wasn't anything the Man-Boy Love Association would like, but it seemed fair to me.

I went to the office ready to get back to business as usual. Kevin Doyle was waiting there when I arrived.

"Nice work," he said.

"And to you. I liked your article in the *Chron*."

He followed me into my office without being asked. "So will you talk to me now?"

"No."

"No? Why not? Reiter's under arrest."

"I never talk about my cases with the press. That hasn't changed," I said.

"Okay," Doyle said, giving up much too easily. "How about your client? You must have a client who asked you to look into Reiter. Would your client talk to me?"

I didn't know. It occurred to me that Joe might very much like to talk with Kevin. It would provide an opportunity to get some publicity about Mitch's murder, and there was always a chance that that might lead to something. "Give me your card again. I'll contact my client, and if he or she is interested in talking with you, they'll call you," I said.

Kevin grinned and handed me a card. "The number on the back is my home phone. Call anytime," he said.

Joe had seen Kevin's article, and after considering it, decided that he would see the journalist. "Just be sure that you don't tell him anything you wouldn't want to see in print," I said. "There is no such thing as 'off the record.' "

I spent the morning putting together a final report on the Reiter case, getting Steve Marley's hours, so I could cut him a check, and dealing with loose ends. At eleven a new loose end popped up.

Carol Bailey from Oakland called. "I think I've found your victim's car," she said. "It's on Felman in the three-hundred block. I got the tip from a gal I busted who finds herself in need of bail money. I haven't checked to confirm it, but I think the tip's good."

"Felman Street? Is that anywhere near Jerry's Bar?"

"No, that's the funny part. It's in the warehouse district above Jack London Square. That's a completely different section of town."

The warehouse district isn't a place you'd leave a car on the way to someplace else, certainly not on the way to Jerry's. I felt the surge of adrenaline that kicks in when a case starts to come together.

Joe was excited by the discovery of the car. It took him only fifteen minutes to clear his calendar so he could go along with me. On the drive to Oakland, he became more somber.

"Does this mean Mitch was murdered by Reiter?" he asked.

"I don't know. Can you think of any reason his car would be in the warehouse district in Oakland?"

He shook his head.

"I'm sure there are explanations, but until we find one it makes Mitch's death look all the more suspicious. That's for sure."

"It's funny," he said. "I hired you to prove that it wasn't a random killing, and now that we're almost there, I wish it was." I kept my gaze on the road. I didn't need to look at him to feel the intensity that I knew burned in his eyes. "If it had been a robbery, I wouldn't be responsible. It wouldn't matter that I didn't help him."

"Don't beat yourself up," I said. "You don't know that it'd been any different if you had helped him." I thought of Mel R.'s comment that "living in the present is hard enough without carrying the burdens of the past along, too." Easier to say than do.

Jack London Square is Oakland's Fisherman's Wharf without the fishermen. It's on an estuary of the San Francisco Bay and most of the waterfront property is devoted to restaurants. Inland from the restaurants and cutesy shops is the warehouse district. The businesslike old brick buildings are still in good repair, and the area is slowly being revitalized as new businesses move in.

Mitch Morrison's old Ford Pinto waited on a street that was on its way up. A couple of the large old buildings had been renovated and turned into office space. The rest were still solid blue-collar structures.

Mitch's car was a black Pinto that was probably no stranger to the want ads. It had a dent in one fender and one tire had gone flat. It was still there because it looked too poor to rob and just respectable enough not to be towed.

The car was locked, but Joe had found an extra set of keys at Mitch's apartment. Inside, the car looked messy, a familiar kind of messy, the kind you generate doing surveillance. There were plastic cups and fast-food containers, a half-empty sack of stale pretzels, a partially eaten bagel, a couple of dirty napkins.

I wore plastic gloves to search, and tried not to move things around too much in order not to compromise the police search. A copy of a newspaper added to the clutter. I checked the date. It was an afternoon paper from the day Mitch died. I found a flashlight, a camera, and an empty thermos bottle. They confirmed my hunch that Mitch had used his car to watch someone or something.

The scraps of paper were mainly food wrappers, but in the space between the driver's seat and the gearshift, I found a piece of notebook paper folded into fourths. On it, JONAH T was printed in block letters, and beneath the name was the number 4736682.

"That's Mitch's handwriting," Joe said. "But he never mentioned a Jonah to me."

"What do you make of the number?"

"It's pretty long. Could be a serial number or the number of a case file or something like that."

It could be damn near anything, I thought. I counted the digits. Seven. It could be a telephone number.

We found another sheet from the same notebook in the glove compartment. Written on it in the same block printing was the name "Reiter," an address which I recognized as his, and a telephone number that was probably his as well.

The word PIPER had been hastily printed on the other side of the paper.

I copied down the information on both sheets of paper and replaced them where I'd found them. They were the only thing in the car that seemed promising. Maybe the cops would have more luck, but I doubted it.

I sent Joe back to San Francisco on BART. The location of the car and its contents were the closest we'd come to finding a clue to what happened the night of Mitch's death, and I wanted to learn what I could before the police arrived to start questioning people. In my experience, uniforms and badges tend to produce severe memory loss in susceptible individuals.

I didn't think it was an accident that Mitch had left the car in this neighborhood. He must have been here for a reason. I had my snapshot of the murdered man and a photo of Samuel Reiter. Now all I needed was someone who'd seen either one or both of them.

In a three-block radius of the car, I found several people who thought they remembered seeing someone who might have been Mitch Morrison. Only one of them seemed sober enough to remember something that happened yesterday, let alone a month ago. That was a woman who worked in a small café a couple of blocks from where the car was parked.

"Yeah, I remember that scar on his hand," she said. "Remember wondering how he got it. He came in here asking about something, I think."

"Do you remember what he asked about?"

"No." She shook her head, then stopped, "Yeah, yeah, it was about a car, I think. Yeah, he wanted to know if I'd seen this car."

"What kind of car?"

She shrugged. "I don't remember, but I think it was an expensive car—you know, fancy. I hadn't seen it around here."

I gave her a business card with a fictitious name on it and the agency's unlisted phone number, and asked her to call if she remembered more about the man. I always feel a bit paranoid using fake cards, but there are times when I prefer not to give my own name and number, especially when I'm looking for a killer.

I headed back to my car and was almost mowed down by a tall, thin young man carrying a large cardboard box. He backed out of a doorway and straight into me.

"Oh, shit, I'm sorry," he said. "Are you okay?"

"I'm okay," I said. "Do you work around here?"

"Huh? Yeah, sometimes." He was probably in his late twenties and had a dark red patch shaped like a strawberry just above the jawline, on the left side of his face.

I showed him the picture of Mitch and asked if he'd seen him in the neighborhood several weeks ago.

"This guy? Why do you want to know?"

"He left his car near here, then he disappeared. His family's anxious to know what he was doing here."

"Oh, sure," he said and studied the picture again. "Yeah, I think I seen this guy, but almost a month ago. Is there a reward or something? And who're you?"

"I'm working for the family, and there is a reward for anyone who has real information. Did you talk to him?"

"Yeah, I did. But I don't remember exactly what about. How much reward?" he asked slyly.

"Depends on the information. Did he ask you about a car?"

"Yeah." He nodded. "Yeah, that's what we talked about, a car. He was looking for a car, but I hadn't seen it."

"What kind of car was he looking for?"

He shrugged. "I don't remember. I guess that's not good enough for a reward, huh? But I'll tell you what, I could ask around. You give me a phone number, and if I find out anything I'll call you."

I pulled out a card and realized as I handed it to him that it was the wrong one. I'd given him a regular business card with my name and the agency address and the phone number on it.

* * *

A seven-digit number can mean just about anything, but the easiest seven digits to check on are a phone number, so when I got back to the office I dialed the number I'd found in Mitch's car. I got a recording telling me that the service was either turned off for the number I was trying to reach or it was out of my service area.

I've gotten that message before. It means you've reached a cellular phone. Jonah T.'s cellular phone? I hoped so. The only problem now was that cellular phone numbers are un-listed and damn near impossible to get ahold of unless you have a court order or know someone at the phone company willing to risk their job to get it for you. I have a source at the phone company, but not that good a source.

I called Inspector Warren at the Oakland PD, and told him about the car and the papers I'd found in it. He was not impressed by my skill at figuring out that the mysterious seven digits might be a telephone number, but he did agree to get the information on the number from the phone com-pany. I restrained myself from suggesting he do it sometime before the end of the decade.

Time to draw on another brilliant investigative technique. I'd have to call the number until I got someone on the other end. I could do that while I wasn't figuring out how to nail Anton Glosser.

Jesse called in just before five. "It's set to go down Friday night. You want in?"

"Tell me about it," I said.

"I'm to leave the side door open and make sure that the boxes are stacked against the wall just down from the loading dock. They've given me a 'wish list.' I make sure the right stock gets in the right place. Then I go home, and they pick up the merchandise."

"Have you tipped the cops?"

"Yep. A couple of them will come in tonight and mark all the stock on the wish list and put transmitters in the boxes. Tomorrow I just follow instructions so everything's right where the gang expects to find it. The cops'll take it from there."

"They're going to wait to make the bust, I hope. We want the person who ordered the theft, not the thugs who're carrying it out. Try to make sure they don't move before the delivery."

"I've already cleared that," Jesse said. "They want the big boys behind this as much as we do. They'll just watch the stolen parts till they get where they're going."

"In the meantime, you'll have to stay on the job," I said.

"I know," he said glumly. "Believe me, I hope they move quickly. You want to be involved in this in any way?"

Part of me wanted to talk to the cops in Sunnyvale, to go back over the operation. Any screwup on their part could blow all of Jesse's hard work and, worse yet, put his life in jeopardy, but I remembered how I'd felt the first time my former boss, Keith Stone, had let me run an entire operation.

"It's your show," I told him. "I'd just be in the way. Just let me know how things are going."

"Will do," he said, and I could hear the smile in his voice.

THE NEXT COUPLE of days held few surprises. Samuel Reiter was released on bail. His cronies who had been so quick to threaten me did not call to apologize. The police found nothing in Mitch s car to whet their curiosity. And the secret of Anton Glosser's finances continued to elude me.

Our client in Sunnyvale was robbed on schedule, and the gang was greedy and careless enough to move the loot straight to the competitor's warehouse. The police had

rounded up the gang, though there was still some question
as to whether they'd gotten the leader. They'd arrested one
highly placed executive in the competing firm, but they were
looking for a bigger fish.

Our client had what he wanted, and Jesse was so pleased
that he had a hell of a time maintaining his pose as Mr. Cool.
It was good to have him back in the office.

Friday morning's *Chronicle* carried a follow-up story on
Judge Samuel Reiter's arrest, again with a byline by Kevin
Doyle. The reporter devoted a good deal of space to the
suspicious circumstances of Mitch Morrison's violent death.
He inserted the word *alleged* at all the right spots, and stayed
on the safe side of the libel laws, but he managed to make
the connection between Mitch's death and his investigation
of Reiter look a lot more solid than I knew it to be.

He did us another big favor. He included in the story a
request that anyone knowing anything about Mitch's activities during his last days contact Doyle at the *Chron*. We had
been unable to locate anyone who knew much about what
Mitch was up to, yet I felt sure that there must be people
who did. Maybe one of them would see the article and call.

Steve Marley telephoned as I was going over Jesse's report
on the Sunnyvale case. "I'm going over to Oakland to take
another look at the stuff from Reiter's boat. You want to come
along?"

Did I want to look through a pedophile's private souvenir
collection? Not hardly. But there was the chance that something in those boxes might provide a clue to Mitch's death,
so I tried to sound grateful as I thanked him.

Steve's buddy from the Juvenile Division looked as if he
wished I'd stayed home, but he found us a room where we
wouldn't be interrupted. It had a long wooden table, six
chairs, and a dirty window that looked out on the freeway.
He fussed a bit and delivered a set of instructions that trans-
lated as "Don't let the civilian screw anything up"; then he
and Steve went to claim the boxes that would send Samuel
Reiter to jail.

The four boxes they lugged in were only part of the total haul from the boat. Steve's buddy dropped his boxes on the table and announced, "They're all yours. Just check them back in when you're through," and hurried out of the room.

Steve put three of the cardboard boxes on the floor, sat the fourth on the table between us and began to sort through it. There were hundreds of snapshots, all of boys. He dropped a pile in front of me. "Let's see how good you are at this kind of thing. What do these tell you?"

I picked up a handful and looked through them, then laid them out on the table in front of me. A few were ordinary snapshots, the kind parents carry in their wallets; but in most the boys were naked. Some struck provocative poses; others tried to look casual, as if there was nothing out of the ordinary about their nudity.

When you looked at them all together, certain similarities emerged. The boys were all about the same age, somewhere between nine and eleven. Their body types were similar— on the small side with little bony chests. All were white, and most were towheads with a sprinkling of freckles across their noses, the kind of kid Norman Rockwell loved to paint. There were a number of redheads and several dark-eyed Latin types, but the majority were strikingly similar.

I picked up a picture of a strawberry blond, freckle-faced youngster who was wearing only a Mickey Mouse T-shirt. He stood with one foot on a tree stump and offered an uncertain, crooked-toothed smile for the camera. He was the kid down the block, the upstart in the fourth grade, Tom Sawyer in the school play. He should have been holding a string full of fish or a baseball bat, not posing for Samuel Reiter's private collection.

"He likes boys between nine and eleven, white, average build, and prefers blonds with freckles," I said. I looked away from the faces and was struck by the vulnerability of the skinny legs and knobby knees, liberally decorated with the scrapes and scabs that are the badges of boyhood adventures.

"Yep," Marley said. "But you missed the backgrounds.

Most were taken in the woods or on a sailboat. We'll check the interior shots; they're probably from his house." He was holding a notebook he'd pulled from the box. "One of Reiter's journals," he said. "You might find it interesting."

Reiter wrote in a spidery, cramped hand, but it was fairly easy to decipher. The first entry described a boy who'd just joined his soccer team. The writing was flowery, like something from a cheap romantic novel. There was no overt reference to sex, but Reiter's infatuation with the boy was apparent.

I flipped to a later page and found an entry with a different tone.

I often wonder if things would have been different if I hadn't met Craig. What if I'd played Little League instead of joining the Boy Scouts? Or what if I'd joined another troop? Would I feel this attraction to boys if Craig hadn't introduced me to it? The "experts" would place the blame on him, but what do they really know? Do they know why he chose me, instead of someone else? Did he see something, know something about me that even I didn't realize?

I showed the journal to Steve. "Reiter was a victim, too," I said.

Steve read the page and nodded. "You'd be surprised how many times I've read passages just like that. I told you that these guys were former victims. In fact, a lot of what we know about peds comes from journals like this."

He returned the journal to me and I read on as he sorted through the contents of several boxes. Pages of self-denunciation and loathing alternated with pathetic, self-serving efforts at justification. At times, Reiter clearly saw the damage he was doing to his "loves" and swore he'd stop, but subsequent passages revealed that not only had he been unable to quit, but he was busy planning the seduction of a new boy.

I followed his infatuation with a boy named Brad who was the son of his law clerk. He described in loving detail con-

versations and outings, the exchange of confidences and other
signs of growing trust and intimacy. There were pages of
descriptions of how Brad combed his hair, his casual gestures
and favorite expressions, the way he sat or stood or ran.

That was the touching, almost sweet, part. There were
also sections so explicit and prurient as to be pornographic.
I skipped those.

Toward the end of the journal I came across an entry that
caught my attention.

> Spent the evening with K. and several of his boys. They
> were so worldly, so unabashed in their sexuality. I was
> both fascinated and repelled.
>
> K. is my dark side. He is the most completely amoral
> man I have ever known. I can't imagine him tormenting
> himself with guilt and remorse the way I do. I don't trust
> him, don't even like him, yet I am drawn back to him like
> a moth to a flame.

"What do you make of this?" I asked Steve.

He read it, then handed back the book. "A buddy. It's not
unusual. These guys find each other. They'll trade pictures,
write to each other about their affairs. Sometimes they even
pass kids along. When a kid gets too old for one guy, he gets
introduced to a buddy who likes older kids."

We spent several hours, and I skimmed through a couple
of diaries, but I found nothing that told me whether Samuel
Reiter had played any role in Mitch Morrison's murder. By
the time we left, I couldn't have faced another page of Reiter's private obsessions.

That evening Molly wanted to go to a party, but when I asked
whose parents would be there, she just laughed. "Parents
don't hang around parties," she informed me. "Even in Palo
Alto, lots of times they go out for the evening."

"And leave a house full of fourteen-year-olds on their
own?"

"Lots of the kids at this party are older."

That's when I realized that interrogation skills might be useful in raising a teenager. It took a lot more questions, most met with evasive answers, to discover that the party was being given by the vampire twins. Molly was indignant when I said no.

I tried to explain the dangers of the streets. She was unimpressed.

"Goll," she said, and rolled her eyes, "you'd think I was a baby. You're so paranoid, Catherine. Not every person out there is a dealer or a pimp or a kidnapper. Most people are cool, like that guy across the street who gave us a ride down to Polk Street yesterday afternoon."

I should have asked, "What guy?" Should have wondered why a stranger would walk up and talk to three girls coming out of my house on a Thursday afternoon. But I was so busy trying to explain the general dangers of urban America that I missed completely a very specific one much closer to home.

The weekend was a disaster. Molly was furious that I hadn't let her go to the party, and the fragile relationship that we'd begun to build when she first arrived had eroded as I spent long hours at the office. She went off with the vampire twins both days and came back spoiling for a fight. Even fairly innocuous requests that she turn down her music or rinse her dishes were met with angry tirades or sullen sulks. I felt like I was living in the middle of a minefield.

Peter was as tired of his role as peacemaker as I was of mine as wicked stepmother. He found more reasons to be away from home. I missed him and was silently furious for his defection.

By Monday morning I was ready to send Molly back to Marion. I'd decided that they deserved each other. I didn't delude myself that sending Molly home would solve her problems, but it would mean that one less person would be miserable, and since that person was me, it seemed like a good plan.

I was figuring out how to effect the reunion of mother and daughter when Arthur Costa called. I know Arthur only in-

directly; Peter's worked for him and has some very enter-
taining stories about Costa's courtroom antics. He is a highly
respected, somewhat eccentric, defense lawyer who has won
more than his share of lost causes.

"Ms. Sayler, I'm representing Joe Girard," he said. He
had a marvelous voice, radio-announcer perfect with the trace
of an accent I couldn't identify. "I understand that Mr. Girard retained you on a matter involving Samuel Reiter."

"Yes," I said warily. A call from Arthur Costa suggested
that the week that had started so poorly was about to get even
worse. "That's correct."

"I wonder if you could manage to see me today. It's a
matter of some urgency. Joe has been arrested for the murder
of Judge Reiter."

It took a minute for the words to penetrate, and when they
did, I felt as if someone had knocked the breath out of me.
"The murder of Judge Reiter?" I stammered.

"Yes. I assume you haven't heard of it."

Monday mornings are hard enough without starting them
off with a dose of the news. I rarely listen to the radio, and
this morning I'd even skipped the front page of the *Chronicle*. "No, I hadn't heard. Can you tell me what happened?"

"Judge Reiter was found dead in his study early Sunday
morning. He'd been struck on the head with a blunt object."

"And they've arrested Joe?"

"Yes. They can place Joe at Reiter's house at eight Saturday night. Death occurred sometime between eight and
ten. Joe has made no secret of his belief that Reiter is responsible for his cousin's death. They have motive and opportunity. Enough for an arrest. They arraigned him this
morning. He's being held without bail."

I tried to make sense of what he was telling me. It was
shocking enough that Samuel Reiter was dead, but the idea
that Joe might have killed him was even more disturbing.
"What does Joe say?" I asked.

"He says he's innocent, that he left the house about twenty
minutes after he arrived, and Reiter was alive at that time."

I didn't ask if Costa believed Joe; it's not a relevant question for a defense attorney. Costa's job wasn't to decide on Joe's guilt or innocence, but simply to provide him with the best defense possible.

"How did they place him at Reiter's?"

"The judge had an assistant who admitted Joe at eight, then left shortly thereafter. He discovered Reiter's body when he returned home this morning."

An assistant. That had to be the tall young man who'd opened the door the night I visited Reiter.

"Joe has asked that I retain you as my investigator in this case. I'm agreeable to that if you're willing to take the case."

"You know that I don't usually do criminal work."

"Yes, and I've discussed that with Joe. He's most adamant that he wants you to continue. Your rates are somewhat higher than my regular investigator's, but I'll pay them."

Very generous, except that Arthur Costa wouldn't be paying my rates, he'd be billing them to Joe. A well-known San Francisco lawyer, when asked how much it cost for a first-degree-murder defense, once responded, "Whatever you've got." I feared that was what Joe's little visit to the judge would cost him.

"I'll take the case," I told Costa. "Did you say that they've denied Joe bail?"

"That's correct. It's outrageous. A combination of bad luck and worse timing. The judge we drew is tough under the best of circumstances, but only a week ago he released a man on bail who subsequently shot his wife."

"But this is a first offense, and Joe's a member of the bar. Can't you appeal?"

"I'm doing that, but since the victim is a public official, it's a special-circumstances situation, and they are within their rights to deny bail. I am not optimistic about our chances of a reversal.

"I'd like you to see Joe today if you can. Take him through his activities on the night of the murder in as much detail as possible. Tape the interview. I can see you at three this afternoon. Let my secretary know if you can't make it then."

I put the phone down and tried to absorb the information

I'd just been given. Reiter's death was a shock, but it was Joe I was worried about. Was it possible that he had killed Samuel Reiter?

Anyone can kill, and Joe had plenty of reason to hate the judge, but I couldn't imagine him as a killer. Joe believed in the law the way Catholics believe in the Eucharist. I just couldn't see him taking it into his own hands.

The thought of Joe in jail filled me with fear. Joe would not do well in jail. In fact, he might not survive it. He wasn't a guy who knew how to back off or keep a low profile, and he had a bad attitude toward authority. He'd alienate the guards, then he'd side with some poor, weak inmate against the more powerful, predatory cons who called the shots. No one would be surprised when he became a jailhouse casualty.

Working for Joe was supposed to help me forget the Orrin Merrick case, but it brought back all my feelings of anger and helplessness. Only this time I wasn't helpless. I made myself a promise that Joe was not going to end up like Orrin.

Joe was being held at the Oakland jail, a formidable square tower with slits for windows that squatted next to the Nimitz Freeway. It's a classic example of the concrete block construction so common to buildings dealing with law and order. I don't know whether the designers wanted it to be ugly, depressing, or intimidating, but they achieved all three.

I checked in, and was taken to the attorney's booth, which was really a glass cage facing another glass cage, next to several more pairs of glass cages. In the cage next to me a small black man in his forties talked with his client, a tired-looking guy who could have had a job on celebrity wrestling. The little guy did a lot of hand waving, but it was all motion and no sound.

I sat in the tiny glass cubicle and felt vulnerable and exposed even though no one was looking at me. Just being this close to confinement made me jumpy. I thought first of Orrin, then of Joe.

As if cued by my thoughts, the door in the cubicle opposite to me opened, and Joe walked in and sat down. He looked pale and drawn. He seemed to have lost weight since I'd last seen him.

"How're you holding up?" I asked.

"I've been in jail before," he said cockily. He waited for a response, then shrugged. "Okay, civil disobedience is different from murder one. And I hate jail, thank you. I've always hated jail. But you want to know something funny, the guards have been nicer to Joe Girard, the killer, than they ever were to Joe Girard, the good citizen." He gave a mirthless laugh. "My roommate is a twenty-year-old who shot two people in a Seven-Eleven. A real nice guy."

I nodded in sympathy. Today's jails are full of the people you'd most like to avoid, and you get to meet them when they're at their most angry and have the least reason to restrain themselves. It doesn't take a lot of imagination to understand why prison holds such terror for the weak and defenseless.

"Tell me what happened the night you went to Reiter's," I said.

"I assume that whatever I tell you is covered by attorney-client privilege."

"It is. I'm working for your attorney," I said, bracing myself for a confession.

"I haven't told the police about what Reiter did to me. They still think that my only connection with him is through Mitch."

"Have you told your lawyer?"

"Not really."

"Joe, there isn't any room for 'not really' when you're putting together a murder defense. Arthur needs to know the whole thing."

"I'm not telling anyone else about it. That's the way it is."

"*Joe,*" I burst out, then lowered my voice, "this is a murder charge, and a very substantial one, that you're facing. If you don't want to spend the rest of your life in jail, you'd better stop worrying about what happened to you as a kid and start worrying about what's going to happen to you as an adult."

The way his jaw tightened and set told me he wasn't about to listen to me. "Telling the cops what happened would just give them a better motive," he said. "It doesn't help my case any."

"You still need to tell Arthur."

"You do it. I don't want to talk about it," Joe said grimly.

"What happened at Reiter's?" I asked.

"He called me around seven and asked if we could meet. I didn't want to. Shit, I've worked for years to put all this behind me. But he was so damn persistent. He said maybe it could help both of us." Joe looked down for a moment and wiped one hand across his eyes. "I don't know why I went. It sure as hell wasn't because I thought it'd help. Maybe I just wanted to see him squirm.

"The assistant was there when I arrived, but he must have gone out because he wasn't around when I left. Anyway, Sam was pretty loaded. He offered me a drink, and I took one. He was refilling his glass before mine was half empty.

"It was all right at first. I mean he wanted to know what I'd done with myself, was pleased that I'd chosen the law. He played the proud father like he'd done when I was a kid. The more he talked, the more pissed off I felt. I was about to tell him he was full of shit when he started telling me it was *his* influence that had made me what I am, how nobody understood that he was really helping 'his' boys. The bastard wanted me to say that what he'd done was okay, that it was really good.

"I exploded. I told him that was bullshit, and that he didn't know how much he'd hurt me. That he'd totally screwed up Mitch. I wanted to tell him the whole thing—the years of therapy, all the relationships I've screwed up just when they were getting good, the loneliness, the never trusting anyone, God, all of it. But he didn't want to listen.

"He started yelling at me. I don't even know what he said, because by then I was so angry I couldn't listen to him anymore. I threw my glass at him—I think it broke on his desk— then I just walked out. I got in my car and drove around for hours before I came home."

"And the next day the police arrested you."

"Yeah. I was there, and I hated him, but I didn't kill him. He was still yelling when I went out the door."

"Was there anyone in the house when you left?"

"I didn't see anyone."

"But he called you; that's why you went to see him?"

"Yeah."

"We'll have to get access to his phone records for that night," I said. "We need to know who else he called."

"You mean he might have called the killer, just like he did me? Why?"

"From what you say, he was distraught, anxious to talk. If he called you, he may well have called other victims or their families. Maybe he got someone who was less able to control his anger than you are."

Joe nodded. "Yeah, that's a real possibility. He seemed to need me to tell him that what he'd done was okay, that it was no big deal." He shook his head in disbelief.

"But you didn't, so maybe he called someone else. Someone he knew could be manipulated to give him the answers he wanted."

"Or someone he knew would blow up," Joe suggested. "As I think about it, he was more than drunk, he was depressed. Maybe he was looking for someone to whack him."

"A cowardly suicide? It's possible," I said, "but I doubt that it'll play well in court. What did you do after you left?"

"I just drove around for a long time, first around Piedmont, then out Highway 24 to Walnut Creek and back. I needed to cool off and get myself together."

"Anyone see you?"

Joe shook his head. "I don't think so."

I took him back through the whole day, from the time he put on his socks to when he climbed in bed. I took notes and got it all on tape. There wasn't much on which to build a murder-one defense.

21

JOE GIRARD HAD asked me to find a murderer three weeks ago; now the alleged killer was dead, and Joe needed his own defense against a murder charge. Another three weeks on this job and maybe *I'd* be in jail. The trend was not in the right direction.

I got back to the city a little before two o'clock, too early for my meeting with Arthur Costa, enough time to check in at the office. Amy informed me that I looked as though my favorite cat had died, and I probably should not see any clients in my current condition. I knew the situation was serious when she offered to fix me a cup of tea.

She handed me four pink message slips. Not surprisingly, one was from Kevin Doyle. I hate to see cases tried in the press, but there are times when access to the media is important, and Kevin had shown himself to be a thoughtful and intelligent reporter. It might be very handy to have him on our side. Still, I wouldn't return his call until I'd talked with Arthur Costa.

I did call the mysterious seven-digit number I'd found in Mitch's car. I'd gotten the recording so many times that I was startled when a human voice answered. The voice was masculine, low and fairly gruff. "Yes."

"Jonah?" I said, hoping the name and number were connected by more than coincidence.

"What? Who is this?" the voice demanded.

"I was trying to call Jonah. Is this the right number?"

"Who's calling?" Suspicion and a hint of hostility hardened the voice. It told me that there was some connection between the name and number. I doubted that the man I was speaking to was Jonah. His reaction to the name was wrong, but he knew Jonah and had some reason to distrust anyone who mentioned him.

"This is Catherine Small," I said, using one of the names I'd developed for situations like this. "Who's this?"

"Why do you want Jonah?"

"I want to talk to him. Can you tell me how to get ahold of him?"

"Give me your number. I'll have him call you."

I gave him the unlisted office number. He wouldn't be able to trace it back to me, and if he called, we'd be expecting him.

I called Arthur Costa's office and was told to come right on over. The address was downtown in one of the skyscrapers that keep sprouting around the Embarcadero. Costa's not a Belli or Hallinan or Erlich, one of those men who create legends and end up in Herb Caen's column for their clever one-liners, but he is well known and highly respected among the legal community. He's been mentioned for the bench more than once, and the next time the powers that be are looking for a Spanish-surname judge, they may well look his way. They'd probably have tapped him much sooner if his sharp tongue and independent mind hadn't made him some powerful political enemies.

I pulled my file on Joe and headed for Costa's office. As I drove downtown I realized that I wasn't looking forward to working for Arthur Costa. I don't work for lawyers. I work for the people who hire lawyers, and that means the lawyers have to be reasonably polite to me. I like to call the shots. I had a hunch Arthur Costa did, too.

Costa's office was decorated in a style I call tasteful-expensive. It comes in modern and traditional, and he'd chosen the traditional version with lots of heavy wood and brass, thick carpeting, and paintings of dogs and horses on the wood-paneled walls. I suppose it makes his clients feel secure to know that their lawyer is so well-heeled. It'd just make me feel poorer.

Costa was in his late forties, and the years showed around his middle but not in the thick dark hair that he left cut just slightly long. His face was roundish and dominated by thick eyebrows that slanted down to the side. Seeing him on the street, you'd take him for a mild-mannered accountant.

He seated me on a large leather couch and took the armchair next to it; his secretary brought us coffee. I do envy unliberated employers who can get away with asking their secretaries to make coffee. Amy would just ask solicitously if I'd hurt my arm.

Costa had me go over my work for Joe from the beginning, and as he probed and questioned the mild-mannered accountant disappeared, and I got a taste of the sharp mind behind his bland brown eyes. I decided that working for Arthur Costa might be fun after all.

When I told Costa that Joe had been abused by Reiter, he restrained himself to a heartfelt "Damn," then demanded, "Who else knows this?"

"Joe's been in therapy for it, so his therapist knows. Beyond that, I doubt that he's told anyone."

"No need for it to come out, then," Costa said. "It just provides the prosecution with a stronger motive."

I finished laying out my investigation. He considered what I'd told him. "I know you're not experienced at this," he said, "but how would you go about constructing a defense?"

"Joe doesn't remember much about where he drove after leaving Reiter's, so there's not much chance of developing a credible alibi. I'm used to looking for the guilty party, so I'd want to know who else might have visited Reiter that night. It was only a few days after his arrest. There must be a number of parents who just discovered that their sons were molested, maybe even some adults for whom the arrest brought back painful memories."

"Reasonable doubt," Costa said. "It's a weak defense."

"There's the wife. Joe didn't see her; he doesn't think she was home, but I'll check on her. And there's the assistant.

If he's the man I met at Reiter's, he's young enough and attractive enough to be a former victim. It's not unusual for a pedophile to continue his relationship with boys after the sexual liaison ends. He could have been jealous or afraid of exposure.''

Costa nodded. I continued. "Then there's the issue of Mitch's death. Two murder victims connected to each other; you have to wonder if the killer might be the same person.''

"But you don't have anything on Mitch's killer.''

"No.'' I had a feeling that Mel R. from AA might know something, but it was too early to tell. "I'd like to keep working on that angle. I might be getting close to someone who knew what Mitch was doing, but I won't know for a day or two, maybe more.''

"Well, one of the things I want you to do is develop alternate suspects. But there are some fairly routine jobs that I'll need from you first. I'll want you to gather the discovery information. You'll need to see Inspector Roselli in the DA's Office. He'll give you copies of the police reports, information from the technicians and the lab, autopsy protocol, photos, taped statements. My secretary will give you a letter authorizing you to receive them.''

I groaned inwardly at the name Tom Roselli. He was an old friend of my ex-husband, Dan Walker. Both Dan and Tom had started out on the SFPD. Dan had stayed and risen to homicide inspector. Tom had left to work for the District Attorney's Office. The DA's Office is a lot easier than working the street. It's as close as you come to a nine-to-five job in law enforcement.

Knowing the inspector in charge ought to have been a help, except that Tom had never recovered from a bad case of male chauvinism imparted by his Italian father. He was capable of making cracks about keeping women barefoot and pregnant without the least embarrassment, and he was the only man I knew who referred to me as "the little woman.'' I could expect him to either refuse to take me seriously or act openly hostile because of the divorce, probably both.

Costa continued. "The way we work, you're my eyes and

ears, you understand. You go to the police property room
and look at any evidence they've got. It's usually just routine,
but maybe you'll see something that isn't quite right or raises
questions. You don't even need to know why it feels funny,
just tell me if it does. A feeling can be the beginning of a
theory.

"I'll want a statement from the assistant. And start digging to see if there's anything to your hunch about him being
a past victim. Get a statement from the wife, even if she
wasn't there that night, and from the neighbors, and anybody
else who might know something.

"I'll subpoena the phone company to provide us with
Judge Reiter's phone records for the last week and to reveal
the name that goes with the phone number you found in
Mitch's car. You can take it down today, and with luck they'll
have the information for us in a day or two. They can try to
quash the subpoena, but I don't think we'll have a problem."

I told Costa about Kevin Doyle and showed him a copy of
Kevin's story in the *Chronicle*. "Do you want me to talk to
him, or should I avoid him?"

Costa pursed his lips and considered it. "He could con-
ceivably be useful at some point—not yet, I think, but maybe
in the future. Try to stay on good terms with him. Don't tell
him anything unless you clear it with me first."

As we were finishing up Costa said, "I get the impression
that you're a friend of Joe's."

"Yes," I nodded. "He's a friend as well as a colleague."

Costa nodded. "Yes, I also consider him a friend. He does
good work, and he's an honest man. I'd hate to see him go
to jail."

"I think jail for a man like Joe could be a death sentence,"
I said, giving voice to a fear that had haunted me all day.

Costa nodded. His expression was grave. "He would make
the wrong kind of enemies, I think."

"On both sides."

"Yes, on both sides. That's why it's imperative that we
keep him out of jail."

"I'll do my best to help you do that," I said, praying that my best would be good enough.

Costa's secretary whipped out the subpoena for the phone company in a matter of minutes, and I made a dash for the Pac Bell building to deliver it before closing. There were no parking places, but then there are never any parking places in this city. Maybe at 2:00 A.M., but never when I'm looking. I left the Volvo in a red zone.

A bored woman in a pin-striped power suit frowned as she scanned the sheet. I groveled rather well as I urged her to expedite the request, and stressed how important it was. She didn't seem nearly as impressed as I would have liked.

Back at the office, Jesse was getting ready to head home. "Can you stay a minute?" I asked. "I may be digging us into a hole; you should probably know about it."

I told him about Joe's arrest and my meeting with Costa. "We've never worked criminal defense. I realized after I agreed to take the case that I should run it by you."

Jesse looked surprised. He was no more used to being a partner than I was to having one. "Hey, it's your call," he said. "What do you want me to do?"

Unqualified support. That was exactly what I needed just now. "You've just done it," I said. "Can you stay on top of our current cases a little longer, so I can concentrate on this one?"

"No problem. I'll even take on the Glosser case if you'd like."

Did I want the albatross off my neck? You bet. Glosser's finances were complex, and I hadn't had the time to trace them the way I wanted to. I was only too happy to hand the job over to Jesse.

I gave him my first full smile of the day. "I'd love it, as long as you feel okay about doing it."

"Vigilante justice is one of my specialties. What do you have so far?"

"Nothing solid. I've been too busy to do much on it. I've

got two companies held as limited partnerships that look interesting. In both cases, the ownership is hidden in a maze of different entities. Then there's Sunnyside Properties and a man named Milton Diesman.''

IF THINGS WERE dicey at work, they weren't any better on the home front. I arrived home at six to find that neither Molly nor Peter was there. Peter had left a message on the machine, saying that he was going out with friends to play music. I usually join them. Tonight I wasn't invited.

Molly hadn't left any message at all, but there was a message from Gil, the teacher who ran Phoenix, telling us that Molly had missed school, and asking us to call him.

"I'm having a hard time getting through to her," he said. "Sometimes an idea catches her interest and she really takes off, but a lot of the time she's just coasting in neutral."

"Do you think she's on something?" I asked.

"No, not at school, anyway. But she's talked about some friends of hers who're clearly into street life. If she keeps hanging out with them, it could happen. That's why I wanted you to know she'd skipped school.

"It's real seductive for a kid like Molly. She's been on her own a lot, and she enjoys the freedom. Living with a bunch of kids sounds just great. No one to tell you what to do. Everybody sharing drugs and booze. She doesn't realize what else goes with that. Your friends put you up for a while, but at some point it's your turn to contribute something for food and drugs, and what does a fourteen-year-old have to sell except her body?''

I felt sick and sat down on the floor so I could lean against the wall. I'd known all this, I suppose, but had refused to think about Molly in those terms. "What can I do?" I asked Gil.

"Just what you have been doing. Be there for her. Let her know you care. You can't live her life, and you can't lock her in a closet. She's a good kid, basically, and smart. She'll make it okay."

He offered me a few more platitudes, then the conversation was over, leaving me sitting against the wall in the dark with thoughts I didn't want to have.

It was just before midnight when Molly came in the front door and tried to sneak down the hall to her bedroom. I had weeks of AA meetings to thank for the fact that I hadn't crawled into a gin bottle during the long hours while I waited for her. I had, however, drunk enough coffee and tea to be running on a caffeine high that probably wouldn't wear off for days.

"It isn't midnight yet," she said defensively. She reeked of marijuana.

"You missed school today," I said.

"Yeah," she said, trying to sound defiant. "It's boring. And the kids are boring. They're not much better than the ones in Palo Alto."

"And the streets are fun."

"Yeah."

"Tell me one thing. Where do your friends get their money?"

"What money?"

"The money that buys the drugs, the booze, the food, whatever else they need."

"I don't know. They get jobs when they need some money, and Cindy has a boyfriend who helps her out."

"A boyfriend? Or a pimp?"

Molly looked shocked. "It's not like that," she said indignantly.

"Isn't it? Does Cindy do dates?"

Molly looked sullen. "Sometimes, but only when she feels like it."

"Or needs the money. Or the drugs."

"You don't understand," she shouted.

"I understand that life at home can be so tough that even the street seems better. But I don't understand why life here is that bad."

"It's not you," she said. "I mean I really appreciate all you're doing. It's just that I enjoy hanging out with Cindy and Rae. I'm not doing drugs or anything. I don't know why you're so uptight about it."

Uptight. It was the ultimate failing when I was a kid, and now I was definitely uptight. "I'm uptight because I love you, and I don't want anything to happen to you," I said. "The streets are dangerous."

I could have given her the litany of dangers I'd spent the last three hours reciting to myself—bad drugs, men who regard an underage girl as a special treat, AIDS, any of the assorted psychos who place no value on human life—but she wasn't about to listen to me. She looked at me with the same expression I'd used on my mother.

And I was sorely tempted to adopt my mother's reaction to that look, which was to send her to her room. Instead, I said, "Okay, this is how it plays. If you want to stay here, you go to school and you're home by six on school nights. That's six in the evening, not in the morning. Understood?"

She started to object.

"Are you living with me or with Marion, or are you ready to join your friends on the street?" I prayed that she'd give me the right answer. I had no idea what I'd do if she chose the street, but I knew that it was time for me to set the rules.

"Shit, I guess I'll stay here," she grumbled.

"Good, and you agree not to cut school or stay out after six?"

"Yeah. Can I go to bed now?"

I'd have liked a hug, some little sign that the wonderful twelve-year-old who used to inhabit that body was still in there somewhere, but she stalked past me and slammed the door.

Peter came in a little later, rosy from too much beer and smelling like cigar smoke. Now that I didn't have to worry about Molly, I was furious at her for putting me through such hell. Peter was a convenient target for all that anger.

I yelled at him; he yelled back. When he delivered his I-just-need-some-space speech, I suggested he could find that at his own place. That's exactly what he decided to do.

I don't like to sleep alone; it makes me grumpy. The next morning, I was not in the best of moods to tackle a visit to the Alameda County District Attorney's Office and Tom Roselli, but I didn't have much choice.

Tom greeted me heartily—a bit too heartily—called me Katie, which I've always hated, and led me down the hall to his office. He delivered his condolences on my divorce with an attitude more appropriate to a diagnosis of terminal cancer, and launched into an enumeration of my ex-husband's virtues.

When he paused for breath, I said, "I'm here about the Reiter homicide. I'm working for the defense."

He chuckled condescendingly. "What's a nice girl like you doing on a case like that?"

I wondered how much you'd get for slugging a cop. Probably too much. So I smiled sweetly and said, "Tom, can we cut the crap and get down to work?"

A dark, ugly look crossed Tom's face. I was not being a nice girl. He was offended. I didn't give a damn. If I wasn't going to get any advantage from being nice, I was at least going to have the pleasure of not taking any shit from Roselli.

"Katie," he said.

"My name is Catherine," I said. "And you would do well to remember that any obstruction by your office can have an adverse effect on the prosecution."

Roselli was looking downright mean. "And you'd do well to remember to keep a civil tongue in your head."

We glared at each other, then I switched tactics and smiled. "How is Anne Marie?" I asked.

That caught him off guard. Anne Marie is his daughter, about Molly's age. She's the apple of her daddy's eye, and when last I knew her, she was driving him nuts by proving her prowess in judo.

Tom can't talk about Anne Marie without smiling. He mellowed noticeably and said, "She's doing fine. Pretty as a picture, boys calling her every night, and straight A's in school."

"That's terrific," I said. "And the judo?"

"She's a purple belt now, and she was a finalist in the national championships this year."

"You must be very proud."

He nodded. "It doesn't seem like anything a girl should want to do, but she loves it. And it'll keep her safe on the streets. You did some of that, didn't you?"

"Aikido. My dad feels about it the same way you do." It wasn't true. My dad had applauded my decision to study martial arts, but I was going to get a lot further with Roselli if he thought of me as an older version of Anne Marie than if he remembered me as Dan Walker's ex-wife.

"So you're working on this Reiter thing. A nasty piece of business all around."

I nodded. "I did the investigation that revealed the child abuse, so I know that part of it," I said.

"Not so hard to understand why your client wanted to kill him," Roselli replied.

"I imagine there were quite a lot of people who felt the same way—former victims, parents of recent victims, brothers, even sisters."

Roselli nodded grimly, his expression indicating that he'd be leading the lynch mob if his son had been a victim. "True, but Girard is the only one we can place at the scene."

I had him walk me through what they'd found, and didn't learn much that was new. The cause of death was a blow to the head. Murder weapon, a heavy brass paperweight. The paperweight had been wiped clean of fingerprints; however,

Joe's prints had been found on a broken glass next to the judge's desk.

"Was the front door locked?" I asked.

"No. Closed but unlocked."

"Joe doesn't know if it was locked when he left. It seems unlikely that the assistant would have left it unlocked. That means someone had to unlock it that evening."

"Could have been Girard as easily as anyone."

"Or it could have been Reiter who unlocked it after Joe left, because he was expecting someone else."

"Who?"

"Someone he called, just as he called Joe. Or someone who'd already arranged to come by."

"We're checking out the phone calls," Roselli said. "But I think you're grasping at straws."

"How about the wife?" I asked.

"In Denver on business."

"The assistant?"

"What about him?"

"Does he have an alibi?"

"He does. Besides, he has no motive."

"Maybe," I said. I gave Roselli my theory that the assistant might be a former victim and possibly a current confederate.

I was on the edge again. The look on Roselli's face told me that nice women did not discuss such subjects with cool objectivity. "You're accusing this man of being a former victim?" he asked tightly.

"I think it's worth checking," I said.

Roselli didn't say he'd do it, but I knew he was too good a cop not to. When I left, he shook hands and said, "Goodbye, Catherine. Good luck on your case."

My mother likes to say that you catch more flies with honey than with vinegar, and it's true, but sometimes it helps to leave the vinegar open, just to make the smell of honey sweeter.

23

I STOPPED BY the jail to see Joe after I left Roselli's office. He looked tense and drawn, and he'd developed a slight nervous tic in his left cheek. He struggled to maintain his former bravado, but there was a brittleness to his manner.

"It's a real kick living with a lunatic," he said. "This guy has the moral awareness of a sea slug, and his hold on reality's tenuous at best."

"Is he dangerous?" I asked.

"Hell, he killed two people. Of course he's dangerous."

"I'll ask Arthur to try to get you a new cellmate."

"Don't bother. This guy's probably no worse than lots of the others, and one thing I'm learning here is that you can always do worse."

It was Tuesday afternoon. I'd been waiting all week for a second shot at Mitch's AA friend, Mel R. With Joe bunking with the 7-Eleven killer, my need to find out more about Mitch had become urgent. Reiter's death might not be connected to Mitch's, but it was the best lead we had right now, and my stomach was tight with tension as I headed for the AA meeting and the man I hoped could tell me what Mitch was doing just before his death.

Mel R. was there, leading the meeting again. I sat with the backbenchers and didn't volunteer anything. I spent most of the time looking at the floor, hoping that Mel would take it as a sign of backsliding. If anything would draw him to me, it was his desire to help.

After the meeting, he headed for me immediately. "So how's it going?"

"One day at a time," I said, smiling slightly. "I almost blew it last night, but I'm still here."

"Good, that's good," he said, giving my hand a squeeze. "That's how it happens, one day at a time."

"I still think about Mitch all the time. His cousin was arrested for murder."

Mel looked surprised. He clearly hadn't heard about Joe.

"The man who molested Mitch—he was a judge—was killed a couple of days ago, and the police arrested Mitch's cousin. But I don't think he did it. See, I think the same guy who killed Mitch killed the judge, and if I knew more about what Mitch was up to, I'd know who the son of a bitch was."

"You have to let the past go," Mel said.

"Easy for you to say. It wasn't your friend who got killed."

"But it was. Mitch was a friend of mine, too."

Bingo. My hunch had been right. "And you don't care about who killed him?"

"He's dead, Catherine, that's all that matters."

The hall had almost emptied. I took Mel's arm. "Can we go for coffee somewhere, just talk a little more?"

"Sure," he said. "Sure, we can."

I hate lying to good people. Scamming sleazeballs and liars doesn't bother me in the least, but lying to someone like Mel makes me feel rotten. Not rotten enough to stop, but rotten all the same.

We found a coffee shop a block away. It was actually a little hamburger joint, and the counterman didn't look at all pleased when we only ordered coffee. He sat the heavy white ceramic mugs down hard enough to make the coffee slosh over onto the table.

"You were his sponsor, I'll bet," I said, when the counterman had gone back to his grill.

Mel looked surprised. He wasn't good at disguising his thoughts and feelings. "Let's just say I was his friend, like you were. And I have to go on, just as you do."

The problem with pretending you're someone you're not

is that you have to tell the truth at some point or give up the chance to get your informant to make a formal statement. I doubted that I could get Mel to talk to the police, but I couldn't even ask him if I didn't admit who I was.

"Mel, I need to tell you something," I said, "but I want you to promise that you won't walk out on me when I do it."

I'm sure he thought I was going to confess to falling off the wagon. That would have been a far safer confession than I had to offer. "Will you hear me all the way through?"

"Of course."

"Only part of what I've told you is true. I wasn't a friend of Mitch's. I'm an investigator working for his cousin Joe. You probably know that Joe refused to help Mitch. When Mitch was killed, he asked me to find the killer and to see that Samuel Reiter was exposed."

Mel's face had contracted into anger and suspicion. I continued. "Mitch didn't have many friends outside AA. Our only hope of finding someone who knew what he'd been doing just before his death was to go to AA."

"So you lied and spied on us," he said, his voice tight with anger.

"I lied. I didn't spy. I'm not about to repeat anything I heard at meetings. But I need to know about Mitch, and you may be the only one alive who can point the way to his killer."

"I told you it's over. Mitch is dead."

"But what caused his death isn't over. The kids in the book aren't dead. They're still alive, and I suspect they need help."

Mel frowned. I was sure now that he knew about the photo book.

"Did he show you the book?" I asked. "Some of those kids weren't much more than babies."

Mel's face clouded. "Leave me alone. I know your kind. You lie and use people. Well, you're not getting anything from me."

It was my turn to be angry. "So you'd rather let someone get away with abusing kids and killing a friend than be caught helping a woman who misrepresented herself at an AA meeting. That's a real interesting set of values, where lying is worse than abuse and murder. I think you're just feeling sorry for yourself and angry that I didn't play by the rules. I don't think you give a shit about Mitch or what he was trying to do.''

Mel looked like he might hit me, and the narrow booth didn't allow much room to maneuver. Then he took a deep breath and closed his eyes. He sat like that—rigid, eyes closed, taking deep, irregular breaths until his shoulders began to relax and the breathing became regular. Finally, he opened his eyes. ''You're lucky. You'd said that to me three years ago, I'd have taken your head off.''

''You wouldn't have reacted so strongly if you didn't care about Mitch. So what's keeping you from helping me?''

He sucked in the edge of his lower lip and chewed on it. I forced myself to sit quietly and wait. The decision was his to wrestle with. At last, Mel said, ''What, exactly, do you want from me?''

''Just that you tell me all that you know about what Mitch was doing and thinking in the weeks before his death. It may be that something you know could lead to the killer and could help locate the kids in the book.''

Mel shook his head. ''You know enough about AA to understand that I can't reveal what Mitch told me.''

''That'd make sense if Mitch were alive, but he's not, so who are you protecting, except the man who killed him?''

Mel stared into his coffee cup as if seeking a solution there. ''You probably know all about the abuse,'' he said slowly. ''Well, Mitch took to following the judge—what was his name?''

''Reiter.''

''He figured that he'd catch Reiter with some kid and convince the kid to go to the police. He had a camera and he was hoping to get pictures. The second night he followed Reiter, they ended up in Emeryville in an area that's mostly warehouses. Reiter met some other guy driving a Mercedes, and the guy got out of his car and went with Reiter.

''Mitch lost Reiter's car when they got on the freeway, so

he went back to the Mercedes. He had boosted some cars as a kid and knew how to get into the Mercedes. That's where he found the photo book.''

''So the book didn't come from Reiter but from one of his friends.''

Mel nodded. ''Mitch waited. They came back several hours later, and he tailed the guy in the Mercedes to someplace in Oakland. He knew that Reiter's buddy must also be a ped, and he figured that maybe he could get them both. He said it'd be a lot easier to stake out this guy's place in Oakland than to watch Reiter's house in Piedmont.''

I nodded, thinking how obvious a man in an old Ford would have been on the affluent and politely deserted streets of Piedmont. ''And then?''

''That's it. That's the last I heard from him. I called several times, and he wasn't there. Recovering alcoholics aren't the most reliable people. I figured that he'd slipped and gone on a drunk. It seems strange now, but I didn't even consider that he might have been killed until you came to the meeting.''

''Did he have a car license or a name or anything to identify the man in the Mercedes?''

''I think he did, a name maybe, but not a complete one. I remember he said it was like AA, where you get the first name and an initial, and that's it.''

''Jonah T.?''

''Yeah, I think that's it.''

''Would you tell the police this?''

Mel shook his head vehemently. ''No cops. I don't get along with cops.''

''How about giving a statement to Joe's lawyer?''

''I don't like lawyers, either. I gotta go now.'' He slid out of the booth. I caught him before he got to the door. I wanted his name and a way to find him, but I knew he wouldn't give them to me. ''I won't hassle you,'' I said. ''But if you think of anything more, will you call me?'' I pressed one of my regular cards into his hand.

He nodded uncertainly and hurried out the door.

I waited a minute, then followed him. There's no way you

can follow someone who knows you for any distance if they're looking for a tail. But Mel was upset, and I hoped he wouldn't be looking too hard or going too far. I crossed the street so I wasn't directly behind him and stayed a block back. He looked behind him a couple of times, but he didn't look across the street.

He'd left his car on a side street a couple of block from the meeting. Unless he made a U- turn, he was going to have to drive right by me. I stepped into a doorway and waited. As the car went by, I got the license number.

Arthur Costa was not nearly so elated as I about Mel R.'s revelation. "I'm not sure how useful he'd be even if he were willing to testify, but without that, we have nothing."

"Not yet, but I'm one step closer to finding Jonah T., and that may put me one step closer to finding out who killed Samuel Reiter."

Perry Mason was probably the only defense attorney to think in terms of finding the guilty party. Costa was clearly far more concerned with building a case that would get Joe off than with finding out who had committed the actual murder. I didn't think we had much chance of doing the former unless I could manage the latter.

I didn't expect the Oakland police to be a lot more receptive to my story than Costa had been. A week ago, when Joe was an interested citizen instead of an alleged murderer, they might have taken a different view. Now, Reiter's mysterious friend would sound like a convenient ploy on the part of the defense.

I pointed out to Warren that I'd given him the name Jonah T. and the phone number several days before Reiter's murder. He thanked me for the information and assured me that he'd check on the unlisted phone number. His tone was polite and distant, and vaguely patronizing. He reminded me of a doctor who once told me not to worry about the pain in my side. That was a couple of days before my appendix ruptured.

As he terminated our conversation he said, "This is a

police matter now. I appreciate your help in finding Morrison's friends, but I won't have you interfering with an ongoing investigation. Do I make myself clear?''

"You do,'' I said, thinking that if the investigation were a bit more ongoing, I wouldn't need to be involved.

Kevin Doyle wasn't one to wait till I got around to calling. The third time he phoned, Amy begged me to take the call.

"I really like Joe,'' he said. "I'd like to help him if there's any way I can. This is a big enough story that the papers are going to give it lots of play. Believe me, you'll do better with me on your side.''

I made the appropriate polite sounds about how much I appreciated his concern and his willingness to help. He interrupted. "I talked to Joe a couple of hours ago. . . .''

"At the jail?'' I asked in surprise. "He agreed to see you?''

"Yes. And he suggested that I call you.''

Oh, great, I thought. Joe had been watching too much television if he thought that enlisting the help of a journalist was the way to solve a crime.

"He said you thought that the killer might be someone Reiter had molested in the past or the parent of one of the victims.''

"Those people certainly have a motive,'' I said cautiously. I was uncomfortable discussing the case with Kevin. I didn't want to find myself explaining to Arthur Costa how quotes with my name on them found their way into the *Chronicle*.

"Look, I'd really like to help,'' he said. "I guess I feel a little guilty. Maybe if I'd gone over that night when he called me, he wouldn't have gotten killed.''

"Reiter called *you* that night?''

"Yeah. He'd seen the story I did on him and he wanted to tell his side of it. I'd have gone, but I must have eaten something that didn't agree with me, and I'd spent the last couple of hours throwing up, so I wasn't in much of a mood to talk, and there was no way I was driving to Piedmont. I told him I'd see him the next day.''

''What time did he call?''

''Jeez, I don't know, I wasn't in much shape to worry about the time. Joe said something about phone records. It'd be there, wouldn't it?''

''Was it before or after eight?''

''I think it was after, but I couldn't swear to it. It was dark. I know that. Does it matter?''

It mattered a lot. If Reiter called after eight, it proved that he was alive when Joe left. Of course, I still had to prove that Joe had left before Reiter made the call. ''Did Reiter sound like he had anyone else there?'' I asked.

''No, I didn't get that impression.''

''Did he seem to have been drinking?''

''I don't know. Maybe. His speech was a little slurred now that you mention it.''

I needed those phone records. I wondered how much longer it would take and made a mental note to call the phone company. In the pause, Kevin shifted gears and asked, ''Do you think the judge's death is connected to Mitch's murder? And do you know any more about that?''

''I might,'' I said. ''I'll call you back on that.''

Kevin didn't want to let me go without the full story, but I didn't give him any choice.

Costa wasn't thrilled that Joe had talked with Kevin, but he agreed that we were better off with the *Chronicle* raising questions about Mitch's death than with it hammering away at Joe. He was cautiously optimistic about the revelation of Kevin's call. ''It could be helpful,'' he said. ''Let me know as soon as you get the phone records.''

Kevin was waiting anxiously for my call. He and Costa were at opposite ends of the energy spectrum. The reporter's energy was so manic that I felt tired just listening to him; the lawyer was so low-key I thought he might have gone to sleep while I was talking.

I told Kevin that we knew Mitch had been following a man who appeared to be a friend of Samuel Reiter and had come into possession of a photo album containing incriminating evidence. We believed that he was following that same man the night of his death.

It wasn't nearly enough for Kevin. He wanted to know about the album and the man and where Mitch had followed him. I've spent too much time with cops to offer anything more than general information. Give out specifics, and you have a dozen confessions and no way to tell if one of them is genuine. Kevin asked if there was any indication that Reiter's friend was a pedophile. I said there was, and that was the last thing he got from me except good-bye.

MOLLY AND I spent a tense evening alone. She arrived home at five fifty-nine, but there was a chip the size of Gibraltar on her shoulder, and she gave me the silent treatment during dinner. I had the evening to reflect that I'd replaced a very desirable lover with a sullen teenager. It didn't seem like a smart move.

Peter and I are well matched in pride and stubbornness. I was the one who'd yelled at him; I'd have to make the phone call. Crow was never my favorite dish, but I knew it only took a few bites to earn dessert.

I was in considerably better spirits the next morning. I'd have liked to share a leisurely breakfast with Peter, but the memory of Joe in jail drove me to the office early.

I called the phone company to see about our subpoena for Reiter's phone records and got a perky young woman who really wanted to help but didn't know anything about the subpoenas. She informed me that the legal department was reviewing whether or not to honor the subpoenas, and they would contact me as soon as a determination had been made. She actually said that—"as soon as a determination has been made." Bureaucrat-speak is an awesome thing.

Waiting around for a determination didn't seem like a hot idea, so I decided to get on with interviewing Reiter's neighbors and his assistant. I didn't expect to find too many of the neighbors home during the day, but on Reiter's street, I might find servants and maybe some gossip.

On Glen Ellen Drive the houses on the downhill side of the street have striking views of the bay and San Francisco. They date from around the turn of the century and are at least twice as large and lavish as their newer uphill neighbors. Their owners all have servants. The uphill houses have cleaning ladies and an occasional cook.

The cleaning ladies spoke a variety of languages, none of them English. They were busy and wouldn't have had time to talk even if they'd understood what I wanted. The servants were far too well trained to gossip with strangers. Two of them were, however, willing to answer a few questions for a legal investigator.

They didn't know a lot about Judge Reiter, but they gave me an earful about his young assistant. Jeffrey Gotelli had made no secret of the fact that he did not consider himself in the same class as the other working people on the block. Reiter's former cook had found him so insufferable that she had quit.

"I don't think the new missus liked him much," the cook next door confided. "She asked him to move out of his little cottage in the back after the judge died. Didn't have any further need for his services. I guess he was pretty upset about it."

I asked what they thought of the charges that Reiter was a child molester. The cook pursed her lips and shook her head. "I don't know where they got such notions, but you'll never convince me. He did have boys around, especially before he remarried, but what's wrong with a man giving a hand to boys that need it? He just wasn't the kind, if you know what I mean.''

I didn't know what she meant. Did she assume that molesters wore dirty raincoats and lurked in alleys? Or was it that Reiter was too cultured, too rich, too wellborn to indulge in such distasteful activities?

Two houses up the street on the uphill side I found Mrs. Braxton-Hancock. She had given the police a long statement and was willing to do the same for me. I'd read her statement; there wasn't much there, since she'd been out the night of Reiter's death, but I hoped to get some background information that the police had been too busy to fish for.

Mrs. Braxton-Hancock was in her sixties, a tiny bundle of energy with birdlike motions. She settled me in a chair in her living room, and made a pot of tea. She was fascinated to meet a woman private investigator and wanted to know all about it. In return she was only too happy to tell me about Samuel Reiter.

She'd lived up the street since he inherited the family home when he was in his early twenties. ''It was a real tragedy, his parents dying like that. A boating accident, I think, on the way to Mexico.''

The first Mrs. Reiter had been a local girl, someone Reiter had known in high school and later met at some social function. ''They seemed the perfect couple,'' Mrs. Braxton-Hancock said. ''Both so attractive and intelligent. She was a painter, I think. But it didn't last very long, five years at the most. She moved away. I don't know where.''

''I thought he was a widower,'' I said.

''Well, I suppose in a manner of speaking. They never really divorced. She was killed in an automobile accident the next year, so he *was* a widower, I guess. It was a real tragedy for him. He must have pined for her, showed no interest in getting married again until a few years ago, when he met his current wife.''

I didn't point out to my hostess that it was unlikely Reiter had pined for an adult woman when his major interest was young boys. She seemed completely unaware of the charges against him. Like the cook, she probably refused to believe them.

"Has he always had an assistant?" I asked.

"Usually. And a cook, I believe."

"And the assistants, have they been young men like the current one?"

She looked at me shrewdly. "Yes. Are you suggesting something?"

"No, not at all. I was just interested in what type of people the judge hired."

"They've all been very nice young men. The last one must have been with him five years at least."

"Were any of them married?"

"No, of course not. The cottage is really only big enough for one."

"I know that Judge Reiter was active in many boys' clubs. Did his assistant participate, too?"

She looked disturbed. "Well, I don't know. I've seen him bring boys to Sam's house, and I think he may have gone along on outings with Sam's clubs. But that doesn't mean anything, you know."

We both knew what it meant, but only one of us was willing to admit it.

Reiter's assistant, Jeff Gotelli, was living in an apartment near Lake Merritt in Oakland. It was a real comedown from the cottage behind the judge's house, but it was nice enough to make me wonder where Gotelli got the money to pay for it. His presence there on a weekday afternoon suggested that he wasn't working a nine-to-five job.

Molly would have described Gotelli as "drop-dead gorgeous." In his mid- to late twenties, he was too old for her, but there are some men you can appreciate at any age. He had the dark good looks of the Mediterranean—smooth olive skin, curly black hair, and large, deep-brown eyes. Many women would kill for the long lashes that framed his eyes.

I was surprised that I hadn't noticed how attractive he was

the night I visited Reiter. In the large, dimly lit entry hall, he'd faded into his surroundings. In his own apartment, he looked considerably more casual and relaxed. There was nothing servile or self-effacing about the way he moved or acted. In fact, it was quite the contrary. If he was the least uncomfortable being questioned by the defense, he certainly didn't show it.

I had him describe in his own words what had happened the night of Reiter's death, and what he'd seen when he entered the study the next morning.

He told me he'd gone to a party that Sunday night. He'd left the house right after Joe arrived and picked up his date in another section of Piedmont at eight-twenty. They'd arrived at the party around eight forty-five. I commented that he seemed unusually certain of the time. "I make it a point to be punctual," he said. "If I tell someone I will be there at eight-twenty, I am there at eight-twenty."

"How did you meet Judge Reiter?" I asked.

"He was a friend of a friend."

"Can you tell me the friend's name?"

"Actually, I can't. I don't remember it. He wasn't a close friend, just someone I knew casually. He knew I was looking for a job and that Sam needed an assistant."

"How long ago was that?"

"Five years."

"So you were how old then?"

Gotelli looked surprised, but he answered. "Twenty-two."

"What exactly were your duties?"

"Mainly assisting him with his business affairs. Most people thought I was the butler or something, but I was really an administrative assistant. I did the other things because he needed someone to do them."

"Did you know of Reiter's interest in young boys?"

Gotelli flushed. "I don't believe that nonsense," he said hotly. "It was lies, made up by people who wanted to hurt him. You know when a man is as successful as Sam, when he has talent and he's also attractive and wealthy, it makes a lot of people jealous."

* * *

At least a dozen people were willing to testify that Jeff Gotelli had been at a party from eight forty-five till after midnight. If Reiter had called Kevin after Joe left, then the assistant had an unshakable alibi. Only the phone records could tell me that.

I stopped by the phone company on my way back from Piedmont. Maybe I'd do better in person than I had on the phone. When it took only three passes around the block before I found a place to park, I figured luck was on my side.

Luck was half on my side. The lawyers had decided to release the name that went with the number in Mitch's car. It was Edward Kohl. They were still considering our request for Reiter's phone records.

Back at the office, I put in a request for motor vehicle registration information for Edward Kohl. I didn't have a birth date or Social Security number and Kohl is not that unusual a name, so I figured I'd have to wade through a bunch of records before I found the right one.

Steve Marley called to ask how things were coming in Joe's case. I gave him a quick rundown, and when I got to the name Ed Kohl, he exploded. "Kohl? Shit!"

"You know the man?"

"Too well. His name's come up in several investigations. He's a slippery bastard, always at the edge of the picture, but never so we can nail him. That's what the Piper is about. Damn it, how could I have missed that?"

"Piper?"

"His nickname is the Piper, as in 'He who pays the piper calls the tune' or the Pied Piper. Word has it he can provide anything your average pedophile or sexual deviant might require, for a price. He claims to be an investment consultant, specializing in real estate. What that seems to mean is that he owns properties which he rents out at above-market rates in exchange for not asking any questions.

"We busted a brothel for underage girls last year. Guess who owned the property. Oh, his name wasn't on the deed.

But he was a major shareholder in the company that owned the company that held the deed. He's one slick operator.''

"Capable of killing someone who got in his way?''

"I wouldn't rule it out. I think the guy's a real psychopath. There's nothing inside, no moral sense, no connection to anything but his own drives. See, he's not like the peds. They do what they do out of compulsion. He's coming from a different place.''

"So he's not a pedophile?''

"Not necessarily. All that I know about him has to do with kids, but that's probably just one of the ways he gets his kicks. And you can figure he's in this for more than kicks. He's a high roller.''

"And the photo album?''

"It's the kind of thing I'd expect him to have. Those photos weren't produced for pornography. Those kids are for sale, and you can bet that a big hunk of their earnings are coming back to the Piper.''

My stomach knotted up and I got off the phone as soon as I could. I didn't doubt what Marley was telling me, but the ugliness of it was appalling. Part of me wanted to just get off this case, but even the little voice that is usually so sensible said, If decent people are too squeamish to deal with this, who does that leave to protect the children?

EDWARD KOHL WAS the break I'd been hoping for. He was a prime candidate for Mitch Morrison's and Samuel Reiter's killer. I called Costa in high spirits.

Costa reacted to my news in his usual low-key manner.

He was very interested in Edward Kohl, but he didn't want me to take my information to the police—not yet, anyway. "I want to decide how best to play this card," he said. "Kohl's name does not appear on the police report's list of people questioned about Samuel Reiter's death. You gave the police the telephone number?"

"A week ago. Of course, I gave it to the officer in charge of the Morrison investigation, but I'd assume that the Piedmont police have talked with him."

"Yes, certainly, but evidently they haven't followed up on the phone number. That could be very embarrassing for the prosecution." I could imagine his sly smile. "Make an appointment to see Mr. Kohl. Find out what he has to say about Samuel Reiter and Mitch Morrison, but don't ask what he was doing the night either one was killed. I don't want to suggest to him that he needs an alibi. As much as the information, which may well be lies, I want your impression of him. What kind of man is he? How will he come across in court?"

I called Kohl's office, but he was gone for the day. I reached him at ten o'clock the next morning.

I'd anticipated some difficulty in getting him to agree to see me, and I was surprised when he suggested that I come to his office that afternoon. He was so cordial I thought he must have misunderstood the purpose of my visit.

I spent the morning wondering why Kohl was so willing to meet with me. It makes me nervous when things that should be difficult are easy. It's often a sign that I've missed something I should be paying attention to, and with an adversary like Kohl, any mistake could be dangerous.

Kohl's office was a block from the place where we'd found Mitch's car and right next door to where I'd nearly been run down by the kid with the big box and the strawberry birthmark. A silver Mercedes was parked just up the street. Its vanity license plate read "Jonah T." That solved the mystery of the name Mitch had written on the paper in his car. He must have assumed, as I would have, that the license bore the name of the owner of the car.

I recognized Ed Kohl at once. He was the man Mitch had sketched with Samuel Reiter in his notebook. Mitch had captured him remarkably well. He looked like an aging fraternity boy—pleasant in a bland sort of way, good features, blond hair, blue eyes, nice straight teeth. It was hard to imagine him as a killer, but I suspect that's true of most killers.

He made small talk; I made small talk. We both watched each other. The whole process reminded me of dogs circling and sniffing. Finally, I said, "Did you know Judge Samuel Reiter?"

"Only slightly," he said. "We met occasionally at social functions. I was shocked by his murder. No one's safe anymore."

"So you didn't know him personally?"

"No."

"And you didn't meet him in Emeryville about a month before his death?"

"No." He lied well, I had to give him that.

"Did you know anything about Judge Reiter's interest in young boys?"

"I knew he worked extensively with youth programs. That's all anyone really knew. Now that he's dead, it seems cruel to speculate on anything more."

Again his execution was flawless. He was the discreet businessman, too well-bred to indulge in unseemly speculation. He would be a difficult witness. I had the feeling that he could be anything he chose to be and that no scruple would intrude to mar his performance.

"Do you drive a Mercedes with 'Jonah T' on the license?"

"Yes, I do. A silver coupe. What does that have to do with this?"

"Did you lose something from that car about a month ago? A black binder?"

"No, I don't think so." He considered for a moment. "I can't think of anything that's missing."

We looked at each other across his desk. I knew he was

lying, and I had the feeling he knew I knew. "Who's Jonah T?" I asked.

He laughed. "A friend. I put his name on my license as a joke."

"Did he put 'Piper' on his?"

There was a reaction, so slight I'd never have seen it if I hadn't been watching, a tightening of the muscles around the eyes. Then he gave me his pleasant, bland smile and asked, "Can I do anything more for you?"

The Oakland Hall of Justice was only a few blocks from Kohl's office. I had more than enough to point John Warren at Kohl, but I'd promised Arthur Costa that I wouldn't do anything until I'd checked with him. As long as there was a chance that Joe might have to stand trial, I'd let Costa call the shots.

The jail was also nearby, and I considered visiting Joe but decided against it. I didn't want to raise his hopes until I could nail Kohl for sure. Besides, since I'd demanded that Molly be home by six, I wanted to be there when she got home.

Traffic was impossible on the way home. A truck had spilled some white powder on the Bay Bridge earlier, and the cops had closed the bridge until they knew what it was. By the time I got there, they'd identified it as harmless and were in the midst of cleaning it up. Those of us who got to sit and wait were not happy campers. In fact, everyone was so frustrated and grumpy by the time they finally reopened the bridge that several drivers promptly plowed into each other and snarled traffic all over again.

I got home at six-fifteen, tired, short of temper, and hungry. No one was there. I poured myself a glass of wine and sat down to wait for Molly.

Peter got home around seven. Still no Molly. I'd passed through irritation and was starting to worry.

"She's probably hanging out with friends and has lost track of time," Peter said.

"The friends are exactly what worries me," I said. "And an hour is quite a bit of time to lose track of."

We had a quick dinner, and by eight, Peter was as edgy as I was. "I just have a bad feeling about this," I said. "She knows she's supposed to be home by six. Do you think she's run away?"

"Did you check her room?"

"Nothing's missing except what she took to school. I have a rough idea where the vampire twins hang out. I'm going to check on them."

"Why don't you let me do it," Peter suggested. "You should stay here in case she calls. Besides, they may be less hostile to me. If I don't get anything from them, I can start checking with some kids I know and some other sources."

Peter had a lot more sources on the street than I did. It made sense for him to go, but I hated like the devil to be stuck waiting by the phone.

It didn't help any that I'd spent my afternoon with Ed Kohl. Kohl was an unnerving reminder that the dangers I'd warned Molly about were all too real.

The hands of my watch slowed down as the hour got later. I wanted Molly home, but I still didn't know what to say to her. I knew we couldn't go on like this.

The phone rang at nine-thirty. "Is this Catherine Sayler?" The voice was female and young, but it wasn't Molly's.

"Yes."

"This is Rae. I was at your house."

"Yes?" I said, my heart speeding up.

"Molly didn't want me to call you, but she's, like, sick, and I think you should come and get her."

"Where are you? I'll be right there."

"She said to make you promise that you wouldn't call the police. She did some drugs, and she's scared you'll turn her in."

"I won't call the police, and I won't turn her in," I promised. "Just tell me where she is."

"We're down near Fifth Street on Bluxome. The number is two twenty-three. It's like this old warehouse, and you can't get in the front door, but there's an alley on the side, and about halfway down, there's this blue door. You can come in there. We're on the second floor.''

"I'll be right down," I said, and there was a click at the other end.

I HURRIED DOWN to my car, torn between concern, relief, and anger at Molly for putting herself and me through all this. As I drove down Divisadero, I wondered exactly what drugs Molly had been "doing," and how sick she was. I prayed it wasn't an overdose or a batch of bad stuff.

At Turk, I almost missed the red light and had to brake to a stop just shy of the intersection. All I needed now was a ticket or a wreck. I resolved to be more careful. But as I turned onto Golden Gate my foot seemed to have a will of its own, and the needle on the speedometer climbed more quickly than it should have.

I had to brake again at Van Ess. The red light glared down at me, stubbornly exercising its power. I realized that my breath was coming in short, shallow gasps, and made a conscious effort to take deeper, longer breaths. Usually, that calms me; today, it simply made me more impatient.

Just as I decided that the light must be broken, it winked green. Getting past the Civic Center and through the Tenderloin took forever, but once I hit Sixth Street, the traffic thinned, and I could make decent time at night, so I cut over to Howard. I hoped to hell that Bluxome Street was where I thought it was.

I found it on the first try, and drove up the street until I found the number, then around the corner and up the alley to the blue door. The alley looked deserted. Years ago its proximity to the train yards would have made it attractive to hobos, but today's homeless weren't railroaders, and they stayed closer to downtown. I wondered how the devil Molly and her friends had found this place.

I parked just before the blue door, pulled the flashlight from the compartment on the car door, and got out.

The blue door bore a faded pink notice that informed me in large letters that the building was unsafe for human occupancy. Beneath the notice, the door stood slightly ajar, its shattered doorjamb mute testimony to someone's contempt for the city's warning.

The door was braced with heavy crossbeams, a clear sign of earthquake damage. This area was full of brick buildings built on fill, which is about the worst combination in a quake. During the quake, a couple of them had lost their outside walls, and many more had been damaged. Some, like this one, still awaited repair or the wrecker's ball.

I pushed the door open, wedged it to keep it that way, and stepped inside. The building was a warehouse, and I was standing in a wide hall. To my left, heavy beams cross-braced an opening the size of a garage door. My flashlight illuminated only a tight circle of space. Beyond its beam was black emptiness.

"Molly?" I called.

A muffled moan answered me from somewhere ahead. I followed the sound.

Yellow light leaked from under a door at the top of a flight of wooden stairs. I picked my way through the rubble and climbed the stairs. The door opened when I pushed. A single low-watt bulb illuminated a small room. Against the opposite wall, a shapeless heap of blankets lay on an old mattress. I hurried toward them, praying I wasn't too late.

I pulled back the blanket to find a pile of rags and felt suddenly sick as I realized that I'd been set up.

"Hands on your head, please." The voice was almost casual, as if the order were just a polite request, but I recognized it at once and knew that Ed Kohl was deadly serious.

I did as I was told and turned slowly to face him. He stood next to a pile of boxes where he must have been hiding. He wore the same bland smile he'd greeted me with at his office, but he was holding a gun.

"Sal," he called. The door behind me opened, and I turned to see the young man with the strawberry birthmark pushing Molly ahead of him into the room. Her hands were tied behind her, and a wad of cloth had been forced into her mouth as a gag. Her eyes were wide with fear.

After all my worries about Molly running away, I'd discovered that there were far worse possibilities.

Kohl made a motion with his free hand, and Sal moved Molly over next to me and pushed her down onto the mattress. He handed Sal the gun, with orders to shoot me if either of us moved, then moved around behind me.

"Put your arms behind you *very slowly*," he said.

He slid my jacket off and checked the pockets. The turtleneck and jeans I was wearing were too tight to hide a weapon, but that didn't stop him from searching for one. When he'd finished, he stepped back and took the gun from Sal.

"Why?" I asked, though I knew the answer.

"Because you wouldn't back off," he said. "A man in my position can't afford to have someone like you digging around. You'd never have pinned that bar shooting on me, but God knows what else you might have come up with. I can't take that chance."

"But you did kill Mitch Morrison."

"Sure. For the same reason I have to kill you. I'm a businessman. You are a liability, so was he."

"And the judge, was he a liability, too?"

"To himself, not to me. There's no way Sam would have even admitted to knowing me, much less revealed that he knew what I did. No, he wasn't a threat to me."

"Then why kill him?"

"You're asking the wrong man. I didn't kill Sam. I didn't need to."

Kohl was perfectly capable of lying, but there wasn't any

reason for him to. He'd already admitted to one murder, why deny the other?

"Where's the book?" he asked.

"The police have it. They found the photos very interesting."

"The other book. The one Morrison stole from my office."

I didn't say, "What other book?" but my face must have revealed what I was thinking, because Kohl said, "So you haven't found it yet. Too bad. I'd like to have it back."

"What are you going to do with us?" I asked. "Dump us behind another bar?"

"No need. This neighborhood will do fine. Your niece ran away, you got into the wrong part of town looking for her."

"You better make it good," I said, "because my ex-husband is an inspector in homicide, and no matter who does the investigation, it's bound to be a personal friend."

"There won't be anything for them to find, just as there wasn't in Oakland. People die all the time in a neighborhood like this."

"Not people investigating murders. Not former wives of homicide detectives. This is a little too close to the killing in Oakland not to look like a setup. You get Dan Walker on your trail, you're going to wish it was only me you were dealing with."

Kohl smiled broadly. "I'm terrified," he said.

"You surprise me. I wouldn't have taken you for a gambler."

He was smiling, but he was also thinking, and that gave me some reason for hope. If he decided to shoot us here, it was probably all over, but if he had to take us somewhere else, there was a possibility that he'd make a mistake and I'd get a chance at him.

"Okay," he said. "No problem. I've got just the place for you. We don't have to worry about the kid, see. You'll be glad to hear that she's not part of this. A cute little piece like that—what is she, twelve, thirteen? There are folks'll pay plenty for her."

If I'd had the means, I'd have killed him right then. In cold blood. I've learned to control fear, but the fury that surged through me pushed me right to the edge.

Kohl laughed, a nasty, evil sound. "Sal'll take care of her. But don't worry, he'll be real careful with her. Go on," he ordered the other man. "You know where to take her. I'll be there soon as I finish here."

Sal started toward us, and I waited for the moment when he'd come between Kohl and me. With my training in aikido, I had no doubt I could take them both, but not with a gun pointed at me. I needed Sal for a shield. Just as he was about to step between us, Kohl barked out, "Don't walk in front of her, dummy, go around behind."

With him coming in behind me, and my hands on my head, there wasn't much I could do that wouldn't get me shot. I forced myself to stand still while Sal pulled Molly up from the mattress and dragged her toward the door. For the first time, I felt truly helpless. There wasn't a damn thing I could do to stop Sal, and even if I did save myself, I wasn't sure I could save Molly.

When they were gone, Kohl said, "We're going to take a little walk down the street, down to those buildings at the end. You're about to become another victim of the quake." He laughed harshly.

I remembered those buildings. The entire outside walls were gone, but the interior ones remained. Metal scaffolding held the floors up. A deep trench surrounded the foundations. Kohl was right. No one would question an accident there.

Kohl picked up an electric lantern with his free hand and motioned me toward the door. With only a beam of light coming from behind me, I could barely see the stairs. It would have been tricky if I'd had the use of my hands, but negotiating those stairs with my hands on my head was nearly impossible. Just over halfway down, I missed a step and plunged forward in the darkness.

I grabbed for something to break my fall and caught hold of one of the poles supporting the handrail. Momentum threw me forward, and a wrenching pain shot through my shoulder. I let go and rolled down a couple more steps, landing hard on the floor at the bottom. Another sharp pain shot through my shoulder and the side of my face slammed against the floor.

A moment later the beam of the flashlight bored into my eyes. "Get up," Kohl said.

I didn't know if I could. I was still in shock, and I couldn't tell how much damage the fall had done, but as my head cleared, I made a decision. "I don't know if I can walk," I said. "I think I did something to my leg."

"Get up," he said again.

I went through the motions, struggling to get on my hands and knees. My left shoulder hurt like hell, and a knife of pain stabbed through my right ankle. As I started to stand I let myself fall again. "I can't," I said. "I think I broke it."

Kohl hesitated. He descended the stairs and stepped behind me. I couldn't see a thing except the blinding light he kept in my eyes. "Get up now," he ordered.

"I can't." I tried to sound desperate.

"Get up or I'll shoot you here."

I'd hoped he'd reach down to pull me up, but he was too smart for that. "Please don't shoot," I pleaded. "I'm getting up." I struggled and stumbled to my feet.

I didn't have to fake the limp. I just accentuated what my body already wanted to do, but as I approached the door I slowed down. I dragged my right foot so that my left foot was always forward.

"Keep moving," Kohl ordered.

I shuffled even slower. "Damn it, move," he snarled. He stepped in closer and jabbed me in the back with the barrel of the gun.

It was the moment I'd been hoping for. I pivoted to my right and spun around, knocking his gun hand to the side. My right hand slid down to grab his wrist. I stepped behind him, brought my left hand around his neck and across his throat, grabbed the collar of his leather jacket and pulled hard.

He struggled against the choke. I'd missed the carotid artery. The pain in my shoulder was almost more than I could stand. I wasn't going to get a second chance. I stepped back and went down on my left knee, bringing Kohl down hard. I slammed his right arm, fully extended, across my right leg. There was a pop as the elbow broke. Kohl screamed, and the gun dropped to the floor.

P AIN STABBED THROUGH my shoulder and ankle, and I didn't know how long I'd have the strength to keep the pressure on Kohl's throat. I gritted my teeth and held tight as he struggled against my arm. "Where's my niece?" I demanded.

"You want your niece; I want my freedom. We can do business," he croaked.

I gave the arm with the broken elbow a sharp yank. He screamed. "Where is my niece?" I repeated.

He made a gurgling sound, and I loosened my arm a bit. Too much pressure and I'd choke him out. He wouldn't be much use to me unconscious. "Tell me," I said, "or I'll twist your arm off." I gave another yank to make my point.

"All right, all right," he cried. "I'll take you there."

"You'll tell me where she is first, then you'll take me there."

He paused. I tightened my grip on his arm. He gave me an address on Del Norte Street.

"Tell me about it."

"What do you mean?"

"What kind of place is it, who's there, what can I expect? I don't want any unpleasant surprises."

"It's a house in the Castro, sort of a halfway house where kids hang out. Runaways. Boys."

"And where will your friend have taken Molly?"

"I've got an office in the back, on the second floor."

My arm wouldn't hold out much longer. I shifted my grip and increased the pressure on his carotid artery until he sagged into unconsciousness. Then I gave him a push forward onto the floor and felt around for the gun near my right foot. I'd only have a few seconds before he regained consciousness. Even though I didn't think he was in any shape to give me problems, I wanted the gun in my hand when his head cleared.

He'd dropped the lantern when I turned on him. Fortunately, it hadn't broken. It lay on the floor in front of us, illuminating empty space while we remained in the dark. I picked it up and shined it in Kohl's face.

His skin was a ghostly white, whether from the light or the pain, I couldn't tell. His eyes fluttered open and stared blankly at me. I shivered, aware for the first time that my back was wet with sweat. "Up," I said.

As Kohl's head cleared, his nasty disposition returned. He swore colorfully if not imaginatively.

"Get up, we're going to get my niece," I said.

"Fuck you," he said. "I'm not going anywhere."

"You're going. With or without a couple of bullet holes in you. Your choice."

He paused and blinked into the light, as if he were trying to see my face to gauge my seriousness.

"I'll do it," I said.

"You don't have to go there," he said. "You could call and Sal would meet you somewhere, exchange me for Molly. That's the safest bet."

I wanted safe, but I wasn't about to let Kohl define it for me. "We're going to my car now," I said. "Give me any excuse at all, and I'll shoot you. That's a promise."

He limped ahead of me out the door. At the car I made

him stop and keep his good hand over his head while I opened the trunk.

"The trunk?" he shouted. "You can't put me in the trunk. I'll suffocate."

"I don't think so," I said. "I don't like vermin in my car. Get in the trunk."

"What about my arm?"

"It too. Move."

Kohl climbed awkwardly into the trunk. When he was inside, I slammed it shut.

The drive to Del Norte Street was one of the longest in my life. All I could think of was how terrified Molly must be and what appalling danger she faced. Kohl's instructions to Sal gave me some reason to believe that she was safe for the time being, but things can go wrong. Sal could panic or she could try to escape.

I tried to force my mind away from such thoughts, but fear sat heavy in my chest, compressing my lungs so it was hard to get enough breath. There wasn't a lot of traffic, but every slow driver in the city seemed to be on the streets tonight and all the lights were red.

I slammed on the brakes to avoid an ancient Volkswagen that pulled out right in front of me. A muffled yelp from behind reminded me that it was a rough ride in the trunk. I didn't give a damn. Kohl wouldn't suffocate, because Volvos have an opening from the trunk to the main compartment for carrying skis. I wanted him alive. Comfortable wasn't a priority.

I forced myself to think about how I'd deal with Sal and the others at the house on Del Norte Street. It was risky to go in alone, without backup. If something went wrong, Molly would still be in Sal's hands with no one to come after her. But it was even riskier to call the police. Their involvement could easily lead to a hostage situation with lots of men with guns and far too much chance that a shot might go astray.

I decided to call Peter. If he was home, I'd use him for

backup. If not, I could leave a message telling him where I'd
gone and why.

I found the address on Del Norte. It was a two-story row
house, third from the corner on a residential street a block
above the commercial district. I drove past it twice to be sure
I knew the layout, then looked for a parking space some
distance away.

I found one three blocks from the address, just up the
block from a small neighborhood grocery. I needed a phone.

The man behind the counter was Asian, probably Korean,
an older man with tired eyes. He was obviously getting ready
to close. "You all right, miss?" he asked. "Your head is
bleeding."

I touched my cheek and discovered that I'd cut it in the
fall. I considered cleaning up but didn't want to take the time.
Besides, this way I could claim to have had some kind of
accident that required Sal's help.

"I fell," I told the grocer. "Do you have a telephone I
could use?"

"There's a pay phone over by the chips," he said.

I reached in my pocket and realized I'd left my wallet at
home when I rushed out to get Molly. The old man handed
me a quarter with a look that said he hadn't really expected
me to have the money.

I called home, hoping to catch Peter but got only the machine. I left a message telling him what had happened and
where we were. I ended with, "If you don't hear from me
by eleven, call the police. Don't try to go in before then."

I limped the three blocks to the address Kohl had given
me, feeling every step in my aching ankle. My stomach had
tied itself into one large, painful knot; and my chest was so
tight that breathing took an effort. I shivered, but the icy chill
in my hands and feet had nothing to do with the cold night
air.

I paused in front of the house, then climbed the steps to
the porch and knocked on the door. The hand in my right
pocket held Kohl's gun. A boy in his early teens, in tight

jeans and a white T-shirt, answered the door. "I need to see Sal," I said.

He looked at me for a moment, then said, "I think he's upstairs."

"Good, I'll go on up."

The kid stepped aside and let me enter. He didn't seem to care much about who I was or why I was there, and my disheveled appearance hadn't bothered him any.

I didn't have to ask directions because there was a set of stairs in the entrance hall. I climbed to the second story and walked toward the back. If Kohl hadn't lied to me, the door at the end of the hall should be his office. I stood with my back to a wall and knocked.

Sal opened the door. Before he could move, I said, "I have Kohl's gun in my pocket. Just walk backwards into that room." He did.

I followed him in and closed the door behind me. Molly sat on an old couch, still bound and gagged.

"Put your hands on your head," I ordered Sal. His eyes were wide enough so you could see the white all the way around. He put his hands on his head. "I didn't hurt her none," he protested. "I ain't touched her."

"It's a damned good thing for you," I said. I made sure he didn't have a gun, then made him lie facedown on the floor while I removed the tape that held the gag in Molly's mouth.

"Oh, Catherine," she gasped.

I reminded myself we weren't out of this yet and kept my tone as cool as I could manage. "We're going to be fine, Molly, but you have to keep it together till we're out of here. Can you do that?"

She nodded and bit her lip.

"Good. We're going to walk right out of here. Sal, you're going to walk ahead of me; Molly, you walk behind me. Be careful not to get between Sal and the gun." I untied her wrists and ankles. "Can you walk all right?"

"Yes," she said in a small voice. I wanted to hug her and

hold her to me, to smooth her hair and comfort her, but this was not the time for that.

I ordered Sal to get up, cross his arms in front of him, and hold his elbows as we walked out. "Be real careful not to say or do anything that might make me feel I have to shoot you," I said. He didn't look so dangerous anymore.

We must have made a strange procession, but no one stopped us as we left the house. We walked the three blocks to the car, and when we reached the corner and I could see it ahead with the trunk still closed, I began to breathe easier.

At the car, I had Sal put his hands behind his back; then I handed Molly the gun, and used my belt to tie Sal's wrists. It's a lot harder than you'd think to tie someone up with a belt, and it took several tries. I was glad I hadn't had to try this maneuver on Kohl.

I put Sal in the backseat of the car, with another warning on the dire consequences of trying to get loose, then I gave Molly the big hug that we both needed. She clung to me but she didn't cry.

"Are you all right?" I asked. "Can you go with me to the police?"

She nodded. "Yes," she said in the same small voice.

I wanted to take her anywhere but a police station. She needed someplace warm and comforting where a kind, loving person would serve her tea and cookies and hold her while she cried. She needed home, but that was a long way away right now.

The Hall of Justice is nearly deserted at eleven o'clock at night, but there are always people at Southern Station, just inside the front door. I pulled into the red zone at the curb and walked up the front steps with my gun in my pocket, my hands in full view, and Sal stumbling along ahead of me. Inside, next to the door, a cop sat behind a metal detector.

Even in the daytime, this building felt cold and cavernous. At night, it was even less hospitable. Dirty yellow light spilled through the slab of bulletproof glass that separated the police station from the lobby, accentuating the gloomy darkness of the outer room.

I stopped in front of the metal detector. "This man kidnapped my niece," I said. "There's a man in the trunk of my car who tried to kill me. I have his gun in the pocket of my jacket."

At the mention of the gun, the patrolman jumped up. He looked like he was about fifteen. He stammered for a minute and then picked up the phone and called for reinforcements.

Two men in uniform hurried out of Southern Station. The older of the two was a stocky man in his early forties. He was about my height and close to twice my weight. His name tag identified him as Emile Alvarez.

Alvarez came around behind me and very gently removed the gun from my pocket. Everyone breathed easier when that was taken care of.

"There's a fair chance that that's the murder weapon from an Oakland homicide about four weeks ago," I said. "The man in my trunk confessed to being the killer, though I'm sure he'll deny it to you."

Alvarez escorted us into Southern Station and sent two cops to retrieve Kohl. "May I see your identification, please?" he asked.

"I don't have it with me," I said. I was in the process of explaining who I was and why I had an injured man in my trunk when they brought Kohl in. He was pale, and his arm hung useless at his side, but it didn't slow him down any. "That woman tried to kill me!" he shouted. "She held a gun on me and locked me in her trunk. I need a doctor, and I want my lawyer."

Alvarez took a look at Kohl's arm and ordered the patrolmen to take him to the Emergency Room at SF General. "These men will take your statement at the hospital," he said. Kohl was still protesting and threatening lawsuits as they took him out the door.

"He's a dangerous man," I warned Alvarez.

"They know he's a homicide suspect. They'll be careful," he assured me. He turned to Molly. "Do you need to see a doctor?'' he asked gently. Molly shook her head. "How about you?'' he asked me.

I shook my head. "I'd just like to get this over with so I can get my niece home.''

He had me tell him my version of the evening's events, then he said, "The inspector will want to talk with you.''

I put my arm around Molly and drew her to me. "Hang in there,'' I said. "It's going to be all right.'' She pressed tight against me, and I held her there.

W E SAT ON hard chairs and waited for the inspector. The light seemed too bright, and the noise made my head ache. I asked to use the phone and called home. Peter was still out, so I left a message telling him that all was well and we were at Southern Station.

I was almost dozing when I remembered something Kohl had said back at the warehouse, something I didn't want to forget. I'd been so concerned with saving Molly that I'd shoved it to the back of my mind. Now I tried to pull it up.

It was a reference to a book, but not the book of photographs, another book, one Mitch had stolen from Kohl's office. I was too tired to think as clearly as I needed to, but I sensed that book was important and I wondered why it hadn't been in Mitch's apartment or his car.

He must have hidden it somewhere or given it to someone. If the book was worth hiding, it was worth finding. It could be connected to Mitch's murder, and even to the judge's. So long as Joe was still in jail, we needed to know everything we could about Samuel Reiter.

My thoughts were interrupted by the arrival of an attractive Asian woman in her thirties, with short black hair. She introduced herself as Inspector Lui and took us upstairs to her office. There she had Molly recount the night's events. I learned that Kohl had enlisted a friend of the vampire twins, a boy in his late teens, to lure Molly to the warehouse. He'd offered her a ride home and claimed he needed to drop something off on the way. The "something" turned out to be Molly.

I also learned that Molly recognized Kohl as the man who had spoken to her in front of my apartment and given her a ride to Polk Street several days ago. I wondered how he'd known where to find me; then I remembered the business card I'd accidentally given to Sal. He must have been waiting to see how close I'd get. My call, or maybe my visit, had set him off.

Molly described her whole ordeal with amazing composure. She was close to tears several times, but she fought them down and went on. When she apologized to me for the second time, I realized that she felt responsible for what had happened. "I should have listened to you," she repeated.

I pulled her to me and held her. "This didn't happen because of you," I told her. "Those men were after me. They just used you." Later, I'd have time to reflect that the hardest part for both of us was feeling responsible for the other's pain.

Lui had Molly go back over several points. I began to relax a bit, and a wave of exhaustion and nausea hit me. The whole left side of my head throbbed. I reached up and touched it gently. The hair on that side was matted and sticky with blood. I must have cut it when I fell. My cheek and the inside of my mouth also hurt, my right ankle ached, and I couldn't lift my left arm without a sharp stab of pain.

But I would heal. It was Molly I was worried about. When Lui finished with her, I asked if I could call Marion to take her home. Molly objected so strenuously that I agreed to let her stay with me, at least for the night.

As we were getting started on my statement, an older man

in a brown suit came in and whispered something to Lui. I recognized him a few seconds before he recognized me, so I was ready when he said, "Say, aren't you . . . ?"

"Catherine Sayler," I said. "Hi, Bill."

Bill Stanton was one of the first police officers I'd met when I came to San Francisco. He reached out and shook my hand with the same slightly awkward gentility that I remembered from years before. "I didn't recognize the name, but I never forget a face. You're Dan Walker's wife."

"Ex-wife," I said. "We were divorced several years ago."

"Oh." He looked genuinely distressed. "I'm sorry to hear that."

Before I could tell him that he'd do us both a favor if he didn't mention my presence at Southern Station to Dan, he said, "There's a Peter Harman out front asking after you. I'll let him know you'll be down in a while."

I thanked Bill, and we returned to my statement. Lui had me take her through the whole evening, including breaking Kohl's elbow.

"You must be very good to have disarmed a man of his size," she said.

"I had a lot of motivation." I didn't tell her about yanking on Kohl's arm or that I'd have shot him if he'd given me any excuse at all. I wasn't proud of the way I'd felt or the things I'd been willing to do.

It was beginning to look as if we'd be spending the entire night at Southern Station, so I asked Lui if she couldn't expedite things and let us come back down and sign the statements in the morning. I doubt she'd have done it for me, but she could see that Molly was exhausted, so she cut some corners for us.

Peter and Dan were waiting in the lobby, and both of them looked considerably the worse for wear. It's a real ordeal for those two to be in the same room together. They both work so hard at being polite that you think their faces are going to crack.

"You guys look like you're waiting at the morgue instead of Southern Station," I said.

They both jumped up, then there was an awkward moment while they waited to figure out what to do next. I went to Peter and gave him a big hug, then turned and gave Dan one, too. Molly followed suit. We both needed all the hugs we could get.

When I pulled away from Dan, he studied my face. "You have a nasty scrape on your cheek and the cut on your head might need stitches," he said.

The thought of going to a hospital tonight was more than I could manage. All I wanted was to get Molly home and to crawl into bed myself. The head wound wasn't bleeding anymore. It could wait till tomorrow.

"I just want to go home," I told him. "Can you drive my car and leave yours here?" I asked Peter. "I don't feel like driving."

By the time we got home, Molly could barely keep her eyes open. I tucked her into bed and stayed with her until she went to sleep.

I was exhausted, but sleep was a long way off. As I sat down in the living room I began to shake uncontrollably. Peter wrapped a blanket around me and held me against him.

"I hate this part of things," I said through clenched teeth. My head throbbed, my stomach was queasy, and my heart pounded. I had held myself together through the scene at the police station and until Molly was safely tucked away, but my body wasn't holding on any longer.

Peter poured me some brandy and steadied my arm while I drank it. I was afraid my stomach wouldn't take it, but it actually helped. "Want me to build a fire?" he asked.

I nodded, anxious to surround myself with every possible source of comfort. When he had a fire going, he wrapped me in his arms again and held me against his chest. "Want to talk about it?" he asked.

I told him the whole story. It didn't get any better for the telling. "The worst part," I said, "was knowing what could happen to Molly. I couldn't stand to think about what Kohl might do to her.''

Peter's arms were so tight that it would have been uncomfortable under other circumstances.

I put my head against his chest and struggled to calm the maelstrom of emotion that seethed inside me. Fear and anger were no strangers, but I'd never felt either the way I had tonight. I could have killed Kohl in cold blood and without regret. But that wasn't what bothered me. It was the intensity of my fear that haunted me.

Nothing had ever frightened me like the possibility of Molly coming to harm. I'd spent years developing the self-defense skills that allowed me to feel safe even in dangerous places, and in one night I'd discovered an appalling vulnerability. Part of me wanted to ship Molly back to Marion immediately, but that was the same part that wanted to bolt whenever Peter got too close. I try not to listen to it.

Peter's heart beat steadily and reassuringly as I lay against his chest. I gave him a hug. ''And you ended up sitting on a bench with Dan Walker. Poor baby.''

''It wasn't so bad. Walker has mellowed some. He didn't even beat me up for leaving you alone to nearly get killed.''

I pulled away and looked at Peter. The lines on his face seemed to have deepened, and he looked exhausted, not just physically tired but emotionally drained. ''Doesn't look like he had to. I have the feeling you did the job for him.''

Peter managed a rueful smile. ''I keep kicking myself for not seeing that it was a setup.''

''Right, you should have seen it, even though I didn't. Is that 'cause you're a man or just because you're supposed to be smarter than I am?''

''Oh God.'' Peter moaned. ''Now *you're* going to beat on me.''

29

T HE NEXT MORNING complaints from various parts of my body indicated that I'd done more damage than I'd realized on my trip down the stairs. A number of ugly bruises had blossomed during the night, and my cheek now looked like a dark blue camellia. My head throbbed dully, and the scalp wound had opened again while I slept, leaving the pillow looking like something for the police lab.

The blood disturbed Molly, who'd ended up in our bed when the nightmares struck. It was reassuring to have her body cuddled tight against me, but it also made sleeping difficult, and I crawled out of bed at seven feeling exhausted and miserable.

My first effort to move my arm told me that a visit to the doctor was definitely in order. But the worst thing I had to face wasn't the physical pain. It was the knowledge that I had to call Marion, and I had to do it soon before she heard about the evening's escapades somewhere else.

The call lived up to my worst fears. When you have to start out by reassuring a mother that her child is alive and uninjured, you're in trouble. Marion's voice rose to a shrill screech, and the pain in my head expanded. I don't know how much of the story she heard. She vacillated between concern for Molly and fury at me.

"I'll be up to get her immediately," she informed me.

"I think it'd be better if I brought her down," I said. "I don't think you want to run into a bunch of reporters, and that'll be a real possibility here."

As I'd expected, Marion wasn't anxious to meet the media. She accepted my offer with a comment about Leonard having a reputation to uphold in the community. It struck me that Leonard's reputation was a heavy burden to lay on Molly's back.

Peter watched me stumble around the kitchen, favoring my right leg and trying not to move my left arm. "I think you'll need me to drive you and Molly to Palo Alto," he said.

"Palo Alto?" Molly howled. "I don't want to go home. Please, last night you said I could stay."

"As far as I'm concerned, you can," I said. "But that's Marion's decision. I don't have any legal right to keep you here unless she agrees to it."

"I won't go back," she said stubbornly. "She can't make me."

"She's worried about you," I said. "And given what happened last night, she has good reason to think that I'm not a good person for you to live with."

Molly fussed and moaned while we ate breakfast. I called Jesse and gave him the short version of the night's adventures. He had more questions than the police, but he didn't get much satisfaction since I needed to cut the conversation short so I could call my doctor. I reached her as soon as the office opened and managed to talk her into working me in first thing.

The phone rang again almost as soon as I'd hung up. It was Arthur Costa. "I hear you had a rather wild evening," he said dryly.

"How?"

"Your reporter, Kevin Doyle, called. He's most anxious to reach you."

Of course he was. He and a couple of dozen other reporters, probably. I'd better get away before they found me. I gave Costa an abbreviated description of the night's misadventures.

"Do you think Ed Kohl killed Samuel Reiter?" he asked.

"I don't know," I said. "He didn't confess to it, but he's a great candidate if he can't come up with an alibi."

"The police will no doubt question him today. We should know soon whether they have enough to charge him. In the meantime, you can expect to be popular with the press. Be careful what you say."

Costa gave me a telephone number for Doyle. "Make sure he knows how this ties in with the Reiter case," he said.

I put off calling Doyle until I got to the doctor's office. She never takes me right on time, anyway, and I didn't want to be home when the members of the fourth estate found my address.

Doyle had gotten the story from the police reporter, and he was most anxious for the details, but his first question was, "Are you and your niece all right?"

I was beginning to understand why Joe liked him so much. I told him some of what had happened, then said, "Look, Molly and I really don't want a lot of publicity. Is there any way we can keep a fairly low profile on this?"

"It's going to be hard," Doyle said, "but maybe I can help. The story can be played several ways. Obviously, everyone's going to love the beautiful-private-eye-turns-the-tables-on-nasty-villain angle, but I think I can persuade my editor that the real story should focus on Kohl as sex merchant to the rich and powerful. I know that will appeal to him, and in that version, you slip from paragraph one to background information.

"I'll just drop a few comments around my colleagues. If I play it right, they'll all believe they figured it out for themselves. But you have to promise to give me the whole story, especially anything that ties into the Reiter case."

"Absolutely," I said. "I'll call as soon as I get back from Palo Alto." I turned to find my doctor watching from her office door. Her forehead was creased with a frown.

"I'm sorry to keep you waiting," I said. "I didn't mean for the conversation to take so long."

"If you're going to go one-on-one with killers and kidnappers, you'll need more than a GP," she said. "Come on in, and let's see how much damage you've done to yourself."

Mary has a sharp tongue but a gentle touch. I stay with her because she takes me seriously. If I say there's a problem, she keeps looking till she finds it. Today she didn't have to look too hard.

The problem with my shoulder was a bad sprain, which was a whole lot less serious than some of the other possibilities. She put me in a sling and gave me an ice pack for it. "I don't suppose you take painkillers," she said.

"I'm careless, not a masochist," I said. "Of course I take painkillers."

She gave me a couple of prescriptions, one to reduce the inflammation, the other for the pain, and ordered me to get them filled in the pharmacy downstairs. "Now," she said as I walked out the door, "not when it's convenient, but now."

She needn't have worried. I was anxious to do anything that would delay my meeting with Marion.

Both the pharmacist and the officers at Southern Station were unusually efficient. I got my pills and signed last night's statement in less than an hour. The traffic to Palo Alto was light, and all too soon we were pulling up in front of Marion's. The Cape Cod house with its immaculate yard had the "right" address in the "right" town. It was equipped with all the "right" things. No wonder Molly didn't feel that she fit.

I suggested that Peter stay in the car. My sister does not bring out the best in me, and I didn't want an audience for our encounter.

"I'd feel like I was driving the getaway car," he complained. "Besides, you could use some moral support." He climbed out of the car and followed me in.

I hadn't gone into a lot of detail with Marion, so she wasn't prepared to see me looking like I'd lost a fight with the Hell's Angels. "Catherine," she gasped when she opened the door. "You didn't tell me you were hurt." Then she glimpsed Molly behind me, and I stepped aside so she could give her daughter a big hug.

It was a long, warm hug, and Marion had tears running down her cheeks when Molly finally pulled away.

Leonard was waiting in the living room. He's stiff and a bit standoffish under the best of circumstances, and today he was almost frozen. Even before we sat down, Molly said, "I don't want to come home. I want to stay with Catherine."

Marion's face clouded. "Now, listen here . . ."

I put up my hand and said, "Whoa, back up. I know you two love each other, but you sure keep it a well-hidden secret."

They both stared at me. "We scared your mother badly," I said to Molly. "She acts angry, but she's really scared because she can't stand to think of what could have happened to you. Tell her, Marion."

Marion stuttered. She didn't seem to know what to say. "Of course I love you, and I was worried sick." This is the point where the mother-daughter reunion should have started to work. They should have given each other a big hug, resolved their differences, and lived happily ever after. They didn't.

Marion said some of the right things, and Molly started to relax and look like she wasn't under attack, then Marion took a dig at me, and I couldn't resist responding in kind. I showed all the restraint of a ten-year-old, and the fourteen-year-old sprang to my defense. Before long, she and Marion were screaming at each other again.

Even with a hefty dose of painkiller coursing through my veins, I couldn't take the noise. I sank down in the couch, and Peter, sensing the need for reinforcements, stepped forward and took Molly by the shoulders. It was an act of reckless courage, like breaking up a cat fight. He could easily have been slashed by both of them.

"Your mother and Catherine need to talk," he said. "Let's go for a walk."

Molly started to protest, but Peter led her gently toward the door. "Let's go for a walk," he repeated in a tone usually reserved for much bigger, tougher people.

With Molly gone, Marion collapsed into a chair. She didn't

look a lot better than I felt. Leonard kept standing there looking uncomfortable and trying to figure out how to take charge. He started to say something, and Marion interrupted. "Leonard, honey," she said with the same phony sweetness she used to use on our parents, "could you give Catherine and me a few moments to talk?"

Leonard was delighted. He fled to the back of the house.

Then to my surprise, Marion began to cry. She doesn't do that often, so I wasn't sure how to respond. "I don't know," she said, blowing her nose. "I've done everything I could with Molly, and she seems to hate me. We were so close when she was younger, but now she can't stand to be in the same room with me. I've been scared to death she'd do something foolish and get herself hurt. I just don't know what to do with her."

"She's working on a hefty case of teenage rebellion," I said, reflecting that my mother could testify to my expertise in that area. "And she feels like she doesn't fit in here."

"She doesn't try to fit in," Marion complained. "In fact, just the opposite—she dresses wrong, hangs out with the wrong kids. She makes a point of not fitting in."

It always amazes me that some people, my sister included, see right and wrong as social rather than ethical concepts, but Marion and I had had that argument before.

"I think she may fit in better in the city," I said. "She seems to get along all right with the kids at school, and after last night, I think the streets have lost their allure. She's still welcome to stay with me."

Marion considered it and, to my surprise, agreed without an argument. "Do you think she'd spend the weekend here?" she asked almost timidly. "Leonard could bring her back up Sunday night."

Molly had cooled down when Peter brought her back, and seemed pleased both by the agreement that she could continue to live with me and by her mother's invitation to spend the weekend. As we were preparing to leave I asked Marion the question I didn't want an answer to. "Did you call Mother about this?"

She shook her head vehemently. "No. I don't run to Mother with every problem, you know." It was the first time I could remember her missing a chance to snitch on me. Maybe there was hope for my baby sister after all.

I RETURNED TO my office with some trepidation and was grateful to see no sign of TV crews as I drove up the street. But my relief was shortlived. I knew as soon as I saw the expression on Jesse's face that we had a more serious problem than the media.

"Joe's been attacked," he said. "Call Arthur Costa."

"What happened?"

"His cellmate went after him. Arthur says the cops claim he wasn't hurt, but it doesn't sound good."

I got through to Costa right away. He'd been in Oakland to see Joe. "It's not as bad as I'd feared," he reported. "Joe's not seriously hurt, and he's in a cell by himself now, but it could have been very bad indeed."

He explained that Joe's cellmate, the 7-Eleven killer, had taken offense at something Joe had said or done, and slammed him against the wall a couple of times. "This is exactly the kind of thing we were afraid of," he said. "I don't know if it was random chance that Joe drew a raging lunatic for a cellmate or if someone had it in for him, but if the guard on duty hadn't been paying attention, Joe could be dead now."

I told myself that Costa was exaggerating the danger, but the tightness in my chest and heaviness in my stomach were truer indicators of what I really believed. It's too damned easy to die in jail.

Costa continued, "The jails are crowded. I don't know how long they'll keep Joe separated. I certainly hope they find evidence linking Kohl to Reiter's murder."

I hoped so, too. But I knew we'd better not count on it. I needed to find Kohl's missing book, but as soon as I was off the phone, Amy brought me a stack of messages from more reporters than I'd have thought we had in this town. I'd have dumped them all in the trash, but I wasn't about to give up any opportunities to suggest a connection between Kohl and Reiter's death.

I called Kevin Doyle first. "I can probably thank you for the fact that your voracious colleagues are calling on the phone instead of staking out my office," I said.

"I think I can safely accept credit for directing their attention elsewhere," he said. "I'll be right over so you can tell me the whole thing in person. I can also help you figure out which of those calls you need to return."

"Give me thirty minutes," I said. "I've got to take care of something else first."

If Mitch had stolen Kohl's book, I had a good idea where I might find it. The problem would be getting my hands on it. I called Steve Marley. My activities of the night before would probably provide his division with enough material for several months. He was ebullient when he came on the phone.

"We busted the house where you found Molly," he said. "Kohl kept an office there, and we seized boxes of papers. We've got enough to put him away for a long time, even without the murder charge."

I told Marley about the other book. He gave a low whistle.

"It fits," he said. "We haven't found much dealing with money or his personal finances, and the stuff we have uses codes instead of real names. A man in Kohl's business has plenty of dirt on his customers. I can't believe that he didn't keep more than we've found. That book could make very interesting reading."

I wanted to help Marley, but I was far more interested in getting Joe out of jail. Right now the book looked like my best chance of doing that. "I might be able to get it for you, but I need some help. I need to borrow your most lurid example of the kind of photograph we found at Mitch's apartment. Something really shocking that would get to a former victim."

"I have some pictures from previous cases. I suppose I could lend you one. You want to tell me what this is all about?"

"I need to get someone's attention."

In California, an investigator can no longer get the address of a citizen from the Department of Motor Vehicles. It used to be that all you needed was a license number, and for a small fee, you could get information on the owner of the plates, but after one careless PI delivered the address of an actress to a deranged fan who subsequently killed her, the DMV has made that information off-limits.

Off-limits to investigators. Not off-limits to those working for insurance companies. I have a cozy relationship with a firm that occasionally needs my services for corporate fraud cases. They were only too happy to get me Mel R.'s real name and address.

Mel wasn't happy to see me when I showed up at the door of his basement apartment that evening. It took him a minute to figure out who I was, and my battered appearance probably slowed down his door-slamming reflexes. I got my foot in the door and stuck the picture I'd gotten from Steve Marley in front of his face.

"Just a reminder of what we're talking about here," I said. "Have you really shut down so tight that you can't feel anything for those kids?"

"What do you know about it?" he exploded. "And who the hell are you to talk to me about abuse?"

"I'm the one who damn near got killed last night because the man Mitch stole that book from was looking for it."

He looked at me with dawning comprehension. "Come on inside," he said.

He watched me warily as I stepped into the room. It was

scrupulously neat and rather Spartan, as if physical comfort and worldly goods were not of great concern to its occupant. In the corner a portable television set was tuned to the evening news and male and female pretty faces chatted with studied animation. Mel walked over and hit a switch and the screen went blank. "You were the one involved in that thing last night," he said.

"Yes, and the man who tried to kill my niece and me is the one who killed Mitch."

"I didn't know his name," Mel said. "I didn't make any connection to Mitch."

"The police think he was a big-time operator. I think his records are in the book Mitch stole, the one he gave to you."

Mel didn't try to feign ignorance. "How did you know?" he asked.

"Because you were the only one he'd have given it to. The only one he trusted enough. He knew that you'd been a victim, just as he had. I'd guess that's why he chose you for his sponsor; he thought you'd succeeded in putting it behind you."

Mel nodded. "But I wasn't the right one for him. He really needed someone to help him get vengeance, and I was never into that. I believe that you have to find forgiveness in your heart. That wasn't what Mitch wanted."

"Is that why you didn't give me the book?"

"I don't know. I didn't see that it would do any good, and it might have done harm. I guess it did harm, anyway. I'm sorry."

"I don't know what that book contains, but I think Kohl killed Mitch to keep whatever's in it secret. If you hide the book, Kohl succeeds. And the people involved in this"—I held out the photograph again—"are safe to continue what they're doing. I can't believe you want that."

Mel shook his head. "No, you're right. There's a difference between forgiveness and irresponsibility. I'll get it for you."

He went into the next room and returned after a minute with an old, black loose-leaf binder filled to overflowing with papers. "This is what Mitch gave me. He was afraid it might be stolen from his place."

He handed it to me, and without seeming conscious of the move, wiped his hands on his pants.

Kohl's missing book did more to take my mind off the pain in my shoulder than Mary's little pills. I brought it home to Peter like a new toy, and we laid it out on the kitchen table and began going through it. Even a brief inspection told us that it would take days to decipher.

Jesse was only too happy to come over when he heard what we had. We spent the entire evening trying to make sense of Kohl's nearly illegible handwriting. It was enough to convince me that penmanship should be a required subject in all schools.

Jesse went home around eleven, taking a section of the book with him. I didn't expect him to get much done over the weekend since he'd informed me his lady love was returning from a business trip on Saturday. On the other hand, with Molly out of the apartment, it was possible that Peter and I would be less productive as well.

We switched from coffee to wine and moved from the kitchen table to the living room when Jesse left. Peter put the Dead on the stereo, and we snuggled on the couch; at least we came as close to snuggling as my arm would allow.

"So what did the doc say about your arm?" Peter asked.

"It's a bad sprain. She advised against rolling down stairs and suggested that I avoid people like Kohl in the future."

"Good advice. How careful do you have to be with it?"

"You mean, do we have to give up our favorite activity?"

"That was a general question, but if you choose to interpret it as a sexual solicitation, far be it from me to correct you."

"It seems the sort of question that would require empirical examination," I said.

"I just love it when you get empirical," Peter said with a grin.

During the weeks of Molly's visit, sex had taken on a

furtive quality that made me feel a bit like a teenager in my
parents' house. There was a delicious freedom in knowing
we had the whole house to ourselves, though making love
with a sprained shoulder requires a certain amount of careful
choreography.

I was stiff and sore Saturday morning, and if anything I
looked worse than I had the day before. The discomfort just
fed my desire to unlock the secrets in Kohl's book. One
section appeared to be written in some kind of code, and we
decided to start there.

The first column contained entries of two, and in a few
cases three, capital letters. One set was SR. I hoped that
stood for Samuel Reiter. Following each set of letters were
other notations, often with dates. It might as well have been
written in Arabic.

Kevin Doyle called at two o'clock to tell us that the Oakland police had charged Ed Kohl with the murder of Mitch
Morrison, but not with that of Samuel Reiter. It seems that
the night of Reiter's death Kohl had been in Sacramento at
an investment seminar where he had been seen by any number of upstanding citizens.

The news was a sharp disappointment. Though I'd been
fairly sure that Kohl hadn't killed Reiter when he denied it
to me at the warehouse, I'd hoped that the police would
charge him with it. I'd have been only too happy to let Kohl
take Joe's place in jail.

With Kohl eliminated as a suspect, we were worse off than
we'd been before the warehouse confrontation. Joe was still
the prime suspect, and we had nothing to point the police in
a different direction. Joe couldn't command a private cell for
long in the crowded jail, and his next cellmate might be even
more dangerous and violent than the previous one. Kohl's
book looked increasingly like our only hope, so Peter and I
spent a frustrating weekend trying to make sense from its
entries.

On Sunday we took it to the copy shop and copied the

entire thing; then I played the good citizen and delivered it to the police.

O N MONDAY MORNING the Kohl arrest was still page-one news. The San Francisco Police had found information among Kohl's papers that led them to a brothel that specialized in underage girls. The story got bigger headlines than the national news.

Page three carried Kevin Doyle's interview of the madam, and it was one of the more troubling pieces I'd read in a while. The woman pointed out she hadn't stolen the girls from a convent. "Everyone is so offended by the idea of these girls selling sex, but no one gives a damn when they're starving on the street or being raped in a back alley. If the churchmen and the politicians care so much for these girls, where's the money to take care of them?"

It's damned uncomfortable to find yourself agreeing with a woman who prostitutes young girls.

I called Kevin and complimented him on the story. "It's terrific. Pulitzer material," I said.

"The worst part is that she's right," Kevin said. "Kids come last in this society. There isn't one major social program that serves kids that hasn't been cut during the last ten years. It's easier to get money for prisons than for schools."

I'd never heard him so bitter. In fact, I was always amazed at how upbeat he could be while covering such painful subjects. "Sounds like this story is getting to you," I said.

"Oops, you caught me on my soapbox," he said. "I'll climb down if you'll have lunch with me."

I agreed and he asked, "What's happening in the Reiter case? Any other leads at all?"

"Maybe. Take me to lunch, and I'll tell you a story."

The mail arrived around eleven and Amy handed me an envelope with no return address. "Looks like it might be personal," she said.

A single sheet of white typing paper fell out when I slit open the envelope. On a manual typewriter with an old ribbon, someone had typed, "If you care about your niece's health, stay away from Samuel Reiter's death."

I stared at the note, and Amy stared at me. "Leave everything on my desk just the way it is. Don't touch a thing," I said. "I'm going to Molly's school to pick her up, then we'll call the police."

All the way to Molly's school I told myself that she wasn't in danger yet. My mysterious correspondent wanted to scare me off, not to hurt Molly. Surely they'd wait to see the effect of the warning before taking further action.

Emotions set little store by logic, and the rest of my body paid little attention to my head. My heart speeded up, my mouth went dry, and I felt exactly as I had on the drive to the warehouse.

Phoenix School had its temporary headquarters in the basement of a church about twelve blocks away. I left the car by a hydrant and ran inside and down the stairs. As I hurried down the hall I could hear Molly's voice from a room up ahead. There was no fear in it, but it had a serious, thoughtful quality that I hadn't heard a lot lately. "Well, I don't think the Trojan War was Helen's fault. She was just an excuse. These guys didn't give a shit about women. They slaughtered them and traded them around like baseball cards. You can't tell *me* the war had anything to do with love."

A thin boy with a reedy voice began to object, but I didn't hear his argument. I leaned against the wall and took several deep breaths before I entered the room.

I'd forgotten that I still looked like recent road kill, but

the kids' surprised expressions reminded me immediately.
"I need to take Molly out of school early," I told Gil.

Molly looked confused, but she gathered her things. One
of the girls reached out to give her hand a squeeze. "What's
going on?" she asked as we headed for the car.

I told her about the note. "Wow," she said. "You mean
that there's someone else, someone besides those guys at the
warehouse?"

"I'm afraid so," I said.

I took Molly back to my office and called the police. Then I
called Peter. Both got there about the same time.

The police took the note as seriously as I had. They bagged
it for the lab and questioned both Molly and me about any
strangers we'd seen around the apartment or her school. Neither of us had seen anything.

"I'd like to be able to assign an officer to watch her," the
investigator said, "but we're shorthanded, and I can't do
that."

I'm not overly impressed by the deterrent power of one
bored police officer following you around, perhaps because
I can think of several ways I'd get past that officer. "I'll get
her out of town," I said. "I don't want this guy to have any
idea where she might be."

"Not home," Molly wailed.

"Definitely not home," I said. "It wouldn't take much to
find you there."

"Your parents?" Peter suggested.

"No, that's still too easy. Would you take her to the
cabin?" Peter owns a cabin in the Santa Cruz mountains. No
one would connect it with me, and it isn't a place you're
likely to meet someone accidentally.

"That'd be neat," Molly said. "I love the cabin."

The cabin is a lot less "neat" in the cold and wet of April
than in the warmth of summer, but I didn't tell her that. Peter
frowned. "It's a good place for Molly, but I'd rather be closer
to home. You could use someone to watch your back."

"It's not my back I'm worried about. It's Molly. Please,

Peter, sending her with you is the only way I'll feel she's safe.'' It took more grumbling on Peter's part and the promise that I'd use Jesse for backup and not go off on my own, but in the end he agreed to take Molly to the cabin.

The police officer issued the required warnings about keeping doors locked and calling if I saw or heard anything suspicious, then departed. Once he was gone, Peter said, ''I can take off work for two or three days, maybe four, if you'll do some work at the courthouse for me. That'll give you time to figure out where to send Molly till this is over. This could go on for months, you know.''

I knew that. I didn't think I could stand months of worrying every minute about whether a killer might be after Molly, and I sure as hell wasn't going to let Joe down. I had to find a way to get to the killer before he got to me.

I'd completely forgotten that I'd arranged to have lunch with Kevin. He arrived at my office just as I was saying good-bye to Peter and Molly. I wanted to wrap the two of them in my arms and hang on for dear life, but I forced myself to let go after a quick hug. I bit back the temptation to issue lists of instructions and warnings and tried to keep our parting light. Peter made no such attempt. ''For godssake, be careful,'' he said as he left.

Kevin and I had lunch at a little place just off Fillmore that has great homemade soup, and while we ate I told him about the note and Kohl's book.

''Have you any idea at all who sent the note?'' he asked.

''None. It makes me think that I must be closer to the killer than I realize. There must be some evidence out there that the killer thinks I have or he's afraid I'll find, something to make him nervous enough to risk threatening me.''

''But what?''

''I wish I knew. I suspect it has something to do with Kohl's book. I spent a good part of the weekend going over it, and I kept a copy I made after I turned the original over to the police. I haven't found a list of names, but he was clearly keeping some sort of accounts. Marley's pretty sure he'll have a list of clients somewhere. I'm hoping it'll lead us to a good suspect.''

"Another pedophile, like Reiter," Kevin suggested. "I've heard something—unfortunately, I can't reveal the source—from a guy who knew both Kohl and Reiter. He says that Reiter wasn't the only one in the criminal justice system who was into kids. Reiter had a friend—he thinks it was someone important—who also liked boys.''

"Did he tell you anything about this friend?''

Kevin shook his head. "No, but it'd be worth looking into Reiter's friends.''

I thought of Reiter's diaries. K. was the only adult friend that Reiter had mentioned, and I assuemd K. stood for Kohl. But other friends might have appeared in other diaries. "I wish I'd read all the way through Reiter's diaries,'' I said.

"Reiter kept diaries?''

"Yes, Art Costa should be able to inspect them. They were hidden on Reiter's boat. Marley took me with him once when he went through that stuff.''

"Wow, what else did they find?''

Kevin's avid enthusiasm reminded me that he was still a reporter and always on the lookout for a good story. "Down, boy,'' I said.

"Sorry,'' he said. "I couldn't help thinking what a great story the diaries might make. What else did they find?''

"The only other thing I saw was a bunch of photos of the kids Reiter had molested.'' I told him of the piles of snapshots, the naked, freckle-faced kids trying to pretend that nothing unusual was going on. "They all looked so young and vulnerable,'' I said. "It was a vivid reminder of how many kids he abused.''

Kevin nodded soberly. "After Kohl's trial, I'd like to try to see those diaries. It's a story that needs to be told, you know.''

"I know, but right now I'm more interested in Joe's story. Will you see if you can get anything more out of your source?''

"Of course, and I'd also like to help you run down stuff

from the book. I'm not worth much as a bodyguard, but the killer's less likely to try something when there are two of us. Besides, you look like you could use some help with driving for a couple of days.''

I didn't feel that I needed a bodyguard, but the idea of having a driver appealed to me. My arm was sore and the hand was weak. It hurt my ankle to step on the brake, and driving to Molly's school and back had taken its toll. I accepted Kevin's proposal with enthusiasm.

''One of the things we've gleaned from Kohl's book is a list of properties,'' I said. ''How about taking a look at the actual buildings that go with the addresses?''

The first was a two-story building just off Clement. Four buzzers beside the front door indicated that it was divided into flats. The only one that answered was for the downstairs apartment on the right. Its occupant was a woman in her midthirties who was working at home but agreed to talk to us for a few minutes.

She knew nothing about her landlord except that she mailed checks to Pacific Coast Properties in Oakland. She gave us the address. It was Kohl's.

The other tenants were all young professionals, and it didn't seem like we had anything, until she complained about George Gillespie's nephews. Gillespie lived upstairs, and she didn't see much of him, but she always knew when he had his nephews over because they made so much noise. The boys were about eight or nine, and sometimes they brought friends. They visited several times a week.

Under any other conditions, we'd have taken the story at face value, but given the landlord, you had to wonder about those nephews, especially when it came out she never saw Gillespie in the morning.

''It sounds almost like he doesn't really live here,'' I said, ''like he just visits in the afternoon.''

''At the rent they charge on this place? Why would anyone do that?'' she asked.

I didn't think she'd really want to know.

* * *

"Nice setup," Kevin said as we got back in the car. "A guy wants a pad where he can entertain boys, but he doesn't want to put it in his own name. Kohl provides it, no doubt at something above market rents. The money's clean because it comes in the form of rent, and everybody's happy."

"The SFPD should be very interested in these addresses," I said, "and maybe somewhere in the list of guys they pick up, we'll find one who knew Samuel Reiter."

"Let's check out the whole list," Kevin suggested. "You never know what else we might find." His blue eyes sparkled with excitement, and his fingers drummed on the steering wheel.

"You really love this kind of work, don't you?"

He smiled, a wide, toothy, boyish grin. "I live for it," he said. "The most fun I ever had was working stories on the IRA. It was like being in the middle of a spy movie. In the end, it turned out to be more talk than action, but there was one guy who really was hooked in to the IRA, and had been collecting money and acting as a courier for them for several years.

"He ran into trouble with the tax man here, and we had to smuggle him out of the country. It was great fun. Robbie Quinn was his name. The U.S. wanted to extradite him, but the Irish authorities never could seem to find him." Kevin gave me a wink and laughed.

As we headed back downtown, he said, "There're a lot of Irish out on the Avenues now, but in the old days we all lived south of the slot. You know what that means?"

"No," I said.

"South of the cable car slot, meaning south of Market. Before the twenties the Irish couldn't live north of the slot. That's why the Mission and the Castro had big Irish populations. They were south of the slot.

"San Francisco was a big Irish city. Most of the men ended up as cops and in other middle-level jobs. The best never made it to the work force. Soon as the Jesuits spotted them, they were headed for the seminary. The rest got sent to the Franciscans to be turned into good citizens. That's why there were so few great Irish leaders here. The bright ones ended up as priests.''

It took only a little prompting to get Kevin spinning tales of the Irish in San Francisco. He was a natural storyteller with a healthy shot of stand-up comic and a mockingbird's ability to mimic voices. People I'd known only as names in the newspaper came alive as he described their quirks and foibles and imitated their speech.

The afternoon went swiftly in his company, and I was grateful to him for making an unpleasant job enjoyable. We checked out addresses all over the city, total score: two more apartments that may have been rented to pedophiles and a house that neighbors described as being like the local boys' club. The other places seemed to be legitimate real estate holdings; no sinister purpose we could discern. Maybe the police would have more luck.

K EVIN AND JESSE and I spent a lot of time together over the next two days, most of it hunched over Kohl's book. When you're trying to catch a thief, it helps to think like one, and we quickly discovered that Kevin had a certain native talent for that sort of thing.

"You have a truly devious mind," Jesse said in response to one of Kevin's more creative suggestions. It was a high compliment.

I kept a close watch for anyone suspicious in my neighborhood, but either he was very good or he wasn't sticking close. Kevin loved being a bodyguard. If I hadn't grown so fond of him, I wouldn't have put up with his chivalric non-sense.

Peter agreed to stay an extra day with Molly if we did some research for him at the courthouse. There were a number of things we needed to check in connection with Ed Kohl, so Jesse volunteered to take care of both assignments. It was a real concession for him to go to the courthouse since he was a firm believer that anything worth knowing was available on computer. I do not share his faith. I'd been bugging him for a week to go to the courthouse to check on Anton Glosser.

Kevin and I spent the day puzzling over the book without noticeable success. Jesse called at four and I could tell he was excited. He didn't want to blow his image as cool, so he restrained himself from whooping, and said simply, "I've got something very interesting for you. Be over after I check a couple more things. Oh, you probably want to send Kevin home before I get there."

An hour and a half later, when he finally arrived, I was just past dying of curiosity and headed for deeply annoyed. "So?" I said. "What did you get?"

"Well, first I learned that technology does indeed have its limits. You were right about the value of going to the court-house to check documents."

I love to be right, especially in an argument with Jesse, but tonight I just wanted to know what he'd learned. "I'm going to strangle you if you don't get to the point," I said.

"Okay, here's what I didn't get from the computer files. Ed Kohl's lawyer is Milton Diesman. The same Milton Dies-man whose name popped up in your investigation of Anton Glosser. Diesman's name is all over Kohl's investments, but only on a couple of Glosser's. Care to guess which ones?"

"The two we've had such trouble tracking and, of course, the one with Diesman as a general partner."

"You got it, but it gets better." Jesse couldn't hide his glee. "The house where they took Molly was owned by West Coast Properties, which is owned by a limited partnership with Ed Kohl as the general partner. And guess who is one of the limited partners in this little company."

"Not Anton Glosser."

"The very same."

I let out a low whistle. What a stroke of luck! We'd have gotten to West Coast Properties eventually, but without the Kohl connection we wouldn't have known what it meant.

I wondered about the connection between Kohl and Glosser. It could be Diesman. The lawyer probably helped Kohl find investors for his ventures, and Glosser would have been a natural choice. But it could be a far darker connection. Anton Glosser could be a pedophile.

I went back to the book, to the coded section we thought held the names of Kohl's clients. There was no A.G. listed. We checked the full list of people who were members of Kohl's various limited partnerships. About a third of them matched sets of initials in the book.

"We need more information," I said. "We won't get anything from Diesman. Did you get names of notaries?"

Jesse consulted his notes. "Yep, and we're in luck. The papers for West Coast Properties and most of the others were notarized by a Jules Valdo. He probably works for Diesman."

"He's worth talking to. We might get something from him."

"And then?"

"Glosser is either a pedophile, in which case I'll happily help Steve Marley build a case to send him to jail, or he's simply an investor who didn't ask too many questions about why he was making such a good return on his money. In that case, I imagine that he's very nervous about the possibility that word will get out of his connection to the house on Del Norte Street."

"As well he might be," Jesse said.

The news about Glosser was exciting, but it didn't get me any closer to Reiter's killer and the man or men who threatened Molly. If the book hadn't yielded an answer in two days, it could be weeks before we broke its codes. Weeks of worrying about Molly and rearranging both Peter's and my lives, weeks of feeling like a sitting duck. I wasn't about to put up with that.

I needed a way to provoke the killer, to force him to make a move. Better to know he was headed my way than to have to wonder where he was.

The first step was to get Molly safely out of the picture. Sending her to any of my relatives meant fessing up to my parents about a number of things. Marion didn't want to explain why Molly was living with me, and I didn't want to explain how I'd almost gotten us both killed. It was a story better told in the past tense, when it was really over and they didn't have to worry about how it was going to end.

It was time to call in a favor, and the person who came to mind was Corinne Case, a longtime friend and former employee who now lived and worked in Boise. "Casey" had teenagers of her own, so she was familiar with their rituals and strange behavior. From stories she'd told me on the phone, Molly would fit right in with her brood.

Casey was delighted to help. She'd rather have been down here trapping the killer, but I told her I needed a babysitter more than a backup person and promised to give her a call the next time something exciting came up. She described the cases she was working; they sounded wonderfully dull.

Peter liked the plan a lot less than Casey did. He whined and fussed and complained about me acting as bait for a killer. He made the whole thing sound a lot more dramatic and dangerous than it really was. Finally, I told him just to put Molly on the plane to Boise, in either Oakland or San Jose, and we could fight about it when he got home.

I spent the evening planning my strategy. If I was going to be the bait, I was sure as hell going to call the shots. That meant setting the whole thing up before I let either Jesse or Peter get involved.

The next morning I called Kevin Doyle before I left for work. I knew that Kevin loved a good scam and wanted to help Joe. That made him just the man for my plan. I explained what I wanted to do. "What I need is something that will make the killer think I'm about to deliver incriminating evidence to the police," I told him.

"A newspaper story," Kevin said.

"That could be very useful."

"A newspaper story in which sources close to the defense complain that the police are not pursuing the case vigorously enough and indicate that an unnamed private investigator has evidence implicating a secret associate of the judge's. How's that sound?"

"Terrific. I don't want this to drag on. Can you suggest that this evidence will be delivered to the police in the next three days?"

"Sure, whatever you want. Pardon me for asking, but isn't this a bit dangerous?"

"It could be, but I don't think the killer is a pro, and I'll have Peter and Jesse watching my back."

"It's your show," he said. "I'll write it up, but you better be sure that Joe's attorney will back you up. And you can expect the cops to be on your case."

The killer, I thought, will be the least of my worries.

Costa didn't like the plan. It was risky. It could cause trouble with the police. It wasn't the way things were done. I pointed out that standard procedure had gotten us nowhere and was likely to continue taking us there. This was by far the most promising approach we had.

Finally, Costa agreed that he'd go along with the plan for four days. He didn't say what he'd do at the end of that time, but I had the feeling the killer'd better be in custody or he'd hand me my head.

Next, I called the law offices of Milton Diesman and asked for Jules Valdo. A secretary with a voice that could cut glass informed me Mr. Valdo no longer worked there. She did not know where I could find Mr. Valdo; she obviously didn't care.

Fortunately, Valdo is not a common name. There was only one Jules Valdo in the phone book. He wasn't at home but his wife was, and she was happy to give me his office number.

Valdo worked as a paralegal for a firm I'd once dealt with on a case. It was a definite step up from Diesman on the respectability scale. I offered to buy him lunch. He accepted.

Jules Valdo was a smallish man with a pinched mouth and a crease between his brows. He looked like he could do the "before" segment of an Excedrin commercial. His voice hadn't prepared me for his pinched appearance. It was rich and mellifluous, the kind that ought to go with a cleft chin and lazy smile.

"You wanted to see me about Mr. Diesman?" he said as soon as I'd introduced myself. No social pleasantries, no meandering around to get to the point.

"Yes," I said. "I understand you used to work for him."

"I did once, yes," he said warily.

The tone was so odd, so guarded. I felt like the grand inquisitor or maybe a representative of the IRS. "Why did you leave Mr. Diesman?" I asked.

"I was not altogether comfortable with some of his practices," Valdo said.

I didn't hop up and do a little dance around the table, but that's sure what my spirits were doing. An unhappy employee is almost as good as an ex-wife when you want to know the dirt. And it turned out that Mr. Valdo did know plenty of dirt. He'd watched Diesman and Kohl put together a number of deals.

"I didn't know exactly what was going on until I read those articles about Ed Kohl," he said. "But I could tell just from the way they talked and the way that things were structured that these were not legitimate businesses. And I don't mean that they were highly speculative. That's just it; they weren't speculative at all, mostly just real estate, good solid properties that should have been a straightforward investment. Yet they were looking for investors who wanted a fat return and wouldn't ask too many questions. That's what I heard Kohl say more than once, 'no questions asked.' "

I told Valdo about West Coast Properties and the house on Del Norte Street. He shook his head in disgust.

"It doesn't surprise me," he said. "Not really. I *knew* there was something going on."

"Do you remember a man named Anton Glosser?" I asked. "He was one of the limited partners on that deal."

Valdo shook his head.

"Glosser is a large man, maybe six two and big boned, not really fat, just large. He has blue eyes and thinning blond hair, which he combs over a bald spot where his hair's receded. His voice is a bit loud and harsh."

Valdo shook his head again. "I don't think I met him. Those limited partners, they didn't know what they were getting into. They were anxious to make a killing, and you don't come to Milton Diesman if you're too concerned about ethical investing, but they didn't know the details."

I probed and questioned, but Valdo did not remember Glosser. He didn't know whether Diesman or Kohl had brought him in on the deal, and that was all-important. Finally, Valdo said, "Wait a minute. I didn't meet him, but there was a man who was head of a computer firm, or maybe it was electronics—I think it was electronics—who invested in a number of Diesman's schemes. That could be your Mr. Glosser."

Several hours at the courthouse confirmed that Anton Glosser had invested in a number of deals where Diesman was the registered agent. I felt fairly sure by now that Glosser was simply greedy rather than predatory. I headed back to the office to see Jesse.

He and Peter were waiting in my office, and they did not look happy. Jesse was irritated that I hadn't told him of my plan, and both he and Peter had a dozen reasons why it was a bad idea. I listened patiently, or at least I pretended to listen. When they ran out of steam, I said, "You're both out of line. Would I fuss like this if one of you had come up with this plan?"

"Yes," they said in unison. It was probably true, but I

wasn't about to let truth get in the way of a good argument. "I would not," I said. "I would assume that you had the good sense to figure things out, and I would back you up."

"Fat chance," Jesse said. "This is crazy."

"Thank you very much," I said. I looked at my watch. "It's too late to change things, anyway. Tomorrow's *Chronicle* has already gone to press, and it contains an article by Kevin Doyle revealing that an unnamed private investigator is about to take the police proof that Samuel Reiter was killed by someone other than Joe Girard."

Peter rolled his eyes and Jesse groaned.

"Your confidence is much appreciated," I said. "Now stop sulking, we have something else more pressing."

"Something more pressing than getting yourself killed?" Jesse asked.

I ignored him. "Anton Glosser," I said. "I think it's time to settle a score." I told them what I'd learned. "I'd like to take care of this tonight, before I have to watch my back every minute. What do you think?"

Jesse considered it. "It can't be blackmail. I mean you can't solicit him directly."

"No, definitely not," I said. "What we need to do is let him know that we're aware of his involvement in West Coast Properties and that we're concerned for the Merrick family. If, as a man of compassion and position in the community, he wants to offer to help the Merricks, we're delighted and would certainly not want to see such a fine man publicly embarrassed. If he doesn't offer, we feed the story to Kevin."

"He won't be giving you any referrals," Peter said.

"But by the same token, he won't be anxious to talk about why he doesn't like me," I said.

33

ANTON GLOSSER WAS a busy man, and he didn't have time to stop by my office after work. Not until I mentioned West Coast Properties and the building on Del Norte Street.

I sent Amy home early and let Glosser in myself. Even before we were settled in my office, he demanded, "What is this all about?"

"I'm sorry to inconvenience you," I said, all sweetness and light, "but I've come across something that I thought potentially embarrassing for you, and I wanted to make sure you knew about it."

He frowned.

"I'm working on a case that involves a man named Edward Kohl. You may have seen references to it in the newspaper." I paused. He nodded. "In examining Mr. Kohl's assets, I discovered that he was general partner of West Coast Properties, a limited partnership of which you are one of the partners.

"Now, I'm sure you weren't aware that one of the properties owned by West Coast, a house on Del Norte Street, was used to recruit underage boys into prostitution. Given your standing in the community and your commitment to upholding high moral standards, it must be particularly painful for you to be involved in such a matter. And potentially very embarrassing."

Glosser didn't look embarrassed. He looked furious. His face was a bright red, moving toward purple. In a few more moments I expected him to resemble a ripe eggplant. "I had absolutely no knowledge of this," he said. "I was merely an investor. My investments are far too extensive for me to be aware of the details of all of them."

"Of course," I said. "I understand that. I just wanted to warn you, since I'm afraid that if the story gets out, there will be those who won't understand."

Glosser regarded me shrewdly. A more honest man would have missed completely the unstated threat, but Glosser was no stranger to subtle blackmail and intimidation. He'd played the game often enough to recognize it when the roles were reversed. "What do you suggest?" he asked.

"I'm afraid I can't help you there. I just wanted to let you know what was afoot. By the way, on another subject entirely, I talked with Maureen Merrick the other day. The family is having a very tough time. I know you were deeply upset by Orrin's misuse of your trust, but I also know you're a generous and compassionate man. Have you considered setting up a trust fund for the Merrick family?"

"No," he said.

I smiled. "Well, I can certainly understand. I won't keep you any longer. I certainly hope that you're able to keep your connection with the house on Del Norte Street out of the press. It would be a shame to tarnish your reputation for an innocent investment." I rose and extended my hand.

Glosser remained seated. "I haven't set up a trust fund for the Merrick family," he said, "but I wouldn't want the family to suffer for the father's misdeeds. How much would you suggest?"

"Oh, I don't know much about those things," I said. "Whatever you think is right."

He regarded me coldly, then gave a mirthless smile. "Of course," he said as he rose to go.

I was in considerably higher spirits that night than Peter and Jesse. They sat around the table after dinner developing elaborate plots to protect me from Samuel Reiter's killer. If I hadn't been elated after my victory over Anton Glosser, I wouldn't have put up with them as long as I did.

They were adding the finishing touches to a plan that would have kept me locked in my house and office for the next three days, when I stepped on them. "Look, you two, the whole point of this is to encourage the killer to come after me. Making that impossible defeats the purpose of the plan. You have to at least let the guy think he has a chance, or he won't make a move."

"And how do you propose to do that?" Jesse asked.

"I'll work late at the office. Send everyone home except me, or at least appear to send everyone home. In addition, I don't want you at the apartment for the next three days, Peter. Maybe our man will try a midnight visit if he thinks I'm alone."

"What if he tries a sniper shot or a drive-by shooting?" Peter asked.

"Or a bomb?" Jesse added.

"This guy isn't a pro. Reiter was killed in a moment of passion, with a paperweight," I said.

"Our man could hire a pro. If Kevin's right and he's in the criminal justice system, he'll have contacts," Peter argued.

"Enough," I said. "I am perfectly capable of taking care of myself under most circumstances. The only reason I need you two is to watch my back and make sure no one puts a bomb in my car. You can sneak into the office through the back way," I told Jesse. "And you can spend the night in my apartment if you can figure out how to get in across the back fence," I told Peter. "But beyond that I don't want a lot of fuss."

There was a lot of fuss, of course, so I went to bed.

The doorbell rang at seven the next morning, just as I was pouring milk on my cereal. I checked the window and found my ex-husband on the doorstep. "Good morning," he said. He was carrying the *Chronicle*.

Peter shouted, "Don't answer that door!" and came flying down the hall as I invited Dan in. Both men stopped and stared at each other like a couple of cats on a fence, then they exchanged greetings.

"Coffee?" I asked. Dan shook his head and unfolded his paper to an inside page and handed it to me. "Interesting story, concerns your case, I believe."

His voice was cool and casual, the way it gets when he's deadly serious. The more serious the matter, the cooler the voice. Right now it was around freezing.

I hadn't gotten the paper yet, so I skimmed the story. Kevin had done exactly what I'd wanted. I handed the paper to Peter. For once his frown was directed at me instead of Dan. I decided I definitely needed coffee, so I led them both back to the kitchen.

"I sure as hell hope you know what you're doing," Dan said. "This looks for all the world like a setup."

"Is that illegal?" I asked.

Dan's voice dipped below freezing. "It's an excellent way to get yourself killed. I hope you know that. Both Oakland and San Francisco are working on this case. No one needs this sort of stunt."

Peter looked up from the paper. "You're talking to a blank wall."

"Cut it out," I said. "Let me refresh your memories. This creep has already threatened me. He knows where I am. By now he knows that Molly's no longer around. That leaves me as the target. I'm just trying to force his hand. It's a lot easier to be careful for three days than for three weeks."

I was right, and they knew it, though neither of them was about to admit it. Dan offered to take the next three days off and help with security. I pointed out that we wouldn't get much action if I was always in the middle of a crowd scene.

Ignoring Peter's protests, I walked to the office. It was going to be a long three days.

Kevin called just after I arrived. He'd taken several pages from Kohl's book, and had figured them out. "I think I've solved the mystery of that album of pictures in Mitch's room," he said. "Those kids are from an orphanage in Mexico. I was looking through some old files and found references one street kid made to 'Club Ped.' He said that there

was someone who could arrange trips to foreign countries—
Mexico, Thailand, Greece—where a ped could be met by a
kid, sex and age of his choice, and the kid would be his
'companion' for his stay.

"There were a bunch of flight numbers and times. I
checked and they're all flights to Mazatlán, plus there are
several numbers, all starting with fifty-two. That's the country code if you're calling Mexico. I called the numbers, and
one was the Los Niños Orphanage."

"An orphanage that's really a playground for pedophiles.
Kohl's a real gem," I said. "Have you called the police yet?"

"This is a great story. I'd like to pursue it on my own. I
thought I'd give the information to you, and you could give
it to Marley. That way I'm not directly involved."

"Sure," I said. "You want me to pick up the notes?"

"I'm at home now. I've got a lot of work today, so if you
could pick them up, it'd help."

He gave me an address in Noe Valley, and I told him I'd
be over in twenty minutes or so. Next, I called Peter, who
had the cellular phone, and told him where I was going. I
told him he didn't need to follow me, but he doesn't hear
what he doesn't want to hear.

Kevin had the ground-floor flat in a Victorian row house with
a three-color paint job. It was on a hill steep enough to qualify as a ski slope, and as usual there were no parking places
within two blocks. No one had followed me, so Peter pulled
into a space in front of a driveway across the street and waited
while I hiked up to Kevin's from my distant but legal parking
spot.

Kevin was barefoot when he answered the door and his
hair was headed in six different directions. "Come on in,"
he said, "I'm on the phone in the bedroom. Make yourself
comfortable. There's coffee in the kitchen."

The inside of the house had obviously been redone when
it got its fancy paint job—gleaming hardwood floors and
white walls gave it a modern feel at odds with its exterior.
Kevin was more traditional in his tastes; either that, or he'd

inherited furniture from his parents. It was a remarkably conservative room for a brash young reporter. The bookcase even had a shelf full of photographs.

I'm a sucker for family photos. Maybe it's the voyeur in me, but I can't walk past a portrait or snapshot without studying the people and wondering about their lives. The self-conscious young couple in a faded formal photo were probably Kevin's parents. He wore a suit, she a dark, tailored dress. I wondered if it was a wedding photo.

There were a couple of baby pictures. They could have been of anyone; then one of a skinny kid in a Mickey Mouse T-shirt. There was something familiar about that one, something that made me stop and pick it up for a closer look.

When it hit me, I felt a shock that went all the way to my toes. There must have been thousands of kids who owned Mickey Mouse T-shirts, and some of those kids had freckles and crooked teeth, but I'd seen this kid before—in Samuel Reiter's private photo collection.

A NOISE TO my right made me turn. Kevin had stopped in the doorway.

I've had plenty of practice at not letting my thoughts show on my face, but I blew it this time. I hadn't been prepared to conceal my reactions, and I just didn't switch gears fast enough.

Kevin had read it all. And he made no effort to play dumb. His expression was grave. "I'd forgotten about the pictures Sam took until you mentioned them. It didn't occur to me that you'd make the connection."

"I always thought you were awfully passionate about the Reiter case."

"Just my passionate Irish nature," he said. "I've always cared about what happened to kids, from alcoholic parents who abuse them to men like Samuel Reiter who use them for their own pleasure." He snorted, a sharp bitter sound that might have been a laugh. "Who knows better; I've done the whole gambit, except prostitution, and my relationship with Reiter was close enough to that."

"Reiter didn't call you about your story that night, did he?"

"You're wrong. He did. He didn't know who I was. I wasn't Doyle when he knew me. I was Kevin O'Farrell, son of an alcoholic Irish father who died one night when he drove into a tree and almost killed my mother and me along with him. I became 'Doyle' years after my mother remarried and convinced my stepdad to adopt me.

"No, he called because he wanted me to tell his side of the story. He'd read my stuff in the *Chron* and thought I'd give him a fair shake."

He crossed the room and walked toward the desk. I moved back toward the door. "I want to show you something," he said, pulling out the top drawer.

I should have made a run for it, but his tone was so casual that there was no hint of menace in it. I hesitated a moment too long, and when he turned back to me, there was a gun in his hand.

"I'm sorry," he said, "I'm really sorry. I didn't mean for anyone to get hurt, not even Sam. I just wanted to tell the story, to make people understand." His voice pleaded for understanding.

My mouth was so dry I could hardly speak. "Put the gun down, Kevin," I said gently. "Put it down before someone gets hurt."

He gave no sign of hearing me. The gun remained pointed at my chest. "I wasn't even going to tell him who I was. I just wanted the interview. I guess I thought he'd say something that would help me understand it all, understand him.

"He was drunk when I got there and full of self-pity and justification. I tried to handle it like a regular interview. Hell, I interviewed a guy who raped kids, and I stayed cool. But then Sam started talking about all he'd done for 'his' boys. He was going on about how before he found them, they were all losers, human garbage, and how he'd shown them how to make something out of their lives.

"I was so steamed that I knew I couldn't keep up the charade. I was getting up to go when he told me that it was really the kids who came on to him. He gave me this horse-shit about how the kids were really horny little bastards, and they were always sitting on his lap and touching him and giving him knowing looks.

"I wanted to smash his face, but I just said something like, 'Maybe what they wanted was friendship; it was you that wanted the sex,' and he grabbed my arm and put his face so close to mine that the smell of the booze almost knocked me out, and he said, 'They wanted it. They loved it.'

"I pushed him away, but he just kept going on about the 'horny little faggots.' He grabbed my arm again, and I hit him. I don't even remember how it happened. The next thing I knew I was standing over him with this paperweight in my hand, and he was on the floor, and the back of his head was bleeding." Kevin looked sick as he described it. His hand began to tremble.

"Kevin, please put the gun down," I said. I took a step toward him.

"Don't move, please don't move," he said. His voice was shrill. He was more scared than I was, but that wasn't much comfort. It doesn't much matter if you're shot by a decent man who's scared or a brutal one who's evil. You're just as dead either way.

"Kevin, you don't want to kill me," I said.

"No, oh God, no. But I don't really have any choice. I can't face prison. I've done stories on what happens there. I know."

"Are you going to let them send Joe in your place? I can't

believe you can do that, let an innocent man suffer. I don't think you're the type." I sure as hell hoped he wasn't.

"Arthur'll get him off," Kevin said shakily. "Reasonable doubt. He's good; he'll make them see there's a reasonable doubt."

"And if he doesn't?"

"Oh God, I don't know. I don't know what I'll do, but I know I can't go to prison. You don't understand."

I did understand, some of it, anyway, enough to realize that there was an even chance he'd turn the gun on himself. "This isn't as hopeless as it seems," I said. "From what you've told me, a good lawyer could get you off with manslaughter. Any jury would be sympathetic to your story."

He shook his head. "I *can't* go to jail. It'd be just like going back to being a kid, only worse. I'm not very big and I'm not much of a fighter, and when the other cons knew my story, I might as well . . ." He stopped, on the verge of tears. "I can't, I just can't, not again."

It didn't matter whether his fears were justified, no more than it mattered whether Orrin Merrick's were.

"I didn't even remember. You won't believe that, but I didn't. I'd just shut it up someplace. But I always had this terrific sympathy for kids in trouble, and this fury about what people did to them. Then a couple of years ago I was doing a series on male prostitutes, and one of them told me this story and I had this flashback."

Talking seemed to calm him some, and it gave me time. "How did you find out about Reiter?" I asked.

"The same way Mitch did, that article on the Good Citizen for Youth Award. And I had the same reaction. I wanted to see the bastard exposed."

"So you started your own investigation, only you planned to expose him through your articles."

"And I found out about you from Audrey Shay at Youth Services. I'd talked to her before and went back to see her. When she told me another reporter had been around, I did some checking on you. I've got friends at the *Bay News*. They didn't know what was up, but they knew you weren't a reporter. When I found out who you really were, I knew I had something.

"I didn't mean for Joe to be blamed for Reiter's murder. I had no idea he'd even been there. I really did want to help him. When you told me about Ed Kohl, I thought we were home free."

"But the police didn't charge Kohl, and you were still worried that somehow we'd figure out your role."

"No, no. I knew I was safe. I was trying to save Joe. I figured that maybe we could still pin it on one of Kohl's associates. And I never, never would have hurt Molly. The note was just to make the police look for someone else, to shift suspicion from Joe."

He was a bit calmer. "You don't want to do this," I said as gently as I could. "You could shoot me, but you couldn't get away with it. Peter's outside. The others know I came here. There's no way you'd get away with it."

A muscle at the edge of Kevin's mouth jumped and he blinked hard. "There's just no other way out," he said desperately. "I can go out the back, through my neighbor's yard to the street behind. My car's around the corner." He was talking to himself, not to me, struggling to find a plan, some hope that he could escape.

I watched that hope die in his eyes, and something in his expression told me that he'd made a decision. He made a soft sound, somewhere between a sigh and a sob, and his mouth twitched several times before he got it under control. I'll never know which one of us he was about to shoot, but I have no doubt that he was preparing himself to pull the trigger.

Aikido teaches you to step out of the path of attack. Maybe that's why I saw the opening. "You don't have to kill anybody," I said. "There is a way out of this. You need to disappear. Go to Ireland."

"What?"

"Go to Ireland. You have friends there, connections who can give you a new identity. You can just melt into the countryside, like Quinn." He considered it. I rushed on. "If you shoot me, you'll be on the run. The police'll be right behind you. You'd have a much better chance in Ireland, and you don't have to kill me to get there.''

"But how?"

"Take the first flight out. Call the airport and find out when the next nonstop flight leaves for Dublin. We'll figure some way to get rid of Peter, and you can tie me up and leave me here. When you get to Dublin, you can call the police and tell them where to find me.''

"But what if the police find you before my plane lands? Or you get free and call them. They could be waiting for me in Dublin.''

"If the police find me, you're a lot better off if I'm alive rather than dead. They'll go looking for you either way, but they'll look harder if they're dealing with murder one. You have my word that I won't call them.''

"Why would you help me?" he asked suspiciously.

"Do you remember the story I told you about a man named Orrin Merrick?" I asked.

Doyle nodded. "The one who killed himself. I've given it a lot of thought,'' Kevin said.

"So have I. It's a mistake I don't plan to repeat.''

The whole plan almost fell apart when Kevin discovered that there were no direct flights to Ireland, but he settled for a one o'clock flight to New York with a short stopover before taking Aer Lingus on to Dublin. He reserved a seat in first class and had them put it on his VISA card. "Might as well go first class,'' he said as he hung up. "That's one bill I won't be paying.'' He kept the gun in his pocket, and he had me sit in a chair where he could keep an eye on me.

I began to worry about Peter. He hadn't expected me to stay long, and at some point he'd get tired of sitting in his car and decide to join us. Even a knock on the door could upset Kevin's fragile composure and lead to a deadly confrontation.

"We have to figure out how to get rid of Peter,'' I told

Kevin. "He's waiting outside, and he doesn't expect me to be here long."

Kevin looked confused. I could tell he wasn't going to be much help. I was going to have to take a whole lot more active role in this escape than I wanted to, but I couldn't risk Peter's life.

"You go out and tell him that I left by the back door," I said. "That I told you I had something I had to handle myself, and I'd be in touch soon. Tell him I said to go home and wait for me there. Play it like you don't understand what's going on; you're just an innocent bystander. Come on, Kevin, I've seen you scam people. You're a master at this."

He smiled. The schemer in him took over; then he frowned. "I should tie you up," he said.

"Let's not get carried away," I said. "I'm on your side, remember?"

He didn't look convinced. Finally, he said, "I could lock you in the bedroom."

"Fine, lock me in the bedroom. Let's just get on with this."

I had enough time in the locked bedroom to reflect that I could be making the biggest mistake of my life, possibly the last mistake. I was increasingly certain that Kevin wouldn't kill in cold blood, but he was none too stable at the moment, and anyone can kill in a moment of panic. There was also a good chance he'd kill himself. And if anything went wrong and the police got a hold of him, I could look forward to being charged with aiding and abetting a fugitive.

Kevin was in high spirits when he came back. "He bought the story," he announced. "Boy, was he mad at you."

My scheme would be harder on Peter and the others than it would on me. I'd have felt a bit more guilty for what I was putting them through if I weren't still irritated with the macho nonsense of last night.

Kevin was almost lighthearted for the first hour as he packed and decided what he wanted to take with him, then as the reality began to seep in, he became more sober and thoughtful. "I'm giving up a life," he said, looking around the room full of familiar things.

I don't know which was more disconcerting, the manic gaiety or the depression. A man with a gun in his pocket is dangerous enough without wild mood swings.

"Yes, but you're getting a new life, too," I said.

He collapsed onto a chair. "I can't do it. I don't think I can pull it off." He pulled the gun from his pocket. "And I can't kill you. There's really only one solution."

"Kevin," I said sharply. "Snap out of it. You're almost there. Give me the damn gun and let's figure out how we're going to make it look like I'm just an innocent victim."

He was immobilized by indecision. I stepped forward and took the gun from his hand. He made no effort to stop me.

We both stared at the revolver in my hand, and neither of us was pleased to see it there. It put an end to any pretense that I was acting in self-defense and made me, instead, Kevin's judge and jury. The decision was surprisingly easy.

"Do you want to go to Ireland?" I asked.

He nodded.

"I can't do the whole thing for you. You're going to have to help."

"What do I do?" he asked.

"Are you set to go? Do you have what you need?"

He nodded.

"Do you remember what you did with Quinn? That ought to help you know what you need to do for yourself. You'll want to get as much money as you can from your bank. I think you have about an hour before you need to leave for the airport."

The blank glazed look was replaced by a thoughtful one. "Yeah, there are things I need to do."

"I'll figure out where I'm going to spend the next twenty-four hours," I said. Twenty-four hours should give Kevin more than enough time to get to Dublin, even with the usual glitches in airline schedules, but it was much too long a time to be tied up.

I've done enough surveillance work to be real clear on the

issues here. If you're going to spend more than a couple of hours someplace, there are certain bodily functions that have to be taken into account. I checked out the bathroom.

Kevin's bathroom was ideal. It had a tiny little window high enough up to make escape impossible and the room was just large enough that claustrophobia wouldn't be a problem. I dragged some blankets and pillows in, raided the fridge and cupboards for food and drink, and searched the bookshelves for several good novels.

Kevin surveyed my comfy little nest with amazement. "This looks awfully comfortable," he said. "Don't you think they'll suspect something?"

It did look awfully good. But instead of giving up any of my treasures, I added another sack of food, including a bunch of things I never eat, and all the books on the lowest shelf of the bookcase. "My ex-husband will testify that I would never have chosen these," I said.

"I think I'm about ready," Kevin said. "Is there anything else?"

"I'd appreciate it if you'd call from Dublin to tell the police where I am, so I won't have to stay locked up any longer than necessary."

He agreed, then I thought of one thing more. "It would help Joe if you'd write a confession to Reiter's murder," I said. "Just what you told me. You can do it on the plane and mail it from Dublin if you want. Oh, and put this gun in a closet someplace." I handed him the now-empty revolver. I'd already removed the bullets and stuck them under the mattress.

"I don't know how to thank you," he said. "I don't know why you're doing this . . ." He looked like he might cry, and that was the last thing we needed. I gave him a hug, and told him to lock me up and get going to the airport.

The hours of confinement gave me time to think about a lot of things. In helping Kevin to escape, I had acted illegally and unethically. The little scam we'd run on Anton Glosser, if not illegal, was surely unethical. Neither one of them was anything I'd want to explain to the police or even a state examiner.

Yet exile seemed a far more fitting punishment than imprisonment for Kevin Doyle; and while I didn't expect Glosser to learn anything from our run-in, he would pay a price for his betrayal of Orrin Merrick and the dead man's family would benefit from it. In the messy world of real life, moral, legal, and ethical aren't always possible. One out of three isn't so bad—as long as it's the right one.

T HE POLICE BROKE down the door of Kevin's apartment and freed me from captivity sometime in the middle of the night. Kevin had kept his promise to call, and I was glad because the bathroom floor was a bit hard for my taste.

Dan came through the door right after the man with the ax. His first reaction was relief that I was alive. Kevin had evidently forgotten to include that detail. Dan grabbed me and gave me a big hug while everyone stood around looking embarrassed. I'd had plenty of time to work out my story, but I almost muffed it because I was still half asleep.

Once Dan was sure that I was all right, his cop instincts kicked in and I could see him checking out the room. He didn't say anything, but I had a hunch he'd have plenty to say later.

They let me call Peter, and from the way he answered the phone it was clear he hadn't been asleep. Now I did feel guilty. I gave him a short version of the story and talked him out of coming right over to Kevin's. I didn't need both him and Dan snooping around the bathroom.

I gave the uniforms a statement, and as is always my policy, I stayed as close to the truth as possible. I gave Kevin credit for figuring out the escape plan; in fact, I even claimed to have been locked in the bathroom much of the time, so I didn't really know who he'd called. I also gave him credit for the very humane arrangements in the bathroom. "He was really very nice," I told them. "From the beginning he kept saying how sorry he was, and when he locked me up, he asked what I'd like to have to make me more comfortable."

The uniforms were very solicitous and gullible. Dan stood in the background except for a short tour of the bathroom to check the window. When it was all over, he took me home.

"You're losing your touch," he said as he started the car.

"What?" I asked.

"Doyle was a real amateur. I'd have thought you could take him easily."

"He had a gun," I pointed out.

"Mmmm," Dan said. "And that bathroom window. I don't suppose it occurred to you to break it and call for help."

"I considered it, but I didn't think anyone would hear me."

He didn't say anything more, and we rode the rest of the way in uncomfortable silence. When he pulled up in front of my apartment, he said, "I'm glad you're safe. I'd like to break your neck, but I'm glad you're safe."

I gave him a kiss on the cheek, still remembering exactly how soft his lips were, and said, "I'm sorry, but there wasn't any other way."

Peter looked like hell when I came in. He grabbed me and held me so tight that he almost reinjured my shoulder. It was clear that my captivity had been much worse for him than for me.

He poured us each a glass of brandy, and we settled down in the living room while I told him the true story of what had happened at Kevin Doyle's.

"So you sent him to Ireland," he said when I finished, and gave a hearty laugh. "What a hell of a solution."

"He couldn't have handled jail."

"No, and he isn't a danger to anyone but himself. I think it was just right. A stroke of genius."

"I feel bad that you had to worry all this time."

"Comes with the territory," he said. "I've done it to you more than once. I was, however, ready to throttle you when I thought you'd sneaked out on me, and Jesse'd been happy to help. I have several lectures on trust and honesty that I was practicing for your return."

"I probably should call Jesse," I said.

"I've already done that. I told him not to come over, because you'd need your sleep. I don't think he was fooled."

"I do need my sleep. I also need a hug and a snuggle, and who knows what else."

"Here's to 'what else,' " Peter said as he finished off his brandy.

Epilogue

I GOT A postcard showing the impossibly green hills of Ireland several weeks ago. It wasn't signed, and the message was just a short quotation from *The Winter's Tale*: "What's gone and what's past help should be past grief." And the words "Thank you" in large letters at the bottom.

Kevin's officially listed as a fugitive from justice, and the Irish police are on the lookout for him. But a friend of his assures me that when the true nature of his crime and the cause of it is known, they won't look too hard.

Edward Kohl is not so lucky. His young assistant, Sal, gave the DA a full confession, and between murder one and all the charges involving juveniles, he's looking at about three hundred years. That is, if he doesn't end up in the gas chamber.

Joe Girard is back to his old job of harassing oil companies and the U.S. government. He had a lot of time to think in his jail cell and decided that his childhood secret had haunted him long enough. In his typical laid-back fashion, he's joined about a dozen children's advocacy groups, begun a research project, and even started speaking publicly on the prevention of child abuse. But the best news is that he and his girlfriend are planning to marry this summer.

Anton Glosser set up a very generous trust fund for the Merrick family. It doesn't square things, but it'll make life easier for Maureen and the kids. I'd like to say that I didn't enjoy my encounter with Glosser, but I did. Immensely. Jesse's right that the desire for vengeance is not a pretty emotion. If I were a better person, I'd probably feel guilty.

Steve Marley broke the codes in Ed Kohl's book, and a number of citizens, some of them prominent, now have court dates. Unfortunately, the city of San Francisco is no more solvent than any of the nation's other metropolises, and the latest round of budget cuts eliminated one juvenile officer. Steve is now in Fraud.

Molly is still with me, though I don't know for how long, and Peter, who only a few months ago got claustrophobic at the mention of cohabitation, is doing remarkably well as a surrogate father. Not that it's all easy—more like three porcupines trying to get close without drawing blood.

About the Author

Linda Grant lives in Berkeley, California, with her husband, two daughters, and two cats. She is also the author of *Blind Trust*, her first book for Ivy.